CRISIS AT THE CATHEDRAL

CRISIS AT THE CATHEDRAL

A Dorothy Martin Mystery

Jeanne M. Dams

This first world edition published 2018
in Great Britain and the USA by
SEVERN HOUSE PUBLISHERS LTD of
Eardley House, 4 Uxbridge Street, London W8 7SY
Trade paperback edition first published
in Great Britain and the USA 2018 by
SEVERN HOUSE PUBLISHERS LTD

British Library Cataloguing in Publication Data
A CIP catalogue record for this title is available from the British Library.

ISBN-13: 978-0-7278-8764-1 (cased)
ISBN-13: 978-1-84751-891-0 (trade paper)
ISBN-13: 978-1-78010-954-1 (e-book)

All Severn House titles are printed on acid-free paper.

Severn House Publishers support the Forest Stewardship Council™ [FSC™],
the leading international forest certification organisation.
All our titles that are printed on FSC certified paper carry the FSC logo.

Typeset by Palimpsest Book Production Ltd.,
Falkirk, Stirlingshire, Scotland.
Printed and bound in Great Britain by
TJ International, Padstow, Cornwall.

FROM THE AUTHOR

I have indulged, in this book, in two literary privileges. First, I learned when I had nearly finished that New Scotland Yard is no more! The building has been sold and the offices moved to a much smaller facility on the Embankment. As a lover of tradition I was devastated, and made the decision not to rewrite the portions of the book that mention the beloved old name. Let Scotland Yard live still, at least in the pages of this book.

Second, the summer-time setting of this book, necessary for various plot considerations, would in real life correspond roughly with the Muslim holy month of Ramadan. I hope my Muslim friends will forgive me for having ignored that coincidence and made no mention of Ramadan and its observance in the narrative.

As always, I owe much to various people who have helped me, but in particular to a Muslim family living here in my home town. They have welcomed me into their home and allowed me to witness their joy when they were sworn in as American citizens. They have all been very kind in helping me to understand their faith and culture, and patiently answered many questions that arose while I was writing. I'm sure I've made mistakes anyway, for which no blame attaches to Husam, Shaymaa, Alaa, Ameer, and Saif. Thank you, dear friends.

ONE

'Greta, do come and sit down.' I patted the chair next to me. 'The rush is over; Rosemary can manage. Tell Peter to come, too, and have a glass of something with us.'

'Do you know, I think I will.' Greta and Peter Endicott, owners of the inn in Sherebury's Cathedral Close, had been busy all evening with a crowd of tourists. The Cathedral, one of England's loveliest, draws visitors from all over the world, and quite a few of them are drawn to the warm atmosphere and superb food of the Rose and Crown. Peter, a Dickensian Mine Host to the life, oversees the bar with genial hospitality (and a sharp eye for potential troublemakers), while Greta, a stunning woman originally from Germany, takes care of the hotel side of the business and keeps an eye on the dining room with the help of the manager, Rosemary, and a couple of students from Sherebury University.

I've known the Endicotts ever since a visit to Sherebury many years ago, with my first husband, Frank. When I moved from Indiana to Sherebury after Frank's death, Peter and Greta were kindness itself, and we've become fast friends. I live now in an early-seventeenth-century house just outside the Close with the dear man I married a while back, retired chief constable Alan Nesbitt, and we've formed the pleasant habit of dining at the Rose and Crown to celebrate any special occasion, or sometimes just because we feel like it. Tonight the perfect evening had seemed a good enough excuse.

Alan, that morning, had seen the expression on my face and begun to laugh. 'You're going to say it,' he said. 'I can see it just about to come out.'

'"What is so rare as a day in June?",' I said, obligingly. 'Well, all right, I was. So there. Laugh at me if you want, but it's one of my favourite lines. And you have to admit, a day like this in England, even in June, is indeed rare, and deserves accolades.'

After living in England for some years, I can no longer
claim to believe it rains all the time, but this spring had been
particularly raw and chilly, with few warm days to tempt one
outside. I like to walk, but not in wellies and Burberry, with
a gusty wind trying to turn my umbrella inside out. The past
week had been moderate, though, and I'd gone out this morning
to find that Bob Finch, my gardener, had worked with the
weather to create magic. My spring flowers, the daffodils and
iris and so on, had gone, but the early summer ones, the
delphiniums and wallflowers and lupines and snapdragons,
were all in bloom, as well as a lot more this Indiana native
didn't know, but loved all the same. And the roses! I'm
convinced that there is no place in the world that roses like
better than England. Mine aren't fancy prizewinners, but under
my gardener's loving care, they seem perfect to me. I called
Alan away from his computer (the memoirs I don't think he'll
ever finish) to bask in the glory.

Our two cats came out with us, of course. Samantha is
only part Siamese, but it shows in her voice at times like
this. She delivered a long oration to the effect that it was
high time we'd done something about the weather and then
went off to sharpen her claws on a tree I'm particularly fond
of. Esmeralda simply yawned, stretched, and settled her grey
bulk in a sunny spot on top of a young snapdragon, to its
immediate peril.

'Sam's going to destroy that mulberry,' I said. 'Nothing I
do keeps her away from it. And I *wish* Emmy would stay out
of the flower beds. I keep thinking she'll get tired of getting
all muddy.'

Alan looked up and then back at me. 'Didn't see a single
pig flying around up there.'

I gave a half-laugh, half-sigh. 'Oh, well, they're cats, after
all. Like the Rum-Tum-Tugger, they will do as they do do.
You're much better behaved, aren't you, sweetheart?' I was
addressing not my husband but our loveable mutt Watson, who
had wandered out wondering where everybody'd gone. As he's
grown older, he becomes anxious when his family isn't under
his eye.

A peal of bells smote the ear. Living practically under the

Cathedral tower, we're used to the bells, but in the clear air they seemed to ring out more urgently than usual. 'Matins?' Alan checked the time on his phone. 'Indeed. Shall we?'

I was wearing jeans and an old sweatshirt; Alan had on his most threadbare corduroy pants and a plaid shirt that was missing a button. 'Should we change?' he asked.

'No time.' We closed the door to the house and headed through the gate into the Close and across to the Cathedral. Watson whined, but stayed behind when we ordered him; he knows the rules about church.

'We'll shock the tourists,' Alan said as we approached the nearest door.

'Tough. They ought to be thinking about the service, not looking at the congregation. We're both clean, just a trifle shabby.'

The verger on duty at that door knew us too well to be concerned. 'There's still room in the choir, if you put on a bit of speed,' he said with a friendly smile, handing us the order of service. 'Even on an ordinary Tuesday morning, it's amazing how they pile in.' So we went around the quickest way and found two seats at the east end of the choir, in the top row, right next to the bishop's throne. The bishop wasn't there, though, so he wouldn't see us looking like a couple of farm hands.

The daily services of morning and evening prayer display to their full glory the unique qualities of the Cathedral choir, which is what draws the tourists, and both Alan and I love the music. But the quiet sequence of readings and Psalms, prayers and thanksgivings, is what keeps us coming back several times a week. At the beginning of a day, it sets a pattern of serenity for the duties that follow. At the end of a trying day, it soothes and comforts. Always it takes us out of the worries and annoyances of twenty-first-century life into the timelessness of the ancient church, the ancient ritual. I often think of the medieval monks who used to pray here at least eight times a day. The choir where they gathered, built in 1220 or so, was destroyed by fire in the fifteenth century, but the space where I sat now was rebuilt quite soon – in cathedral terms – so I could imagine an almost unbroken thread of prayer and praise here, in this very place, for something like eight hundred years. The idea puts my annoyance over a malfunctioning dishwasher into perspective.

'Coffee?' Alan suggested when the service was over. Margaret Allenby, the dean's wife, had followed us out of the choir, and he included her in the invitation. So we began to walk across the Close to Alderney's, my favourite tea shop.

When I first visited England, I was taken aback by the idea of commercial establishments actually within the precinct of many cathedrals. My mind flirted with images of tables being overturned at the temple. But the more I thought about it, the more I could see the sense of it. The great medieval cathedrals were, after all, places of pilgrimage for centuries, and though the abbey foundations could offer bed and board to a limited number of pilgrims, when they came in droves they had to have some place to eat and sleep, and the nearer the church, the better. Hence the inn.

The tea shop, on the other hand, was a much more modern institution, since tea wasn't introduced to England until the mid-seventeenth century. By that time Sherebury's monastery, along with all the rest in England, had been dissolved, and the Cathedral had fallen into disuse, but tea was fast becoming a mania among the English, so establishments serving tea and coffee and pastries sprang up all over. A wealthy wool merchant had built a fine half-timbered house near the erstwhile Cathedral, but when he became less wealthy he prudently sold it to a tea merchant, one Matthew Alderney, who turned the ground floor into a shop and the first floor (second, in American terms) into a café. In fine old English tradition, the business has remained in the hands of the same family over the centuries and has become one of the most popular attractions of Sherebury.

Margaret was happy to accept Alan's invitation, but she looked with dismay at the crowd of tourists streaming out of the Cathedral. 'Alan, you're wearing sensible shoes, and have good knees. Do you think you can sprint ahead and find us a table? Will your ankle stand the strain?'

For Alan had broken an ankle rather badly last year, and although it had healed well, he is, after all, not a young man. 'I'm sure it would,' he said, 'but I've a better idea.' He pulled out his phone and made a quick call. 'There. Now we can stroll with dignity. I asked for a corner table, Dorothy, in case you're still worried about our clothes.'

'You were the one who worried. I think we're perfectly respectable, although Margaret may not want to be seen with us.'

'Caesar's wife, you know. I have to dress up a bit, even for the daily office, but I don't impose a dress code on my friends.'

So we had our coffee, and I couldn't resist a toasted teacake. Alderney's has their own special recipe, which includes raisins and cinnamon, and they're served drenched in butter. I've never been able to resist them, and regularly thank the Lord that my arteries are still in good shape. Though I can't say the same for my waist! I'm sure I had one, once.

We didn't linger. Our table was needed, and the lovely day was beckoning. We took our time strolling home, fed the animals (all of whom complained bitterly about our wanton neglect), thought about taking a little drive to the seaside, and took a nap instead.

After a late salad lunch, Alan went back to his computer while I did a little very mild gardening. Bob Finch doesn't appreciate my interference with his creation, but he allows me to pull the odd weed now and then. He has carefully (and not too patiently) taught me which ones *are* weeds, after I pulled up some violas he'd just planted.

Bob and his mother Ada are two more of my treasured friends here. Ada is one of a dying breed, a true Cockney char transplanted from London, whom I met over a very odd case of murder. Probably in her eighties, she works harder than anyone I've ever known, can talk the hind leg off a donkey, and is a treasure of integrity. She helps me keep my house clean, no easy task when a place is over 400 years old. She also keeps house for her son Bob, who works nearly as hard and is just as trustworthy, though far more taciturn, but who has an unfortunate drinking problem. When he's sober he can get through an amazing amount of back-breaking work, and when he goes on one of his periodic benders those of us who employ him just muddle along with our gardens until he comes back full of remorse and, usually, with peace offerings in the form of rare plants for our borders.

I can't really do a lot of gardening, since my titanium knees don't allow me to kneel for very long, and I can't sit back on my heels at all. There's a limit to what I can do bending over or sitting on my little gardening bench. Besides, the sun was really almost hot. So I went in, washed up, and sat with a favourite Dorothy Sayers novel, the animals disposed around me, until Alan gave up on his writing and came into the parlour, yawning and stretching.

'Were you planning on doing something about a meal?' he asked.

I looked at the clock on the mantel. 'Oh, good grief, look at the time! No wonder I was beginning to feel a little empty inside. It stays light so late in midsummer.'

'Nevertheless, it's nearly nine, and *my* inside has been complaining for some time.'

'And I truly don't feel like cooking. It's been such a perfect, lazy day, I don't want to spoil it.'

'Then why don't we celebrate the day at the Rose and Crown?'

'Won't it be overrun with tourists?'

'Probably not this late. I'm sure Greta can find a corner for us somewhere.'

So it was that we ended the day happily with a superb meal. The Endicotts have a chef any Parisian restaurant would love to steal – several have tried, in fact – but he loves what he does and where he does it, and continues to produce perfect food, both French and English, with his own special touches. We finished with a crème brûlée just tinged with a hint of hazelnut flavour and, sated, invited our host and hostess to join us for an after-dinner drink.

'Whew,' said Peter, putting down a tray of glasses and assorted bottles, and sinking into a chair. 'What a day! The weather brought them out in force. It's all good for business, of course, but we're both getting too old to work this hard. The drinks are on us, by the way. Whatever you like.'

'After that meal, I should abstain, but I'm not going to,' I said. 'A small cognac, please.'

'I thought you might like to sample the Calvados. It's a new one, to me, anyway. Only just available here.'

Alan and I had learned to enjoy Calvados, the famous apple

brandy of Normandy, during our recent stay there, but I shook my head. 'Not for me. Some other time. This has been a perfect day, and I want to end it the perfect way.' The others made their choices, and I raised my glass in a toast. 'If there is a paradise on earth, it's in Sherebury. Here's to the Cathedral, and the Rose and Crown, and the gardens, and lovely, lovely friends!'

I would have been happy to sit for a while, basking, but Greta saw a party appear at the front desk and went to make sure Rosemary was coping. 'Shall we, my dear?' said Alan, and offered me his arm to get out of the chair.

I was a bit bemused by Greta's new guests. Sherebury attracts tourists of all sorts and nationalities, especially in summer, but I didn't somehow expect a Muslim family to book into an inn so near the Cathedral. A tall, imposing man in a tunic and cap, with a full beard, a woman in a long tunic and lovely, embroidered hijab, and two children in more conventional Western dress, looking tired, but behaving beautifully; these would have been a common sight almost anywhere in England, except perhaps just here. The father ruffled his son's hair and gave his daughter, who was leaning against him, a hug, saying something quietly in Arabic (I presumed) to both of them. I noted that he spoke to Greta in perfect English and seemed entirely at ease both with the language and his surroundings.

'The world is growing smaller by the moment,' I said as we started for home.

'And more interesting,' Alan agreed. 'And what interests me most right now is my bed.'

TWO

What with one thing and another, it was Friday morning before I made it back to the Cathedral. I had slept too late for Matins, but I wanted to buy a book I'd seen in the Cathedral shop as a gift for a friend in America. She's a great admirer of stained glass, so a lavishly illustrated guide to some of the finest glass in England was perfect for her birthday. As usual, I couldn't simply make my purchase and leave. The shop carries an amazing variety of beautiful things, at prices to match, of course. I was trying to decide, in fantasy, between a small crystal model of the Cathedral, meant as a paperweight (£200) and a sterling silver bud vase (£110), when Margaret Allenby appeared at my side. With her were the couple we'd seen at the Rose and Crown.

'Dorothy, I'm so glad I saw you. I'd like you to meet some visitors. Mr and Mrs Ahmad are visiting here from Iraq, with their two children. This is my friend and neighbour, Dorothy Martin.'

'Oh, yes, I saw you checking in at the Rose and Crown a few days ago. How nice to meet you!'

'But – you are surely American?' said the man, his voice questioning. 'Forgive me, but your accent . . .'

I laughed. 'I am indeed American by birth. I've lived here in Sherebury for quite a long time, but I never seem to lose the accent. And I hope you don't mind my saying so, but you seem to have no accent whatever.'

It was his wife who answered, smiling. 'We have what I believe is known as an international accent. My husband does a great deal of travelling for his business, and as the children and I often go with him, the edges have got a bit smoothed out.'

'The thing is, Dorothy, these two lovely people are most interested in our Cathedral and would like to attend a service. Unfortunately neither Kenneth nor I will be able to take in evensong today, so I wondered if you and Alan were planning to be here.'

Her manner was as smooth as always, but I caught the undertext. Relationships in Sherebury between Muslims and adherents to other religions, especially Christians, are reasonably amicable. The small mosque, a fairly recent development, is tolerated by its neighbours and welcomed by some, and many people patronize the halal food store, not just because the foods are acceptable under Muslim dietary laws, but for Middle Eastern delicacies unavailable elsewhere. However, a couple of recent terrorist incidents in London and other English cities had raised tensions even in our small city. There are always people prepared to believe the worst when hatred and fear have dimmed reason. A Muslim family attending a Christian church service might cause some consternation, or worse. Margaret wanted to make sure the Ahmads were properly chaperoned.

'Of course! We'd be delighted to come with you. Will your children be coming, too?'

'If you think they would fit in, they would like to come,' said Mrs Ahmad. 'They are old enough to be interested in the differences between groups of people, nations and religions. You see, Islam is a religion of peace, though the extremists have tragically abandoned that fundamental teaching. We teach peace to our children, and we believe very firmly that the best way to ease tensions between Muslims and the rest of the world is through understanding, so wherever we go, we try to involve the children in the local culture and traditions and religious practices. So they will come with us, unless you think the service would be too long for them. They are reasonably patient and well behaved, but . . .?'

'This afternoon it will be rather shorter than usual,' said Margaret. 'Jeremy's been overwhelmed with getting ready for the festival, so he's doing a very simple Psalm setting and a short anthem the choir knows well. And Canon Lewis is taking the service, and he always keeps things moving right along.'

'So you see,' I said with a smile, 'it's the perfect day for you to come. Suppose Alan and I meet you at the south door a little after three, and we can show you around a bit before the service starts.'

'That will work out well,' said Mr Ahmad. 'Friday prayers will have ended by then, so we can all go to pray again – with you.'

'I wonder,' I said to Alan over lunch, 'if they're just interested in seeing what Christian worship is like, or if they have some interest in converting.'

'I'd think conversion an unlikely scenario. Most Muslims are quite devout, and you heard the husband mention their observance of Friday prayers. No, I think Mama is being entirely frank about it. Teach the children tolerance by way of understanding. I don't suppose you got any idea of what Mr Ahmad's business is?'

'I didn't have any more conversation with them, and Margaret had to leave, so I have no idea, except that they look very prosperous. My guess would be oil, but it's just a guess. They're beautifully polite, anyway, so I hope we'll get a chance to know them better.'

'How long are they going to be here in Sherebury?'

'No idea. Could I have a little more salad, please?'

We got to the south door before three o'clock. Neither of us wanted the Ahmads to have to wait for us and endure the curious and possibly hostile looks of other visitors. We had taken a little more care with our dress this time. The Ahmads dressed so well, we didn't want to look like poor relations.

When they arrived, I introduced Alan, and the parents intro-duced the children. Aya, the girl, looked to be about nine years old, the boy Rahim a little older. Aya was, this time, wearing a tunic and long slacks, and a simple white hijab. They were both very self-possessed, not apparently at all shy about meeting two adult foreigners. Rahim shook hands gravely; Aya gave us both a brilliant smile. I admired Mrs Ahmad's hijab, which was beautifully embroidered, and she smiled an acknowledgement.

'Right,' said Alan briskly. 'I imagine Mrs Allenby gave you a quick overview of the building, and we have only about fifteen minutes before we need to find a seat. Is there anything in particular you'd like to see first?' He addressed himself to

Mr Ahmad, and I remembered that in Muslim families, the husband is still very much in charge. But the man consulted his wife with raised eyebrows.

'Are there some of the small chapels – what are they called? – donated for private prayers for the dead?' asked Mrs Ahmad.

'Chantries,' I replied, 'called that, I think, because the prayers were chanted. Yes, there are a few, but most of them were destroyed in the fire. Mrs Allenby told you about the fire?'

'Yes,' said Mr Ahmad, shaking his head. 'A terrible thing. So many fine buildings were lost to fire over the ages.'

'Yes, it was a terrible scourge, and the great medieval cathedrals are still vulnerable. They look indestructible, built of solid stone, but so many of the roofs are timber-framed. Look at what happened to York Minster in the 1980s! But anyway, by the time Sherebury was rebuilt around 1485, the practice of endowed chantries to speed the way of the donors into heaven was almost extinct, so the only ones remaining here are up in the choir transept.'

We made our way up the aisle, and Aya was awestruck by the stained glass, brilliantly lit by the sun at this time of day. 'They are so beautiful,' she said, 'but why are they pictures of people?'

'They were put there hundreds of years ago,' I said, going into school teacher mode, 'to tell stories from our scriptures to people who couldn't read. Our religion allows pictures of people and all living things in our churches, although I believe yours does not?' I made it a question, and she shook her head.

'No. But our mosques are beautiful, too.'

'I'm sure they are. Are Christians allowed to visit?'

'Not in Iraq, I'm sorry to say,' said her father. 'Or at least, it would not be safe. Alas.'

Alan had been leading us up the south aisle, and we came to the choir transept.

'You are familiar with cathedral architecture?' I asked of both adults. 'The basic layout in the shape of a cross?'

They nodded. 'But here you have two sets of transepts?' asked Mr Ahmad.

'Yes, it's fairly unusual,' Alan replied, 'but not unheard of.

And since this particular transept, here on the south, was the only part of the Cathedral to escape the fire, the old chantries are still here. They are not, as in some cathedrals, separate little rooms, but simply dedicated altars.'

Neither of us mentioned the tragedy that had unfolded around one of these chapels, where I had quite literally stumbled over a body, my first Christmas Eve in Sherebury. Nor did we talk about the ghost that was said to haunt this area, though I firmly believed in him, had seen him, in fact. No, the darker stories could wait until later, if ever, when the children weren't around.

'The chantries are quite interesting,' said Mr Ahmad politely, 'and quite beautiful, though I find their reason for being somewhat obscure.'

'Do people of your faith not pray for the dead?' I asked.

'Yes, of course we do, but our prayers are rather different. There is no intent to – I believe you said –"speed their way into heaven".'

I laughed. 'Well, that idea has rather gone out of favour for Christians, too, at least for Anglicans. Nowadays it's more like reminding God to look after those we love who have gone before. Not that we exactly think He needs reminding. It's a bit complicated, actually. At any rate the chapels are, as you say, beautiful, and many people find it a great comfort to kneel here and remember their beloved dead.'

The bells outside began their call to the service, and Alan began to shoo us toward the choir. 'We can sit in the nave if you'd rather, but you get a better feel for the service up with the singers.'

We found seats in the back row, near the choristers. I began to explain in an undertone what would happen. 'Have you ever attended evensong before?'

'No,' said Mr Ahmad. 'We have been to Christian Sunday services, in America and other countries, but never to any church in England.'

'Well, this is a service of prayer and praise, most of it sung by the choir. All the words are in the service leaflet here. We join in some of the prayers and in the hymn, if there is one. Ah, yes, I see there is, at the end. There's a good deal of standing and kneeling and sitting, but you don't need to do any of that if you don't want to. It's perfectly okay just to sit and watch and listen; lots of tourists do.'

'Thank you,' said Mrs Ahmad quietly. 'We are comfortable doing what others do.'

Well, that was fine with me, though I did wonder what the rest of the congregation would make of an obviously Muslim family participating in the very archetype of Anglican worship services. Then I mentally smacked myself. The reaction was none of my business, and doubtless God would sort it out.

Once the service began, I forgot about our guests, lost in the sheer beauty of it. 'Worship the Lord in the beauty of holiness,' says the Psalmist, and for me a fine English choir worships in nearly perfect beauty. Jeremy Sayers, our organist-choirmaster, believes firmly in the less-is-more theory of church music. Except on the big festivals, he chooses simple music and directs it simply, no big contrasts of dynamics, no fireworks, just the boys and men singing perfectly the notes and words set before them, their goal to convey the meaning of the words to the congregation so that we can worship as we listen.

When it was over and we had left the Cathedral, I asked the family to come to our house for coffee. 'Or tea, or whatever you prefer,' I said a little hesitantly. This was the time of the afternoon when I wanted tea, or perhaps some sherry if it had been a difficult day, but I knew Muslims didn't drink alcohol, and I wasn't sure about other restrictions. To my relief, the adults said they'd love some tea, and if there was fruit juice for the children?

There was, of course, so I bustled around in the kitchen while they settled themselves in the parlour, and when I came in with a tray they looked very much at home, the children entranced by the animals and the adults talking with Alan.

'So I'm eager to know how you liked the service,' I said as I poured tea and distributed the drinks.

'I liked it,' said the boy – Rahim, I remembered. 'I liked the way the boys sang, high like girls, but different.'

'They are a very fine choir,' said Mr Ahmad. 'I had not understood how fine they would be. Tell me, are only men and boys allowed to sing in church?'

I smiled. 'Not at all. In the great cathedrals, paid male choirs were the standard for centuries, but even that is changing now. And parish churches – that is, the small churches all over the country – have always had mixed choirs, volunteers from the village. I never thought about it till this minute, but I suppose it goes back to the days when the cathedrals were monasteries, and of course the monks and novices did the singing. Chanting, it mostly was back then, and usually with no accompaniment; the big church organs came later.'

'Ah, yes, Gregorian chant,' said Mr Ahmad. 'It can be very lovely, but I think I prefer the polyphonic music your choir did this afternoon.'

I looked at him in some astonishment. 'You are very well informed about music, sir.'

'Oh, Husam has always been mad for music,' said his wife, 'especially Western music. Our musical traditions are quite different, of course, and we have little opportunity to hear good Western music.'

'I would like to sing in a choir,' Rahim announced, 'if I could sing high like that.'

Mrs Ahmad smiled. 'You would not be able to do that for very much longer,' she said gently. 'You are eleven. In perhaps two years your voice will start growing to be like a man's. It is only young boys who can sing like those boys this afternoon, and only, I think, after considerable training.'

'Yes, they go to the choir school here,' said Alan, 'studying music along with all the other subjects. They have in-born talent, of course, but they have worked very hard to develop it. We're quite proud of them.'

'You know, I've had a thought,' I said. 'You may have heard Mrs Allenby mention the festival earlier. The Cathedral holds a major music festival every year; it's always quite an event. Or series of events, really. You may have seen posters around town. The thing is, it's next week, and the highlight, the most important concert of all, is a performance of Handel's *Messiah*. You may know it?'

It would have been a silly question to ask any music lover in the Western world, but I would have assumed that Iraqis would not know the work. It was only because of Mr Ahmad's stated love for Western music that I ventured to ask.

'But of course! It is magnificent. I have heard it performed only on recordings, however.'

'Well, then – if Alan and I can still get tickets, would you like to be our guests? The only thing is, it's in the evening, and it's rather long . . .'

'We would leave the children at home,' said Mrs Ahmad decisively. 'At the inn. No, Aya, Rahim. You enjoyed this afternoon, but a long evening concert you would not enjoy. Mrs Endicott will help us find someone to look after you, and perhaps their grandchildren might come for you to play with. Mrs Martin, we would be delighted to come, if you can get tickets. We will pay for them, of course.'

'Well, we can argue about that later,' said Alan smoothly. 'I think we can manage a couple of seats, though they might not be with ours. It should be a splendid performance. I think you'll enjoy it.'

THREE

Alan was able to get two tickets for *Messiah*, but as he had expected, they were in a different part of the church, halfway down in the north transept. He offered to trade our seats in the nave, but the Ahmads wouldn't hear of it. 'We will be able to see and hear perfectly, I am sure,' said Mr Ahmad, 'and you are sitting with your other friends. We can talk about the performance afterward. Mr and Mrs Endicott have very kindly helped us arrange a little party at the inn when the concert is over.'

'Oh, we'd thought you might like to come home with us,' I said.

'We don't like to leave the children for too long,' said their mother, 'though I know they'll be well looked after. And if your friends can come, too, we'd be pleased. We have met Mr and Mrs Evans, of course, but we have had little chance to talk with them.'

Nigel Evans had married Inga Endicott some years ago and they had produced two delightful children, who were, along with the Ahmad children, going to spend the evening at the Rose and Crown under Greta's supervision while Nigel and Inga enjoyed the concert with us. Nigel was himself a fine musician, a tenor who had sung briefly at King's College. He now made his living as a highly skilled computer technician, but still loved singing when he could and listening to music of all kinds, especially choral music. Our other companion at the concert was to be Jane Langland, our next-door neighbour and dearest friend. Jane has the face of a bulldog (her favourite canine breed), a keen mind, a gruff manner, and a heart of marshmallow, and I know no one in Sherebury who doesn't love her. She's getting up in years, and has put on quite a bit of weight, to the risk of her heart and general well-being, but I don't even want to think about a time when Jane might not be around. She's the kind who contributes time and talents to every charity in town, takes soup to friends who are ill, looks after our animals when we have to be away, provides a willing ear to anyone with troubles, and in short is indispensable. I looked forward to introducing her to the Ahmads.

Our spell of perfect summer weather came to an end the morning of the concert. We woke up to a gloomy sky and the sort of rain our part of England seems to specialize in, a steady drizzle that looked like carrying on for days.

'Drat!' I said. 'Friday the thirteenth, and the weather is living up to it. And I did so hope the weather would be nice for the concert.'

'The rest of the festival has fared very well, love. Which is a good thing, considering those two concerts in the Close.'

'I do think anyone who plans outdoor events in this country is either very brave or very foolish.'

'You've quoted Mrs Major to me often enough,' he said with a smile. Years ago I'd attended an event sponsored by the Dorothy L. Sayers Society, at which Norma Major, wife of the then prime minister, unveiled a plaque at one of Sayers's childhood homes. There was a reception on the terrace, with wine and snacks, and a chilly light drizzle falling. I made some comment to her about the weather, to which she replied, 'My dear, if we waited for fine weather to do anything, we'd spend the whole summer in front of the fire, wouldn't we?'

'Yes, well, I suppose bad weather isn't confined to any country. I remember once back in Indiana when a planned outdoor commencement had to be hurriedly moved inside when a thunderstorm arrived and drenched everybody. Anyway, we'll only get wet getting there this evening; the Cathedral roof is lovely and sound. Is there more coffee?'

The drizzle persisted all day and into the evening, but it wasn't too bad when we set out for the concert. Jane went with us, carrying her own sturdy golfing umbrella, and we got only slightly damp. Nigel and Inga were waiting for us and took their seats while Alan and I went with Jane to find the Ahmads and make sure they were comfortable. We performed introductions and Jane accepted the invitation to their 'little party' afterward. 'Oh, by the way,' I said, 'it's customary for the audience to stand for the Hallelujah chorus. Nobody is really sure how the practice got started, but it's a venerable tradition.'

They nodded and smiled. 'We understand. Where shall we find you after the concert?'

'We could meet by the west door. Or we could just walk over to the inn,' Alan suggested.

'That might be best. It would be easy to lose one another in this crowd.'

We agreed, and took our seats with great anticipation, just in time for the usual announcements about silencing mobile phones.

The performance was all we could have hoped for, and more. All the musicians were splendid. I got teary-eyed when 'There were shepherds abiding in the field' was sung by a boy soprano from the choir, in that heartbreakingly angelic voice, and again when the contralto sang 'He was despised' with such feeling and passion that I truly felt Christ's humiliation. I read somewhere that the first time that aria was sung, in Dublin at the premiere in 1742, a clergyman stood and said to the soloist, 'Woman, for this be all thy sins forgiven thee!' I could understand.

As lovely as it all was, the chairs began to feel very hard after a while, and I think everyone was glad to stand for a rousing 'Hallelujah!'. As we settled back down for Part III, I tried to look for the Ahmads, but their seats were just beyond my range of vision, so I sat and listened eagerly for some of my favourite parts, the brilliant 'The trumpet shall sound' and the glorious final 'Amen'.

The applause went on for a long time. I clapped till my hands were sore, and continued to shout 'Bravo!' until all the performers walked off for the last time. Then we made our way (slowly) to the great west door and out through the small portals cut into them.

The rain, still coming down with dreary persistence, discouraged many of the attendees from heading for the inn, for which I was grateful. I was sure Mr and Mrs Ahmad would have booked a private room for their party, but it would be much more pleasant not to have to inch through hordes of customers.

Peter was doing a good business at the bar, enough that he

was glad when Inga shed her coat and slipped behind the bar to help him. She had been a big help to her parents before she married and even after her little boy was born, but when the sister came along, she found caring for two young children quite enough to do.

'Mum okay?' she asked as she pulled a couple of pints. 'Kids behaving?'

'Last time I checked,' said Peter, 'the big ones were mothering the little ones, and the little ones were eating it up. And the dining room is under control. So you can relax and enjoy the party, as soon as your hosts get here. Meanwhile, what will you all have to drink? On the house, of course – or rather on the Ahmads' tab for tonight.'

That surprised me a little. 'They're serving alcohol?'

He chuckled. 'Husam said to give people anything they wanted. They don't drink themselves, but he said, and I quote, "I have no right to impose my religious views on my friends."'

'They are remarkable people, I think,' I said. 'The world could do with more of that sort of tolerance. I really look forward to getting to know them better. They should be here any minute, I imagine, so meanwhile I'll just have a very small tot of Jack Daniel's.'

Jane has learned to appreciate American sour mash as well, so she joined me, and Alan and the Evanses stuck to beer. I sipped my drink slowly; I was still so 'high' from the music that I didn't need much in the way of any other stimulant. 'What was your favourite part?' I asked Nigel.

'I think the part that began with "Comfort ye" and ended with "Amen",' he said with a grin.

'Well, I liked the whole thing, too, but would you care to be a little more specific?'

'Really, it's hard to pick out any one bit. Everything was perfect – the choir, the orchestra, the soloists. This may be the best performance I've ever heard.'

'You say that every time,' said Inga, shaking her head in mock despair. 'What I want to know is what our Muslim friends thought of an evening devoted to prophecy and praise about Christ.'

'I want to hear that, too. Of course I know that Muslims

do revere Jesus, but not as the Saviour.' I looked at the clock over the bar. 'I wonder what's holding them up. The crowd must have dispersed by now.'

Alan moved to the front door of the inn and peered out. The Cathedral was only a couple of hundred yards away. 'Nobody's near the door now. It's not the sort of weather to encourage people to linger.'

'Maybe they stopped to talk to the dean,' I said. 'They might have wanted to thank him for scheduling such an outstanding programme, or maybe Jeremy for pulling it all together.'

'Perhaps.'

There was a note in Alan's voice that made me look at him sharply, but he raised his glass to drain it, which hid his face, and I thought I was imagining things.

A couple of minutes later the Allenbys came in, the dean shaking himself like a wet dog. 'Goodness, it's really pouring down now!' said Margaret. 'We positively ran here, but we got frightfully wet.'

'There's a fire in the lounge,' said Peter. 'I know it's June, but it's cold enough for March. Let me take your wet things, and go on through.'

'Are the Ahmads in there seeing to things?' asked the dean.

'We thought they were with you,' I exclaimed. 'Or I thought that. We haven't seen them. Are they still talking to Jeremy?'

'Jeremy's gone home, worn out, poor dear,' said Margaret. 'Exalted, you know, after that glorious music, but quite exhausted from all the work putting it together. The only ones left at the church, so far as I know, are two of the vergers and the sexton, just making sure all the lights are out and the doors locked and so on.'

'But then – where are the Ahmads?'

Alan exchanged looks with the dean. 'Kenneth, I hate to ask you to go back out in the rain, but I think we need to make sure nothing untoward has happened. If you'll come with me – or you could lend me your key, if you prefer . . .'

'I'll come, of course. I'm sure it's some simple mistake, but of course you need to check.'

The rest of us drifted into the lounge, usually devoted to the use of residents, but reserved tonight for the Ahmads and their party. A generous cold buffet was laid out, looking most appetizing, along with a serve-yourself bar. The fire made the room beautifully warm. We stood around awkwardly, no one wanting to eat or drink anything. No one could think of anything to talk about, either, except the absence of our host and hostess, and we didn't want to speculate about that. It's the old superstitious feeling that talking about something might make it happen. No one really believes that – but one can't be too careful.

It seemed an hour, but was really less than half that time before Alan and the dean returned. Alan shook his head. 'We checked all the places where they might have been accidentally locked in, or might have fallen or otherwise hurt themselves. There is no sign of them. Their coats and umbrellas are gone, and their programmes for the performance. They're gone.'

'But . . . but where would they go?' I hoped I didn't sound as panicky as I felt. 'This was home for them, temporarily. And we're here as their guests. They wouldn't have just left us.'

'Not to mention their children,' said Peter grimly, 'who are upstairs asleep at this very moment. Greta just came down to tell me they were settled for the night.'

'Did they have a hire car?' asked Alan.

'Yes, a dark blue Bentley. Very nice car. I took the number when they signed the register. It's parked at the back.'

Alan left without a word and went through the bar into the kitchen. He was back in a moment. 'There is no Bentley in your car park.' He took out his phone and punched in a number he knew by heart. 'Hello, Alan Nesbitt here. I'd like to speak to Derek, please, and if he's not in I must ask you to find him for me. This is an emergency. Two missing persons.'

FOUR

The sky was still quite light. Darkness comes late to England in mid-summer. But the persistent drizzle made it a little hard for Husam to see, when they pulled up at the railway station.

'Is that the one?' asked his wife, pointing to a young man just boarding the train.

'I believe so. Quick, park the car for me, and I will try to stop him.'

But before Husam could reach the train, it uttered its beep of departure. The doors closed and the train glided silently out of the station.

'This is not good, Rana.' Husam motioned Rana out of the driver's seat and got back in the car.

'Shall we go back?'

'No, I prefer to go on to London. We can get there quickly by car at this time of night, and I believe this is a slow train. We should be able to intercept Fahd at the station. I am very worried about him. He's unstable, and has fallen under the influence of some very persuasive men. He could get into great trouble in London – and could cause great trouble. You remember that tomorrow is the day they mark the queen's birthday, with great celebrations, a parade and so on. It is an invitation to terrorism.'

Rana sighed. 'Yes. That name he chose – Panther! He thinks he is so ferocious, but he is so small, so slight. He could be killed. I understand why you are worried. But Husam, the children!'

They had left the station car park and were driving down quiet streets, headed for the motorway and London. 'We were able to get away without observation. I think. I hope. It would be unwise to go back, or to delay. We will be gone for only a few hours. The children will be asleep.'

'We must still phone and tell the Endicotts where we are. They will worry.'

'If you wish.' Husam took one hand from the wheel and felt in the pocket of his tunic. He frowned, switched hands, and explored the other pockets. 'Rana, did you pick up my phone, back at the church?'

'No. You used it, taking that call.'

He uttered some words in a low voice, words that Rana was too ladylike to notice. 'Then, my wife, I have left it behind. It will not be lost; someone will find it and return it to us when we go back to the inn.'

'But we cannot call the Endicotts.'

'Not until we get to London. There will be public telephones there, and we will be there in less than an hour. Try not to worry. The children are being well looked after.'

Rana's only reply was a look, which Husam decided not to see.

Derek Morrison, trusted assistant to Alan back when he was chief constable for the county of Belleshire, was now the senior detective inspector on the force. He was at home when Alan called, which was only to be expected late on a Friday evening. However, the very fact that he wasn't working meant that nothing desperately urgent was requiring police attention at the moment. Which was a good thing, because Alan was about to ask for a good deal of attention.

He returned Alan's call immediately. 'Derek, thank God. I'm sorry to disturb your evening, but we have what could be an explosive situation here.' Alan had turned away and was walking out of the room, but I could just hear that remark. He turned away from his phone for a moment and spoke to me, gesturing with his head to the others in the room. 'Dorothy, tell them they needn't stay. We know none of them could have anything to do with whatever's happened, and Derek can question them later about what they might have seen and heard. Yes, Derek, the situation is this.'

I went back to the others. 'Alan is talking to Derek. Of course the actual orders will have to come from higher up, but Alan hopes Derek will be put in charge of the investigation.'

'I thought,' said Inga, sounding puzzled, 'that a missing

persons report couldn't be filed until someone had been gone for at least twenty-four hours.'

'There are extenuating circumstances,' I said, sighing. 'For one thing, they left their children behind. I've only met them a couple of times, but they seem like loving parents. I can't imagine what would make them just leave them, without a word. And of course the other thing is . . .' I stopped, unsure of how to continue.

'The other thing is that they're Iraqis,' said Jane bluntly. She usually spoke in a kind of telegraphese. The full sentence underscored the gravity of what she was saying. 'Any number of reasons for going. None pleasant. Some frightening.'

'Lord, have mercy,' said the dean, and it was clearly a prayer.

'Anyway, he said you can all go home. Derek's minions will probably talk to you tomorrow, in case you saw or heard anything that might help explain . . .' I shrugged helplessly.

'We do need to get the children home,' said Inga. 'I hope we won't wake them. I don't want to answer any questions they might ask. Time enough for that when they start wondering why their new playmates are upset.'

Peter, who had been in and out, keeping one eye on the bar, put a hand on Inga's shoulder. 'No need to worry about that, pet. They're deep asleep. Nigel can bring the car round and I'll carry the Nipper, if you can manage Greta Jane. They'll never know they've been moved.'

Jane, who had taken a seat in one of the squashy leather chairs, simply shook her head. Plainly she was staying. The Allenbys consulted each other with a wordless glance, and then the dean said, 'I'll stay, I believe. I'd like a word with Alan. Margaret's a bit tired and will excuse herself with thanks.'

She smiled, kissed her husband on the cheek, and went out into the rain.

Alan came back into the room and accepted the presence of Jane and the dean without comment. 'Derek will be here in a moment or two. Meanwhile, I might as well ask the obvious question. Did any of you see or hear anything at all that might be relevant to the situation?'

I shook my head. 'As you know, Alan, we couldn't see the Ahmads from where we were sitting. I tried to crane my neck when we were sitting down after the Hallelujah chorus, but I still couldn't see that far back. So I saw absolutely nothing of them after we showed them to their seats. We were early enough that they were the first ones in that row, so I don't even know who sat next to them. They seemed perfectly normal then, don't you think?'

Alan sighed. 'Assuming we know them well enough to know what "normal" is for them. They seemed grateful to us for arranging the tickets, and excited about the concert to come. Just what one would expect, in short. Dean, you were sitting up front. Could you see them?'

'Only just, and only for a few minutes before the programme began. I might not have recognized them but for Mrs Ahmad's headdress. I caught no more than a glimpse, but they seemed to be chatting amicably with their neighbours on either side.'

'I don't suppose you saw them leave.'

'No, and I should have done if it had happened during the concert. They were in the centre of the row and would have had to disturb several people to get out. That wouldn't have gone down at all well with our group of dedicated music-lovers. They must have gone immediately after the last chorus, when everyone was standing and applauding.'

'There's another possibility,' I said. 'The Hallelujah chorus. You wouldn't have noticed if they slipped out when everyone was sitting down after that. People would have thought they were going to the loo. A bit unusual for both at once, but not impossible. Or they might have thought that the Muslims had got tired of Christian music. I think that unlikely, but people who didn't know them – who knows? And when they didn't come back, it might have been thought they'd stayed at the back so as not to disturb anyone.'

Jane leaned forward. 'Why leave?'

'Yes, that's rather the point, isn't it?' said Alan. 'It looks as if they left of their own free will, taking their coats and so on with them, taking their car, and yet leaving their children. What compelling reason would cause them to do that? Ah, Derek! I've been meddling in your business here. Over to you.'

Derek nodded and cast his glance quickly over the small

group of people. 'I take it that none of you saw or heard anything unusual?'

We all shook our heads.

'I've people searching the area near where they were sitting, and we'll have to question those sitting near them, of course. I've put some men on that, since the matter might be very serious. There were only a very few tickets sold at the door, so the booking office has the names and seat numbers of almost everyone who attended. On computer, fortunately, or looking up particular seats would have been a nightmare. Your booking secretary wasn't best pleased at being hoicked out at this time of night, dean, but we persuaded him that it was urgent. My men are phoning people even as we speak.'

'Won't make them popular,' said Jane.

'No, well, the police are often unpopular. Now, Alan, just to make sure we're on the same page, tell me what possibilities you have in mind.'

'You don't need to be told, but very well. The Ahmads might have seen something, or someone, that caused them to leave so precipitately. It might have frightened them. Anti-Islamic prejudice is not as rampant here as in some parts of the world, but it exists, and recent events haven't helped.

'Or the stimulus, whatever it was, might have spurred them to action of some sort. That is, someone they know might have come to tell them there was something urgent that they must do. Or, of course, it's possible that they might have been lured out of the Cathedral by some ruse, and then abducted.'

'Tale about the children,' said Jane.

I nodded. 'Yes, some story about the children would have done it. Someone could have come in claiming to bring a message from Greta – one of the kids ill, or a bad fall, or something. They'd have gone like a shot.'

'Your thinking parallels mine,' said Derek. 'I think we must adopt that scenario, at least for now. If they were abducted for ransom, we'll hear something soon. He's a very wealthy man.'

Jane shook her head firmly. 'Would have taken kids, not parents.'

'Yes,' said Derek, 'if the yobs were planning to get ransom

from the parents. But what if they were expecting to hold up Ahmad's employer – or the Iraqi government? He is a very important person to them, very highly-paid, critical to the prosperity of the company and, one gathers, of the country. Yes, Dorothy,' he said in response to my look of amazement, 'we do keep a security file on VIPs visiting the country. It's quite necessary in this age of terrorism.'

'Other possibility,' said Jane, sounding grim.

'Yes, that hadn't escaped us. We can't avoid wondering if these apparently lovely people came to this country to engineer a terrorist attack.'

'Not with their children!' I cried.

'What better cover?' said Alan. He sounded infinitely discouraged, and suddenly very old.

The dean looked at Alan and opened his mouth, and then closed it again. There was a long silence before Jane said, 'Kids can't stay here.'

Peter, who had closed the bar, was sitting in a corner. He said, 'I'm afraid you're right. Greta's quite happy to be a temporary childminder, but she can't take on the job full-time. And we're not certain about the dietary restrictions for the children. Rana and Husam have been advising us, and providing some of the food themselves.'

'I'm too old,' said Jane, before anyone had the temerity to suggest that she take on the task. 'Walter.'

Walter Tubbs was Jane's grandson, though she hadn't known of his existence until quite late in her life. I had met him when he was working as a volunteer for our small local museum. He had since finished his degree, landed a job with the Museum of London, and married Sue, a delightful girl who worked at the Museum of Childhood in Bethnal Green. They lived in a small but pleasant flat in a London suburb and as yet had no children.

'He and Sue would be perfect, but do they have room for two kids? And what about their work schedules?'

'Young. Work it out. Won't be for long.'

I was nodding in agreement when a knock came at the door. It was one of Derek's men. 'Excuse me, sir, but I thought you might want to see this. We found it under a chair near where the Ahmads were sitting.' He was handling it with a handkerchief.

It was a mobile phone. Derek took a quick look. 'I'm guessing this belongs to the Ahmads. Peter, have you some plastic gloves?'

He supplied them, and Derek pushed a few buttons on the phone. 'Hmm. There appear to have been no recent calls. Peter, I imagine you and Greta have their phone number?'

Greta went to the desk and came back with a slip of paper. 'Alan, call it, please.'

The phone in Derek's hand began to ring.

'This is theirs, then. It's a little hard for me to believe they have taken no calls since –' he looked at the display on the screen – 'since the middle of May. The records seem to have been wiped out.'

No one made any comment, but the unspoken words were clear. Why would they erase phone messages unless they had something to hide?

'There is no place to leave the car. Rana, take over, please, and drive around the area until I come back. With Fahd, I hope, though the traffic made us rather 'late.'

Rana had made only one circuit of the complicated one-way system around Victoria Station when Husam waved her to the kerb. He was alone.

'The train has come and gone. Fahd was nowhere in sight.'

'What are we to do?'

A policeman was approaching them, stern purpose written on his face. 'Quickly, Rana.' They changed seats and Husam drove off before they could be reprimanded. He found a quiet side street where they could stop for a moment or two.

Rana spoke. 'My husband, I will go where you go, but I would prefer to return to the children.'

Husam shook his head. 'How can we do that? It would defeat our purpose in coming to England. I know it will be difficult to find Fahd, but I must try, if not tonight, then early tomorrow morning. He is in great danger. And I regret, but there are no more trains to Sherebury tonight, or I would be happy to send you back.'

They looked at each other. Rana sighed. 'Then we must find a place to stay for the night. There are many hotels near here.'

'I suspect they are all fully booked. The palace is only a short walk away, and with the ceremony tomorrow . . . however, I can phone and ask.'

'No,' said Rana, 'you cannot. You have misplaced your mobile. I will drive again, and you will go to the biggest hotel, the Grosvenor, and ask. If they cannot give us accommodation, you will use a public telephone to call Uncle Abdullah. You know his number, do you not?'

'I do. That is a good idea, Rana.'

She drove as near as she could to the Grosvenor, and dropped him off. 'I will meet you here when you return,' she called after him as he got out of the car.

This time she drove for some minutes before Husam returned and took over the driver's seat. 'There are no rooms available anywhere. The desk clerk was very pleasant and rang some other hotels. It is no good. I then called Abdullah, who will be happy to be our host for the night.' He pulled a paper folder out of the door pocket, consulted it, and entered an address in the satnav. 'Abdullah suggested we return the car, which is a liability in London. His chauffeur will pick us up at the car hire.'

Rana sighed again, but said nothing. It was usually easier to let Husam believe he was in charge of matters.

'I wish I shared Jane's optimism,' I said when Alan and I were finally getting ready for bed. 'I'm sure Walter and Sue will take good care of the children, but even so, it seems to me there are any number of possible endings to this drama, very few of them happy.'

'Derek will do his best,' said Alan wearily.

'Of course he will, and his best is very good indeed. But if he's not dealing here with ordinary criminals but with international terrorists, he could be out of his depth. Should he maybe call in MI5, or whatever it's called now?'

'Still MI5, and he'll certainly do that if he feels the need. There are also many other agencies, branches of the police for the most part, that deal with terrorist threats. For now, though, a low profile is needed. You do realize we could be talking about an international incident?'

I shuddered. 'I'm thinking more of the disrupted lives of two charming children.'

Watson, who had been asleep in our bedroom when we came home, had grown more and more agitated about the worry in our voices. Now he clambered (with some difficulty, owing to his weight and age) out of his basket and up onto our bed to deliver reassuring face licks all round. I hadn't thought I could sleep, but between Watson's gentle snoring and Alan's warm, comforting bulk beside me, I was out in a very few minutes.

FIVE

No great city ever really sleeps. London, on the eve of a major royal occasion, teemed with life and vibrancy even in the small hours. It was well after midnight before Abdullah's chauffeur negotiated the snarled traffic and deposited the weary Ahmads at the home of their host. Abdullah was, in fact, a distant cousin of Husam Ahmad, but was regarded as a benevolent uncle by the whole family. His home, a handsome Georgian edifice in one of London's most affluent neighbourhoods, was furnished in tasteful luxury, and his welcome befitted the setting. He greeted Rana and Husam with hugs and sat them down at once with tiny cups of very strong coffee and a plate of sticky-sweet pastries.

'Now, my little ones,' he said, settling his bulk on a comfortable couch and helping himself to a piece of baklava, 'explain to me the trouble. You told me very little on the phone.'

'You know why we came to England,' said Husam.

'This is to do with your mission, then?'

'Yes. A young man from the mosque in Sherebury was showing great promise, but he became involved with a group of people who, we fear, turned him in the wrong direction. He came to London tonight, we think because of the ceremonies tomorrow, and we are very worried. We tried to intercept him, but he evaded us.'

'It is hard to know what to do,' said Rana. 'The children are back in Sherebury, at the inn. We could not phone to tell them where we had gone, because—'

'Because I stupidly left my phone behind, at the Cathedral. We went to a concert there, but before it had ended the imam called, and we left in a hurry to catch the train. But we were too late.'

'So the children do not know where we are, nor do our host and hostess at the inn. Nor, indeed, anyone in Sherebury. They have been very kind to us. We *must* phone them!' Rana put down her untouched cup of coffee.

'But perhaps not until morning,' said Abdullah, his round face showing compassion. 'Forget your fear and think, Rana. It is very late. The children will have been put to bed long ago, and your friends will be asleep as well, I suspect. From what you have told me of them, they sound like sensible people. Yes, they will be worried. Yes, they will wonder where you have gone, and why, and probably will have imagined unpleasant possibilities. But they will know that very little can be done in the dead of night. Better, I think, to wait until morning, when you can phone and set their minds at rest. Meanwhile, what are your plans?'

Husband and wife consulted each other with a look. 'I wish to start early tomorrow to look for young Fahd. Rana wishes to return to the children as soon as possible.'

'And how do you propose to find one young man in a city of some nine million people? Not counting the thousands, perhaps hundreds of thousands, who crowd in from all parts of the globe, especially when something colourful is to happen among the royals. Are you gifted with the eyes of a magician, or the instinct of a hunting hound, or the second sight, to see into the mind of this young hothead?'

Husam smiled. 'No, but I am gifted with a certain amount of common sense. Fahd has come because of the Trooping the Colour. He will be found near the palace or along the parade route, but I think near the palace. So that is where I shall go.'

Abdullah shook his head sadly. 'There are times, my child, when I wish I were not faithful to the rule about strong drink. I think some wine would ease my feelings just now. First, you plan to be near the palace. You and many, many thousands of other people. There is a saying about a needle in a haystack. You know it, perhaps?'

He didn't wait for Husam's reply to the obviously rhetorical question. 'Second, are you not aware, my idealistic friend, that there are people in this country and in this city, organized groups of people, who are aware of your activities and would do anything, up to and including murder, to stop you?

Fahd is not the only hothead in this world. You have embroiled yourself in a gravely perilous undertaking, and what is more, you have also brought your wife into it. That I find hard to understand or forgive.' His face, which was made for good cheer, was twisted into a frown that accorded ill with his jovial figure or the peaceful surroundings.

Husam started to speak, but Rana held up a hand. 'No, Abdullah. I cannot let you think ill of my husband. Yes, he has perhaps allowed his enthusiasm to lead him into more danger than he had anticipated. But I came with him of my own free will. Where he goes, I go, even if I do not always agree with him.'

The older man held up his hands. 'Then I give up. You will stay with me for what is left of the night, and in the morning—'

'Early in the morning,' Husam said.

'Very well, early in the morning, we will decide what is best to be done. And now go to bed and let an old man get his sleep.'

Morning dawned very early, and the birds woke me. The rain had moved away, and the midsummer sun was brilliant by quarter past five. I was not. I got up to go to the loo, waking Watson in the process. He instantly decided it was time for breakfast, and his confident *woof* brought the cats upstairs, loudly sharing their agreement with his point of view.

I gave up, shrugged into the disreputable old terry-cloth robe I should have thrown away years ago, and went down to the kitchen. I knew I couldn't get back to sleep, anyway. The minute my eyes had opened, the squirrel in my brain had started frantically racing round and round on its wheel. What had happened to the Ahmads? What was going to happen to their children? What were Alan and I going to do about it? Could we have been wrong about them? Was it conceivable that they were terrorists?

I fed the animals and let them out, and then made a pot of very strong coffee and brooded over cup after cup of it until Alan came down.

He poured himself a cup and sat down next to me. 'Toast?' I suggested half-heartedly.

'Not just yet.'

We sat in silence until Alan's phone rang. I looked at the clock on the wall. 'Alan, nobody calls at this hour with good news!'

'Unless it's Derek. He would know we wouldn't be asleep. Hello?' He put the call on the speakerphone.

'Alan, I hope I didn't wake you.' Not Derek. Peter Endicott.

'No. Dorothy's been up for quite a while. Do you have news?'

'Only that Jane has settled the question of the children. They woke up about three and discovered that their parents weren't here, and were of course frightened. Jane spent the night here against that very emergency, and handled them with her usual calm common sense. She told them their mother and father had had to go away unexpectedly, and that they, Aya and Rahim, were going to stay in London for a little while with two people who would take them to wonderful museums and the zoo. She went on listing the marvellous things they could do in London, in such a calm, quiet voice that they went back to sleep. At first light this morning she phoned Walter and Sue, who agreed instantly to take the kids. She's packing them up even as we speak, and a taxi's waiting to take them all to catch the first up train.'

'And Derek's agreed to all this?'

'With great relief, I think. It's one less thing off his list of worries. If the parents have been carried off, for whatever reason, the safety of the children comes into question. Of course he took Walter's address and phone number.'

'I would have thought London would be a far more dangerous place than Sherebury,' I responded dubiously.

'In some circumstances, yes. But Walter and Sue have no connection whatever with the Ahmad family. It could take a very long time for someone to find the children in Bexley.'

'One hopes,' Alan sighed. 'Thanks for letting us know, Peter.'

'And you'll pass along anything you hear?'

'Of course.' He ended the call. 'Trust Jane to cope.'

'Jane is an ever-present help in time of trouble. And oh, Lord, Alan, but is this ever a peck of trouble!'

* * *

'I have some bad news for you.' Abdullah's face was once again set in an unaccustomed expression of worry.

'The children!' gasped Rana.

'No. But several men I know, men who keep their ear to the ground, have phoned this morning. They have heard that you have come to London, Husam. I don't know how,' he said, forestalling the question on Rana's lips. 'They have also heard that certain people also know, men who do not wish you well. It is as I said last night. You are both in danger. None of the dangerous groups seems to know as yet exactly where you are, but they will work it out sooner or later, and by that time you must no longer be here.'

'I must go back to the children.' Rana's voice was firm.

'No, Rana, you must not.' This time it was Husam who issued the order. For order it was, and Rana's temper broke.

'You are my husband and I always obey you, but this time I will not! I will go to them!'

Husam took hold of her hands, which she was waving wildly. 'My wife, listen to me. You are the delight of my heart, and so are Rahim and Aya. I cannot see you walk into danger, danger that would encompass them. Do you not see that you could lead this people, our enemies, straight to them? You must not do this. Abdullah, you say we must not stay here, either. What are you suggesting?'

'There is one place in London that is almost as well protected, almost as secure, as Buckingham Palace. And that is your place of employment, Husam.'

'UniPetro?' He considered. 'Yes. I had not thought of it in those terms, but it is a fortress, well guarded against terrorism. It has had to be, as an Iraqi company in a city not always friendly to the Middle East.'

'And as a company whose strategic importance to both East and West can hardly be over-estimated. Oil, my friend, is the lifeblood of today's civilization in both war and peace. Yes, the headquarters building is as safe as any place can be in today's world gone mad. It is where you should go until the current crisis blows over. My chauffeur is very good at circuitous driving. I will make a phone call or two, and you can leave in a few moments.'

'We have no extra clothing,' said Husam. 'We had not planned a stay in London.'

'This London is not a desert, my son. We can obtain clothing and toiletries for you, and my chauffeur can deliver them.'

'And you trust him, this chauffeur? He has been with you for a long time?'

'I trust him with my life,' said Abdullah, relaxing into a smile. 'He is my cousin. Now take some coffee while you wait for him to bring the car around.'

'No,' said Rana, the fire still in her eyes. 'First I must speak with my children.'

Abdullah, very gently, said, 'My dear, it is not yet six in the morning. It would not be kind to wake them. I will phone to the Rose and Crown after you are safely away from here and explain as much as the proprietors need to know. I will not tell them where in London you are. In this situation, the less anyone knows about you, the better. You can phone later, from a mobile that cannot be traced back to your location, and speak to them.'

Husam sighed. 'It has never before been this difficult, this dangerous. Are you sure you are not exaggerating?'

'The world changes, my child. You think people are like you, their hearts and minds on the right paths. They are not. Perhaps I do exaggerate. Is it not better to do that, and be safe, than to underestimate the danger?'

'Yes. You are right. Nevertheless, I cannot go into hiding. There is a young man whom I must try to save from himself, and other people whom I must try to save from him.'

Rana drew in a long breath, but said nothing. Abdullah's face showed his sorrow. At last he said, 'Then go with God, Husam, and may you be safe.'

'In shah'Allah,' Husam replied quietly.

SIX

The animals came racing back into the house, loudly proclaiming that they were worn out from chasing wonderful smells (Watson) and grasshoppers (Emmy) and voles (Sam) and required immediate sustenance. Breakfast? That was *hours* ago.

So Alan put down a second meal for them, telling them all the while that they were getting fat and didn't need it, while I decided that we also needed some sustenance to help us get through the day, and assembled a boring breakfast of cereal and fruit. Alan and I usually enjoy our food, but there are times when one eats to live.

The next call was from Margaret. 'Dorothy, have you seen the news this morning? On the telly, I mean?'

'No, we don't usually switch it on before evening. You're *not* saying . . .'

'Sadly, yes. How *do* they get hold of these things so soon?'

'Osmosis, I think. Is it bad?'

'Frightful! Two different groups are already claiming responsibility for an abduction, but since they differ on just what has happened, and what the point of it is, Kenneth and I think they're both telling a tale. The bishop is about to issue a statement of concern for the Ahmads and support for all our Muslim brothers and sisters, and of course that will start a new row, but what else can we do?'

'Nothing else. It's the right thing to do, but the extremists on both sides will howl. Sorry, Margaret, someone else is trying to call me. Come over and talk if you get the chance.'

I clicked off just in time to lose the other call, but before I could call back, my phone rang again. So did Alan's.

It was like that all morning. Derek called to say they'd reached nearly everyone who'd sat near the Ahmads, and no one admitted to seeing or hearing anything unusual, though several had been a bit huffy about Muslims daring to come to a concert in a Christian church. A list of those had been kept for possible follow-up. 'The couple sitting next to them, to Mrs Ahmad's left, said they went out just after the Hallelujah chorus, and they don't think they came back – but they're not sure. Wrapped up in the music, apparently.'

Jane called to report that all was serene in Bexley, the children apparently accepting the situation. 'Rahim not as happy as Aya. Smells a rat. Not talking about it.'

'He seems to be a very mature child. I imagine he doesn't want to alarm his sister, though how he'll manage if the parents aren't found soon, I don't know.'

'Keep 'em busy. May not be back for a few days. The dogs . . .'

'We'll look after them, of course.'

About mid-morning, Greta called, and her news was enigmatic and disturbing. 'Dorothy, I wanted you to know about this, though I'm not sure what it means. Peter says it means nothing, but I'm not sure.'

I waited with what patience I could muster. When Greta is in distress, she often talks round and round a subject until she can bring herself to the point.

'It was a phone call. We were very busy serving breakfast, and I only just had time to tell you about it.'

'Greta, who called?'

'That's just it, you see, we don't really know. It was a man who said his name was Abdullah. No surname. He said he was calling from London, and that the Ahmads wanted us to know they'd had to go there in a hurry, and that they were safe and well. And then he wanted to speak to the children, and before I thought about it I said they weren't here. And then I realized I didn't know anything about the man who was calling, who he was or anything, and when he asked where the children were, alarm bells went off, and I hung up.'

'Wait a minute, Greta.' I repeated what she had said, and Alan took the phone from me.

'Greta, did your phone display the number of the caller?'

'Yes, and we looked it up, but it was a public phone box in London.'

'I see. Then Peter's probably right, and it's a crank call.

Let me have the number, though, and I'll pass it along to Derek.'

We mulled that over for a little while, but couldn't make any sense of it. And the phones kept ringing. The media called and came to talk to us. Newspapers, local and national. Television, ditto. We perfected a script that sounded cooperative without saying much, and finally locked the door and checked the phones carefully before answering.

Friends called, offering sympathy and asking what they could do to help. (Keep your eyes open, call the police if you see anything.) 'Though what good that will do, I don't know. The police will get flooded with reports of men sporting beards and women wearing hijabs. To some people all Muslims look alike.'

'The police will sort it out,' said Alan. 'They're used to that sort of thing. Happens every time a public appeal goes out. Once in a million times, something useful comes of it.'

'So much for keeping a low profile,' I groaned. 'Now I suppose MI5 *will* get into the act.'

There was no possible reply to that. I brooded for a while longer, and finally got up and began to pace. (Both cats were sitting nearby. Offended, they got up and stalked to the back door, where they pushed through the cat flap with as much noise and drama as they could produce.)

I followed them, though not through the cat flap. 'I can't believe the day is almost gone already. I'd love to take a nap, but it's time to take Jane's dogs for a walk. Come with me, will you? I can't handle them all myself.'

Of course Watson woke up at the magic word, so we ended up with five dogs, leaving them on leads until we reached the small park where we could let them run.

'They can run off any troubles,' I said enviously. 'Not that they really have any troubles. It must be lovely to have the mind of an animal. If there's food and a warm place to sleep and a human to love, all's right with the world. Alan, what *can* have happened to the Ahmads?'

'So many possibilities, most of them dire. It's hard to see a happy solution to this.'

I looked around. There were a good many other people,

some with their dogs, some with children in strollers, a couple with infants in prams. Nobody was paying the slightest attention to us. I sat down on one of the uncomfortable benches and rummaged in my handbag for the notebook I always carry. 'Let's see if we can work it out. Not where they are, I don't mean, but at least some of the possibilities. Alan, I can't just wait around for Derek and his forces to find them! I have to feel at least a little bit involved. If nothing else, it'll give me something concrete to pray for.'

'I don't imagine God needs specific instructions on how to handle problems, but if it makes you feel better, go right ahead.'

Early that morning, Husam, clad by way of disguise in old clothes belonging to Abdullah's chauffeur-cousin, made his way to the Knightsbridge Underground station and from there, by a slow and devious route, to the St James's Park station. With the crowds already growing to mammoth proportions, that was as close as he could get to the palace by public transport. Now he would have to walk.

He had kept his eye peeled for Fahd at every stage of his journey. Here, so near to the parade route, was the most likely place to find him, but the station was full of people. A tall man, Husam was able to see over most of the heads, but there were so many of them.

There! At the other end of the train, just getting off. Surely that was Fahd. Husam tried to press through the crowd, but it was dense and unyielding, all bent on reaching the stairs, the only way out of the shallow station. A large handbag, slung over a woman's shoulder, banged him on the elbow as she pushed her way forward. Husam made an involuntary cry of pain, and eyes turned towards him.

Eyes, including those of Fahd. The boy saw him, and turned away, twisting through the crowd like an eel. Husam tried to follow, but he was bulkier than Fahd and was, by nature, more courteous. He made little progress, while the boy gained the stairs and hurried up them, regardless of the wake of angry protest that followed him.

Husam got to the exit in time to look up and see Fahd take off running down the street. Saw him trip and almost fall – straight into the arms of a burly policeman. The crowd divided around them, like a stream around a boulder, and allowed Husam a good view of what happened next. The policeman was joined by another, and together they restrained the struggling youth, while one of them patted him down efficiently and found a gun in a pocket, a very professional-looking gun.

Husam could not hear what was said, but he saw the hand-cuffs that were placed around Fahd's wrists, and saw him being led away.

Well, that was that. Whatever Fahd had planned to do on this day of national celebration, he would not now do it. Husam's immediate worries on that score were put to rest. Now to concentrate on getting back safely to his wife. He found a public telephone and called Abdullah to report what had happened.

'Yes,' said Abdullah when he had heard. 'That is the best thing that could have happened, for the young man, and for you. Now that he is in the hands of the police, he is safe from others who would do him harm. And you, my friend, are also safe for the moment since they know that you cannot influence the young panther. They have other reasons to hate you, but just now they also have, as the English say, other fish to fry.'

'That was my thought, also. So perhaps now Rana and I can go back to the children. That will make her happy, and me as well.'

'Ah. There is a problem, Husam. I have not yet told Rana, but . . . the children are no longer in Sherebury.'

'What! Where are they? Has someone taken them? Oh, we should never have left them! Rana will—'

'Stop. Calm yourself. I do not believe they have come to harm.' He explained, 'I did not tell Mrs Endicott when I called the inn who I was because, first, our relationship, yours and mine, is complicated and she might not understand the importance in our world of even remote family ties. And second, I did not want her to be able to trace me too easily. But my reticence meant that she did not trust me, and would not tell me where the children were.'

'How, then, can you say you believe them to be safe? You have no idea what has happened to them!'

'That is not correct. I do have an idea; I do not have exact knowledge. First, there was no sound of distress in Mrs Endicott's voice when she said they were not there. Second, if they had been abducted, *she* would have asked *me* where they were. She would have sounded frantic. Therefore I believe that the children have been taken to a place of safety by someone the Endicotts know and trust.'

'But we must find them!'

'Indeed. And I have begun to do some research into the matter. You often forget, Husam, that I am more than simply a genial old man. I have contacts. And I have the money to pay experts. We will find your children. Now. You must buy a mobile phone as soon as possible, so that I can stay in touch. Call me and give me the number. I must go.'

And he hung up the phone, leaving Husam in a state of furious frustration.

SEVEN

settled myself more comfortably on the bench. 'Right. Now I'm operating on the assumption that they are the good people they seem.'

'Not sound police practice, you know.'

'I'm not the police, and I refuse to believe the woman who gave us her views about tolerance and understanding is a terrorist. So. They are innocent of any wrongdoing, but they have disappeared. There are only two basic explanations for that: either they left of their own free will, or they have been abducted. We have a hint, though it's unreliable, that the first is more likely, so let's explore that scenario. Why would they go away suddenly, without even leaving word for the children? They're loving, caring parents, Alan. That stands out a mile.'

'Fear. They saw or heard something that made them fear for their lives. Which, given the setting, seems somewhat unlikely.'

If I hadn't been so worried, I would have laughed. My husband has lost some of his English ways since marrying me, but the habit of understatement remains. 'Somewhat,' I agreed. 'But they could have had a threatening phone call.'

'Phones shut off for the concert.'

'Or muted. Set to vibrate only.'

'Mmm. Possible, I suppose, though I wonder if they would have noticed that during the concert. If they did leave just after "Hallelujah!", as now seems possible, could they have heard, or rather felt, the call during that powerful chorus?'

'Who knows? If they did get a call, someone might have seen one of them take a phone out of a pocket. Husam, I suppose. Do Muslim women have pockets in their trousers, or whatever they wear under those stunning tunics? Anyway, posit a phone call, or at least a text. *Something* had to pull them away. It could easily have been a threat of some sort. And oh, Alan! That would explain why they erased the records of incoming calls, and didn't tell anybody where they were going or why. They had to keep it a secret, for the sake of the children.'

Alan frowned. 'I don't follow that.'

'Oh. It's quite clear in my own mind, but I'm not sure I can explain it. Someone has threatened them – the parents, I mean. The bad guys are coming to get them, so they have to get away fast, and they have to go to a place where they can't be found, and no one must know where it is, not even Peter and Greta, because they might accidentally let something slip, and then . . .' I trailed off. 'Oh, well, no, I guess it doesn't quite hang together, does it? Maybe they were just afraid that there was no time, that if they went to get the children, the bad guys might catch up with them all.'

'Perhaps. There could be other reasons, of course. They could have had a message that urgently required their presence elsewhere.'

'Like what? A family member desperately ill or in trouble? They would have taken the time to get the kids, or at least tell Peter and Greta what was happening. Alan, I wish Jane were here. She's so sensible. I go off tilting at windmills, and she brings me back down to reality.'

'But she isn't here, so if we're to go on speculating, we have to rely on ourselves to stay grounded. Now, have we exhausted the reasons why they might have decamped?'

'I suppose. Anyway, I can't think of anything else right now. Oh, Watson, NO!'

Led by the bulldogs, he was trying to get into a dense clump of gorse, I suppose after a bird or a small mammal of some sort. The bulldogs, smaller and with a much shorter coat, could get through. Watson, who is mostly spaniel, with long fluffy ears, could not, not without scratching himself badly and collecting hundreds of thorns in his coat. Alan took off after him, with a turn of speed impressive in a man his age with a recently healed ankle, and got his collar just before he sportingly hurled himself into the thicket.

'Now, sir! What do you mean by playing the fool? That is a *very bad dog*!'

Watson knew perfectly well that he'd been naughty. He flattened himself into a remorseful attitude and looked up with the liquid eyes that make it almost impossible to stay angry with him.

I stood. 'He managed to collect quite a few thorns, just getting that close. I think it's time to round up the others and go home.'

Alan had a few treats in his pocket. He whistled for Jane's dogs, shaking the bag, and they came trotting up, drooling.

Having dealt with all the dogs, a lengthy process involving feeding everyone and cleaning up Watson, Alan poured me some bourbon and himself some Scotch. We checked the phones for any possibly important messages, and took ourselves out to the back garden.

'It looks so peaceful,' I moaned. 'Only a few days ago I said it was paradise.'

'You forgot about the ever-present serpent.'

'Yes, and it doesn't do to forget about him, does it? Ah, well, where had we got to in our uninspired analysis?'

'I believe we'd exhausted our ideas about why the Ahmads might have left voluntarily.'

'We didn't come up with anything brilliant, did we? And truly, I hate to consider the other alternative.'

'That they've been abducted. We need to face it, Dorothy. That's by far the most likely scenario, the mysterious phone call notwithstanding. Gone without a word, with only the clothes on their backs, and leaving their children – it's hardly reasonable to suppose they'd do that if they weren't operating under duress.'

'I suppose. Well, then, why would someone steal them away?'

'As Derek said, ransom. His firm would presumably pay a great deal to get him back unharmed.'

'But there's been no demand for ransom. Derek would have let us know.'

Alan shook his head. 'That's often the way kidnappers work, Dorothy. A brief interval before the demand is useful for increasing tension, increasing the likelihood that the victim will meet the demand without question, because he's so terrified of what might happen if he does not.'

'And one of the demands is always "Don't tell the authorities, or we'll kill."'

'And sometimes they do just that. In fact, usually they have planned all along to kill.' I shuddered involuntarily. 'Sorry, love, but there are a good many evil people in the world. But of course in the case of as important a person as Husam Ahmad, there's always the other reason for taking him and his wife.'

'Hostages. I'm afraid I've been thinking that all the time, but I thought maybe if I didn't let it come to the surface, it wouldn't be real. Silly, but you know what I mean.'

'I imagine it was the first possibility to cross Derek's mind. Honestly, it's the most likely, love. Wealthy, peace-loving, squeaky clean politically—'

'What does that mean? And how do you know?'

'I looked them up, of course, just after we met them. If we were going to be neighbours for a few days, and perhaps friends, I wanted to know what we were getting into. Don't look at me that way! No, I was not "profiling" them because they're Iraqis. But their nationality makes them to some extent an unknown quantity, and where you are concerned, my dear, I take no chances. So I did some fairly thorough research into both of them, concentrating on him because—'

'Because the Middle Eastern world is a man's world even more than the West. I need a refill, please.'

When he handed my glass back to me, I said, 'Okay. So what did you find out?'

'In brief, that he is a highly-respected businessman, both in Iraq and in the West. You were right; he works for an oil company, UniPetro. He makes an impressive salary, and there has never been the slightest hint of any shady dealing in anything he's put his hand to. He has never expressed any political views of any stripe, and in Iraq, that's most unusual; I gather infants imbibe political views with their mothers' milk. The country is extremely politicized, and is said to be rife with corruption, but no taint of any of this has touched the Ahmad family. He does his job, and does it extremely well, and practices his religion with devotion. She looks after her household and her children, and her neighbours have only good things to say about her. Squeaky clean, as I said.' He sipped his whisky. 'And that makes them obvious candidates for hostage-taking. "We're going to take these well beloved

people and hold them in unpleasant conditions until you . . ."
Fill in the blank.'

I put my glass down. It would be all too easy to find comfort
in oblivion, but there was no ultimate solution in a bottle. 'I'm
going to make coffee,' I said, standing up and ignoring glares
from both cats. 'Clear thinking is what's needed right now.
And then we'd better have something to eat. I can't remember;
did we have any lunch?'

'I don't think so, but it's been quite a day. Is there something
in the freezer? You shouldn't have to cook.'

'And with my mind in the state it is, I'm not sure I could,
anyway. Yes, the last time I made cottage pie I made a spare.'

'Excellent. It'll take a while to defrost and warm up, so I'll
start that process while you make coffee.'

We settled once more in the parlour. It was far too warm for
a fire, which was a pity, because nothing is quite so calming as
watching a fire. Petting cats comes close, but our two were
annoyed with us – too much time away from them, too jumpy
and unsettled. They had gone off somewhere, probably to find
something breakable and/or messy. Watson settled with us, of
course, but that just reminded me of Jane's dogs, which reminded
me of Jane and our missing friends.

'Because they have become friends, haven't they? In such
a short time.'

Alan is used to my remarks that begin in mid-paragraph,
as it were. 'Yes, and that's rather remarkable, if you think
about it. We come from such different cultures, and yet we
seem to have so much in common.'

'You know, I've been thinking about that. The externals are
different, but honestly, I think people of good will have basic-
ally the same ideals and the same goals. We may differ on the
ways to practice those ideals and achieve those goals, but we
want the same things, in the end. I keep thinking about Rodney
King. You remember Rodney King?'

Alan nodded. '"Why can't we all just get along?", right?
I'll tell you why.' He put down his coffee cup with some force,
and his tone of voice made Watson look up, worried again.
'The trouble comes when not only the goals but the means
are in conflict, and that begins with "I'm right, and because

you differ from me, you're wrong, and you have to conform to my ideas, or else!'"

'But that's what I meant when I talked about people of good will. Part of that is respecting other people's points of view. I don't agree with some of what I know of the precepts of Islam. But I respect the right of Muslims to live their lives their own way, and I expect them to respect my right to do the same. As long as we can do that, we can be friends with the Ahmads, and share our love of music with them, and even our love of God, knowing that we have different ideas about him. But when people abandon good will, then yes, you're right, hatred comes in, and then chaos and anarchy.'

Watson, who was sitting at Alan's feet, got up laboriously and lumbered over to lick my hand, his cure for human distress.

'Dorothy,' Alan mused, 'why are we getting philosophical about all this?'

'To avoid thinking about what might be happening to the Ahmads.'

As if on cue, Alan's phone rang. I jumped; Watson whined. His people were not happy, so he was not happy.

Alan mouthed, 'Derek' at me, and then listened, saying very little.

When he clicked off, I said, 'Well?'

'Abdullah, I was not able to find a phone in any shop nearby. I am in a call box. Have you learned anything?'

'Yes. We think the children have possibly gone with a friend named Langland, Jane Langland. She is an elderly lady who loves children. She lives near the Cathedral, but is probably not able to care for active children herself. She has family, young people, who live in a London suburb called Bexley. She is a good friend to the Endicotts and to Mrs Martin and Mr Nesbitt, and attended the concert last evening. She would have known of the situation and would have wanted to help the children. Her family, a grandson and his wife, are named Mr and Mrs Tubbs. The English do have peculiar names, do they not?' He read off an address to Husam. 'No one has phoned them to make sure the children are there, again for reasons of security. Now, here is how you can find their house . . .'

EIGHT

Alan sighed. 'They've had a demand.'
'Oh, no!'
'It was bound to happen.'
'From whom, and a demand for what?'
'A great deal of money, and the release of prisoners from one of the Islamic terrorist cells.'
I drank some of my now-cold coffee. My mouth had gone dry. 'I suppose there's a deadline.' How horribly ominous that everyday word sounded when it meant exactly what it said.
'Yes. And that's one of the things that make them sure the communication is bogus.'
'Bogus!'
'Yes. The deadline is tomorrow at sunrise. The money is to be paid in cash. Anyone with any sense would know that it's impossible to obtain several millions in twenty-pound notes in such a short time, especially with banks closed over the weekend.'
'Maybe banks operate differently in the Middle East, or they thought some bank manager might be persuaded to open, given the emergency situation.'
'Perhaps. But the real giveaway is that two of the prisoners they are demanding in return for the Ahmads were in fact extradited back to Iraq last week. It was kept very quiet, but a real terrorist group would have known by now.'
I sank back into the sofa cushions with a sigh. 'Then we know no more than we did.'
'Exactly. Come on, love. Let's have our meal.'
The cats condescended to reappear when we went to the kitchen to dish up our supper, probably drawn by the smell of food rather than any desire to forgive our neglect of them. Of course I got out food for them, too, and then of course Watson had to have some, so what with one thing and another we were in a somewhat more normal frame of mind when we finally sat down to eat.

'Thank God for the animals,' said Alan, slipping Sam a spoonful of mashed potatoes under the table.

'They do keep us focussed on the basics, don't they? Food and shelter.'

'And love,' he said with a smile, gently pulling one of Watson's long silky ears.

We didn't talk about anything in particular until we were tidying up the kitchen, but mindless activity leads to conversation, and of course we couldn't keep away from it.

'I keep feeling like we should be doing something, but I can't think what,' I said as I loaded the dishwasher. 'This is such a big deal, not like the problems we've usually encountered, with people we knew, or at least an atmosphere we were familiar with. This is all so unfamiliar. International politics, religious differences – it's so obviously beyond our scope.'

'You forget, love,' said Alan tolerantly, 'that I was involved in a good deal of high-level consultation back when I was a working cop.'

'You know, I had forgotten. That time you went to . . . was it Zimbabwe?'

'It was, and you may also remember that it was for a conference on terrorism. Of course things have got much worse since then.'

'Yes, and it doesn't help that world leaders, even, keep meeting hatred and bigotry with reprisals and more hatred! Can't *anyone* see that's like trying to put out a fire with kerosene?'

'Paraffin, darling, on this side of the Atlantic. And the answer is that it takes a great deal of patience and diplomacy to find ways of dealing with conflict other than using military force.' He sighed and put down the salad bowl he was drying. 'I'm afraid those qualities are sadly lacking in some leaders on both sides of the battle.'

'And here are our friends, lovely, reasonable people, caught in the middle of the mess! I'm scared, Alan! This could all blow up into something horrible.'

'I'm afraid you're right, love. Let's plan to go to the early service tomorrow.'

The early Sunday service at Sherebury Cathedral, and many

Anglican churches, is a simple service of Holy Communion, with no music, no frills. It's usually held in one of the chapels, since it doesn't draw the tourists who are looking for the spectacular, only those parishioners and a few visitors who want time to pray and meditate in peace and quietness. 'That's an excellent idea. Good for what ails us. But it means we'd better get to bed pretty soon.'

I looked out the kitchen window. At almost nine o'clock, the sky looked like late afternoon. Not exactly conducive to sleep, even though it had been an exhausting day. Oh, well, I could pretend I was getting ready for a nap.

Alan's phone rang just as I was dropping into that first delicious sleep. He doesn't usually bring it up with him, but in the middle of a crisis he likes to keep it close by. He answered it sleepily, just as I turned over and snuggled into my pillow. But at his first sharp 'What!' I was wideawake.

He listened intently, asking one or two questions. As soon as he ended the call, he got up and began to pull on clothes.

'What is it?'

'That was Jane. Rahim has disappeared.'

It was a long and tiresome journey to Bexley, which was not on the Tube line. Husam didn't think it wise to call attention to himself by taking a cab for what would be a very expensive trip, even had he been carrying enough cash. Nor did he think a visit to a cashpoint was a good idea. These things are easily traced. So he made his way to the nearest mainline station where he could catch a train to Bexley. The distance was not great, but the train was crowded with those who had come into town for the royal festivities. Husam had to stand, and he was weary enough with worry to make that irksome. Nevertheless, he kept a close watch on his fellow travellers. None of them seemed to be paying him the least attention, but he was careful. Abdullah thought the danger was now minimal. Husam was not at all sure, and he dared not lead enemies to his children.

At least the house where he hoped the children were to be found was not far from the station, and he was able to follow Abdullah's excellent directions on foot. His way led, on occasion, down narrow alleys or pedestrianized streets, the better to confound anyone who was trying to follow him in a car. No one was, so far as he could tell. He reached the house, said a brief prayer, climbed the steps, and knocked, hoping at any moment to hear the excited voices of his children.

He heard nothing. There was no sign of life about the house at all. He knocked again, and rang the bell. He tried to peer through the lace curtain that covered the window next to the front door.

No one answered. There was no sound. Plainly no one was at home.

Eventually, his heart sore, he went back down the steps in search of a public phone. He couldn't find one closer than the railway station, and then he discovered he was nearly out of change. The phone accepted credit cards, but he was wary of using one. He was also, he discovered, extremely hungry. He left the station, bought a stale sandwich and a candy bar at a small shop next door, and paid with a twenty-pound note, requesting his change in as much silver as the shopkeeper could spare. The shopkeeper was not best pleased, but he handed over the cash in heavy pound coins that weighted Husam's pocket and made his trousers sag alarmingly. The sandwich he viewed with some distaste. He wasn't sure what was in it, but it was almost certainly not halal. Perhaps he should eat only the candy, though that might also contain forbidden products.

His stomach made alarming noises; he felt himself dizzy. It had been a long and trying day. He begged Allah's pardon if he was about to sin, but it was, he felt, a case of necessity. He ate, tidily threw away the wrappings, and returned to the station.

'Abdullah, no one is there. I am sure it was the right house, but no one is at home. Have you any suggestions?'

There was a considering silence. Then: 'The two young people, Mr and Mrs Tubbs, are both employed at museums, the man at the Museum of London and the woman at the Bethnal Green Museum of Childhood. It is possible that they have taken the children to one or both, to keep them amused. Take the train back to London Charing Cross. From there go to the Bethnal Green Tube station, and they can give you directions to the Museum of Childhood. That is perhaps the most likely, and you will have time to visit only one, for they both close in about an hour and a half. Hurry, man!'

The crowds impeded him. He tried to be inconspicuous, and keep an eye out for anyone who might pose a danger, but it wasn't easy. He just missed a train into London and had to wait for the next, and then when he got to Charing Cross and discovered he would have to change at Tottenham Court Road to get to the Central Line and Bethnal Green, his anxiety mounted. What if he was too late, and the museum had closed before he could get there? What if the children had never been there at all? How could he tell Rana that their children were somewhere in Greater London, among its teeming millions?

Before today, it had been a long time since Husam had used public transport, and he fumed at the delays. He dared not seem to hurry. That had been Fahd's mistake, calling attention to himself by running, in his desperate attempt to get away. But he couldn't help looking at his watch every few moments. So little time. Such a slow train. What if he couldn't find them? Horrible possibilities kept presenting themselves to his imagination; he couldn't drive them away.

At last, at last, he reached the Bethnal Green Station. Signs pointed him toward the museum; he was grateful he had not had to ask. Only a few minutes until they closed, if Abdullah had been right. And Abdullah was usually right. He reached the street and set off at the slowest pace he could make himself take.

NINE

Alan called Derek as I dressed hastily and filled a Thermos with coffee. Then we went to the car and he explained to me as he backed the car out of our minute garage. 'Walter and Sue took the kids to the Museum of Childhood today. Sue thought Aya would like the dolls' houses, and there's a good deal there for boys as well. Jane went along, determined not to let the children out of her sight, no matter what.'

'She's not a young woman. Trailing after children in a museum would be hard on her feet and her stamina, but she's stubborn. But what *happened*?'

'It was after they'd seen the displays and had a snack in the café, just before the museum closed for the day. They'd come by Tube since it's so hard to park. They were walking to the station very slowly because the children were tired, and suddenly Rahim shouted, tore his hand away from Walter's and ran as fast as he could. The streets were crowded, and by the time Sue and Walter reacted and Walter ran after him, he'd lost himself in the crowd.'

'But what did he shout?'

'It was in Arabic, love. They didn't know what he'd said until they'd given up the hunt and gone home. They'd found a bobby on the beat and asked his help, but there was no sign of the boy. Sue was busy trying to console Aya, who was crying as if her heart would break. Jane, of course, was beyond upset. And when they got back to the flat, the child finally quieted and told them that her brother had cried out "Father!".'

'Oh, dear heaven! He'd seen his dad?'

'Or thought he had.'

It took me some time to process that. The night flashed by, not yet dark on this June evening. We drove through a few villages, quiet except for some activity around the pubs, and then the lights of London began to appear.

'All right,' I said with a sigh. 'Go on.'

'Dorothy, that's absolutely all I know until we get there. Is that coffee you have there? I could use some; we're going to hit London traffic any minute now, and it will be frightful. Today was the official queen's birthday, you know.'

'Oh, *no*! I'd forgotten all about it. That's going to complicate everything.'

Alan didn't even bother to reply.

Queen Elizabeth was born in April, but (English weather being what it is) her birthday is celebrated on the second Saturday in June, so there is a better chance of sunshine for the ceremonies, including the Trooping the Colour, the big parade. I usually watched the proceedings avidly on television, but crises had driven it right out of my mind.

I made a quick call to Margaret, asking her to round up volunteers to look after the various animals we were deserting. Then I clicked off and shut up, the better to let Alan concentrate on driving.

The traffic was horrendous – the big city at the end of one of the biggest royal events of the year. Fortunately Walter and Sue lived in a suburb, and on the southeast, so we didn't have to negotiate central London to get there, but it still took much longer than I could easily bear. My nerves were stretched to the limit by the time Alan pulled up in front of their flat. 'I'll be with you the moment I find a parking spot.'

'Yes. Meanwhile, I'm going to call Jonathan.'

'Splendid idea.' He waved and moved away.

Jonathan Quinn is an old friend, a policeman who was awarded the George Cross for heroism in the incident that left him too badly injured to continue his career. For some years now he's been a private detective operating out of London, and had been instrumental in helping Walter out of a nasty mess some time ago. Rahim might be easily found. He might be home by now. But if not, we were going to need all the help we could get, and Jonathan was our man.

Walter was waiting for me at the door. 'No news?' I asked, though I could see the answer in his face.

He shook his head. 'Sue and Gran have finally got Aya to sleep. Gran is beside herself. She blames herself for not taking better care of the boy.'

'Which is nonsense. She brought him to you, where, of all places, he ought to have been safe.'

'I've been trying to tell her that. Come in. Maybe she'll see sense if you say it. I'm still a kid to her.'

'I'll try, but first I'm going to call Jonathan. I hope I have his number on my phone.'

Walter smacked his head. 'Why didn't I think of that! We've stayed in touch; I have his number, both the office and his mobile.'

Alan came in while Walter was finding the number on his phone. He handed the phone to me and I passed it along to Alan. Jonathan and I had a good relationship, and he'd listen patiently to me, but I was not his revered mentor, as Alan had been and to some extent still was. When Alan spoke, Jonathan snapped to.

'Walter, where's Jane?'

'In the kitchen, making a pot of tea.'

'Of course.'

I took a deep breath and headed for the kitchen. Jane was usually the one to comfort me, or brace me up as the occasion demanded. I wasn't sure I was up for the role reversal.

Jane was stumping around the kitchen, finding a tray, cups, and sugar, while Sue sat and told her where to look. I looked at both of them in surprise. Sue wasn't the type to let someone else do the work, nor was Jane accustomed to taking over another woman's kitchen.

Sue patted another chair at the kitchen table. 'Dorothy, sit down. We're all pretty well done in by what's happened.' She lowered her voice. 'And Jane feels better when she's doing something useful.'

I nodded, seeing Sue's wan face, and then something made me look at her more closely. 'And that's not the whole reason, is it?'

She grimaced. 'How did you know? I'm still in regular clothes.'

'I have a lot of nephews and nieces, who in due course have produced great-nephews and -nieces, and great-greats. There's a look, even early on. When are you due?'

'Not till late November or so. I've been feeling like nothing

'Yes, I agree. It's ridiculous and counter-productive, but there it is. Alan says there was a time when the different branches of law enforcement worked together fairly peaceably, but things like politics and budget cuts have undermined that. Duncan is sure to throw his weight around and try to boss the others.'

'Alan can't be bossed,' said Sue. 'He's retired. And Jonathan isn't in the police anymore, either.'

'He has a license, though, which can be revoked. He'll have to be careful not to tread on official toes.'

'Up to us,' said Jane.

'We're not under any authority, are we? Except the law, of course.'

Jane barked a laugh. 'Never held you back before.'

'I've never actually broken any laws! Well – no important ones, anyway, and all for the sake of justice. But I've never been up against MI5 before. Scares me to death, if you want to know.'

'Doesn't matter. What about the kids?'

Jane taught school for many years. She adores children of all ages, and is ruthlessly single-minded about them.

'But Jane, it does matter.' I took a deep breath. 'Yes, Rahim must be found. But so must his parents. When word gets out that they're missing – and it will get out, very soon – all kinds of hell will break loose. Extremists on both sides will start spouting rhetoric and planning action. Alert levels will go up. All the security agencies in the country will gird themselves for action. Rahim and his parents could become pawns in the hands of a lot of powerful people, including Mr Duncan in there. So the sooner they're found, the better. And I don't have the slightest idea how to go about it.'

'I have an idea,' ventured Sue shyly. 'I mean, I've never done anything like this before, but I think the official police will start looking in Bethnal Green, since that's where he ran away.'

'And where he saw his father. Or thought he did.'

'Yes. And the MI5 people will be looking for the father. But I think – I mean, this is just my idea – that Bethnal Green is the very last place either of them will be found.'

Jane and I looked at her intently.

'Because they're neither of them stupid. I never met the father, but Rahim is a very intelligent little boy. He would know everyone's looking for him, and so would his father. So they'll go elsewhere. At least I think so.'

'Probably right,' said Jane, 'but . . .?'

'But there's an awful lot of "elsewhere" in London,' I said, sighing. 'That's even if they're still *in* London.'

'Mainline station nearby,' Jane contributed. 'Go anywhere from there.'

'Oh!' My exclamation made them both jump. 'But we're forgetting Mrs Ahmad. She's with her husband, or at least they left Sherebury together.'

'Don't know that. Left Rose and Crown together.'

'Blast it all, Jane! You're complicating matters. You're right. They could have separated. But as that leads us nowhere, can we agree for the moment that they're probably together?'

Jane shrugged. 'Then still in London. No idea where.'

And there we stuck. Greater London, including the suburbs like Bexley, is home to well over eight million people. Not to mention the thousands upon thousands of tourists who throng the city at almost any time of year, but especially in summer and most especially for royal spectacles.

'If I were a horse, where would I be?'

The other two just looked at me.

'Didn't someone say something like that? Maybe I've got it wrong, but the idea is, if you're looking for something, you imagine you're that something, and figure out where you might have gone. The trouble is, it doesn't work for me this time. I can't imagine myself a Muslim couple in an alien land where lots of people think I'm weird, at best, and a mortal threat, at worst.'

'Back to front,' said Jane.

This time I was the one giving the funny look.

'Change places,' she said impatiently. 'An American in Baghdad, hated and feared. Where do you go?'

'Well. Gosh. I suppose to a church, a Christian church, if I can find one.'

'That would be very dangerous, Dorothy,' said Sue. 'I've

been reading a lot about Christians in the Middle East, since the last few terrorist attacks here. I don't know if Christian visitors are persecuted, but Iraqi Christians can be killed – a lot have been – or deported.'

'But – but that means it could be dangerous for the Ahmad family to visit Christian churches even here in England!'

'Yes,' said both Jane and Sue.

I was shaken. 'I knew they were courageous people,' I said, 'but I had no idea . . . why, they could have been taken by their own people and . . .' I couldn't go on.

'Point is,' said Jane, 'might go to a mosque.'

'I suppose there are mosques in London,' I said dubiously.

'Hundreds of them,' said Sue. Her tone was gentle, almost the way one would talk to a mentally-challenged child.

'Oh, good grief. Of course there are. I think I need to go home to bed. My brain is not responding, like some of my computer programs now and then. Except – Jane, wouldn't Sue's argument apply here, too? Anyone, friend or foe, who was looking for them might expect them to go to a mosque, so perhaps they wouldn't risk it?'

TEN

We had reached that stage in our unproductive reasoning when a small sound from the other bedroom roused Jane. I, who never had children, am not as attuned as almost any mother to the sound of a child in distress. But Jane, who had only one child many years ago, and had to give him away because an illegitimate child in those days was a black disgrace – Jane is easily the most motherly person I know. She got to her feet as fast as her age and bulk would allow, and padded into the other room. With the door open, I could hear the sobs of the little girl, and Jane's soothing murmur. With adults she could be abrupt and caustic, with children, never.

Alan came to our door. He raised his eyebrows in question when he saw that Jane was missing. 'Aya woke up crying,' I said, and didn't need to explain further.

'The investigators would like to speak to you, Sue, if you're feeling up to it.'

'I'm fine,' she said in the slightly irritated voice of one trying to convince herself it's true. 'Just a bit tired.'

Walter appeared in the doorway. 'I've told them you need to get straight to bed,' he snapped. 'I'm damned if I'll let someone else's missing boy do anything to hurt you and our baby.'

'Yes, darling, I'll tell them I don't know anything and then go to bed.' She gave him a peck on the cheek and went into the sitting room.

'I suppose you've been plotting a course of action.' Alan tried to sound severe.

'We tried, but honestly we couldn't think of a thing to do. How in the world can anyone search for three individuals amongst perhaps nine million?'

'That, of course, is where the resources of the Met and MI5 can be useful. Every single man and woman on the force will have pictures and descriptions of the three of them by tomorrow – or they may do by now. Teams will be actively searching the Bethnal Green area and then fanning out from there. They'll search all the mosques thoroughly.'

'But you see, those might be the least likely places, because they – the Ahmads, I mean – would expect a search there.'

'Dorothy.' Alan was very tired and growing a bit testy. 'We are talking here about trained investigators. They have actually taken that idea into consideration. It is necessary to eliminate the obvious places before the search can be carried into the whole of London. Do you know how many miles of roads there are in Greater London?'

'No.'

'Neither do I, precisely, but it's well over nine thousand. Searching every building in every one of those roads is a monumental task.'

'And – I do hate to say this, Alan – but there's little reason to believe they're still in London. Rahim saw his father – and I for one do believe he really saw him – hours ago. If we're going to resort to statistics, how many miles of rail line are there on this island? And you don't have to show identification to get on a train.'

Alan was silent.

'Look, love, there is one tiny ray of sunshine in all this. If Husam Ahmad was abroad in Bethnal Green, in broad daylight, it means he and his wife were not abducted. He was free to move about.'

'Yes, I agree with your reasoning, but not with your optimistic view. His freedom of movement may prove he left Shrebury of his own free will, but we don't know what happened after that. This Abdullah person called to say he was safe, which may or may not be true, and we don't even know who "Abdullah" is. He could be a friend of the Ahmads, or an enemy – even a terrorist. Or it could be an alias. It's a very common Middle Eastern name.'

I knew Alan was right, and that didn't make me feel one bit better. I knew that the Ahmads were people of goodwill and integrity, but that made them, perhaps, even more likely targets of terrorists. The MI5 people had a responsibility to imagine a worst-case scenario, and the safety of the family might not be their primary concern.

Alan sat down next to me and took my hand. 'I know it's hard, love. I don't care for Duncan's manner, either. But he has an almost impossible job to do: try to stop terrorism before it happens, and at the same time respect everyone's rights. And recent events have made matters much worse. People have died, Dorothy. Questions are being asked in the House. Duncan can't afford to overlook any suspicious behaviour.'

I took a deep breath. 'Okay you're right, but . . . anyway, it's long past bedtime for this old lady. I can't think anymore. What are we going to do?'

'We are going to wait here until everyone who wants to ask you any questions has done so. Then you and I are going to try find a hotel for what's left of the night.'

'But the animals!'

'I've already phoned Greta to say we might not get back. Between her and Peter and Nigel and Inga, our animals, and Jane's, will be well looked-after for as long as we need to be away. And before you ask, our friends will also run into town with whatever we need if the stay is prolonged. I'm sure for one night a hotel will provide us with toothbrushes, and we can rinse out underwear and so on. And London is not exactly a desert island; it is possible to buy almost anything one might need.'

As tired and distraught as I was, the thought of substituting a hotel bed for my own brought me close to tears. Before they could roll down my face, though, Derek poked his head in the door. 'They've extracted everything they can from Sue, poor dear,' he said in a conspiratorial whisper, 'and as she's ready to drop, I thought they might take you on, so Sue can have her bedroom.' He took a closer look at me and said, 'Buck up, old thing. It'll all look better in the morning.'

Derek is an old and very dear friend.

Sue came in, looking indeed ready to drop, and after a hug to reassure both of us, I left her to her plainly much-needed bed and went out to face the barrage.

Carstairs and Duncan were weary, too, and showed it in different ways. Scotland Yard in all its glory was inclined to pomposity. MI5 was terse and not overly courteous. They took me through everything I knew about the Ahmads, which was certainly little enough. When Duncan started on a second round of exactly the same questions, I'd had enough.

'So far as I am aware, sir, I am not under suspicion of any wrongdoing. I have answered your questions, and that is enough. I am far older than you and nearly ready to collapse. If you need me tomorrow, I'll be in London. I don't know at which hotel, yet – Alan will doubtless let one of your staff know – but we will certainly attend church and will be unavailable until noon at the very earliest. Good night.'

Alan followed me out the door, closing it on the stunned silence within. 'And you're not even wearing one of your Queen Mum hats. I expected him to bow.'

'So did I. And so he ought. Alan, let's walk to the car together. If I wait for you to come and pick me up I'm afraid he'll have second thoughts and snare me again, and I swear if he does I'll finish the "Father William" misquote.'

'"Be off, or I'll kick you downstairs,"?'

'Exactly.'

It was so late that the drive into central London wasn't too bad. Most of the tourists seemed to have left town, or gone to ground. Miraculously, we got a room at the Grosvenor, in Victoria Station, and I barely had time to get out of my clothes before falling into bed and into sleep.

I didn't sleep well, though. For one thing, the only room available had twin beds, and I missed Alan's comfortable bulk beside me. Another was that the hotel, like most places in England, had no air-conditioning. On a June night, with the windows wide open, the traffic noise was obtrusive, even though we were on the side facing away from Buckingham Palace Road. The first time a big truck went past, I woke out of my first exhausted sleep and couldn't drop off again for worry about the Ahmad family – fruitless worry, for I couldn't think of a thing I could do to help them.

I eventually fell into a troubled doze full of chase dreams. You know the ones. You're trying to run somewhere, and it's vitally important, but your feet have turned to lead and your way lies through molasses, and you can hardly move. I was actually relieved when Alan shook me.

'Mmph. What time is it?'

'Nearly half nine. I hated to wake you, but given our worries, I thought you might like to take in the Eucharist at the Abbey, and it's at quarter past eleven. I went down to the station and got your favourite almond croissant, and the water's just boiling for coffee.'

'Ugh. My eyes feel like someone's sandpapered them. And I only have jeans to put back on. Wrinkled jeans. Not fit for the Abbey.'

'There's an iron in the closet. Darling, I don't think God cares how you're dressed, and we can sit at the back. Into the shower, now, and I'll have coffee for you when you're ready.'

God might not care how I was dressed, but I cared, and the thought of going into the church of the royal family dressed like a hick from the sticks really bothered me. I was fuming when I got out of the shower, ready to tell Alan I'd skip church this morning, for once.

I had reckoned without his administrative ability. I emerged wearing a towel to see him flourishing, not just the cup of coffee I so badly needed, but a large carrier bag bearing a logo.

'Wha-at?'

'You're very fetching in that attire, my dear, but this might be more to your liking. Sit down and drink your coffee while I show you.'

He took out of the bag a pair of black slacks, a white shirt, a black-and-white scarf, a lightweight black jacket, and a set of undies. 'I should know your sizes after all this time,' he said smugly.

'But how – where . . .?'

'There's a new shop in Victoria Place. They're opening early on Sunday for a few weeks. The concierge told me about it, and a helpful shop assistant did the rest for me. I couldn't do anything about shoes, I'm afraid. One doesn't buy shoes for someone else. But those black things you wore yesterday will be fine, with . . .' And he pulled the last rabbit out of his hat, a small tin of black shoe polish.

'You are amazing.'

'Of course, love. Drink your coffee and eat your pastry, and get a move on. I'll polish your shoes. We need to catch a cab in less than half an hour.'

Alan has the annoying habit of being right much of the time. I had been sure I wasn't in the mood for prayer, but the service in that splendid church was just what I had needed. The choir was perfect, of course. One comes to expect perfection in an English cathedral. The sermon was well thought out and well delivered; the preacher had a voice that could have held me enthralled had she been reading the London telephone directory. But the bit that moved me most, almost to tears, was when we all recited the Lord's Prayer.

That's the one prayer that's common to almost every Christian worship service, of almost any denomination, in almost any country. And since Westminster Abbey draws crowds of tourists, there were people around us from a host of different countries. And they all said that prayer in their own languages. A couple right behind us spoke French. A little farther away I heard German. Those I recognized, but there were so many others I didn't know. A somewhat sing-song rendition might have been Chinese.

Thoughts flashed across my mind. 'One Lord, one faith, one baptism.' 'He's got the whole world in his hands.' 'There is one God, and Muhammad is his prophet.'

Alan pulled me back down into my seat, where everyone else was quietly waiting to go up to the altar for Communion. 'Far away, darling?'

I nodded, not yet trusting my voice. This was universal, this worship. Even the non-believers in the church, and there were certainly many of them, were caught up, for that brief time, in the spirit of oneness, of tolerance and understanding, the spirit that Rana Ahmad thought so important. And I was right back to our great worry, but now with the absolute assurance that in the end, good and right would prevail.

ELEVEN

Of course the first thing that happened, when we had left the church and were walking down Victoria Street toward our hotel, was that I tripped over an uneven paving stone and ran into a passer-by, who sported gold rings in several unlikely places and told me in bright purple language exactly what he thought of me. 'The aura never lasts long, does it?' said Alan when he had caught my elbow and made some more-or-less civil reply to my abuser.

'Hardly ever. But that doesn't make it any less real.'

'No. Now, shall we find something to eat, or go back to our room and make phone calls to find out what's happening?'

'Food first. I have the feeling that as soon as we turn our phones back on, we'll get briefings.'

There are several good pubs near the Abbey. We popped into one, got our pints and ordered our food, and turned our phones on. Before we had time for more than a sip of our drinks, Alan's phone rang. He grimaced and took it outside where he wouldn't disturb others, and I turned mine off. Let Alan deal with it for now.

He wasn't away for more than a minute or two. 'Derek reporting that there's nothing to report. The search is on, all hands to the pump.'

'And Aya? Any word on how she's doing?'

'He didn't say.'

I took a thoughtful pull at my beer. 'Alan, I've been thinking. Are there Muslims on the London police force?'

'Yes, certainly, a great many.'

'Women, as well?'

'Yes. They wear a specially-designed hijab, edged with the traditional black-and-white check. Why?'

'Aya needs a safe place to stay. Tomorrow Walter and Sue have to go back to work, and Jane is well over eighty. She's a fierce fighter for what she holds dear, but she would be no match for anyone who tried to harm that poor little girl. What if Aya could be housed temporarily with a Muslim police family? She'd feel more at home with them than with non-Muslims, I'd think, and she'd be safer.'

'Hmm. But there's the same problem. The working members of the family would be away most of the day.'

'But not necessarily at the same time. Surely it would be possible to find a family where the parents work different shifts, or there's a teenager at home most of the day when the parents aren't. And with one or both of the parents in the police, they'd have training to protect the child. And don't you see, you'd have two problems solved at once – Aya's safety, and a foot in the Muslim community here, to help find the rest of the Ahmads.'

'Right,' he said decisively. Alan the chief constable on the job. 'Brilliant. I don't know why someone didn't think of it before.'

Our ploughman's lunch arrived, but Alan pushed it aside and made a quick couple of phone calls before tucking in. 'Carstairs and Jonathan are on it. Carstairs approved, and Jonathan is still in touch with his former colleagues. Between them they'll find the right family. And Jonathan is going to phone Walter to tell him the plan.'

'They'd better include Jane in the discussion, or . . .'

'Indeed.' He turned off his phone and cut a chunk of Stilton to put on his bread. 'I'm going to get outside this before yet another crisis comes our way.'

'I wish you hadn't said that. Now I'll be thinking up horrible possibilities.'

Amazingly, the Sunday peace continued for the short time it took us to eat our meal. I debated about indulging in some sticky toffee pudding, which has to be the most extravagantly decadent dessert ever invented, but the tight waistband of my new slacks decided me against it. (Alan, bless him, had some-what underestimated my girth.)

'Alan,' I asked, having finished my beer, 'is there any reason for us to stay in London? I do love this city, but I'm getting claustrophobic. So many people, so much noise. I can't think here, and really, there doesn't seem to be anything useful we

can do. Or at least, anything I can do. You're trained for police
work, including searches. All I can contribute is an idea or
two.'

'And you've been doing splendidly in that department thus
far, but I agree that the frenetic atmosphere here isn't the best
for constructive thinking. I think I'd best stay for a bit, though.
Let's go back to the hotel and station and get you on the next
train to Sherebury.'

'I'll phone Jane first and see if she wants to come with me.
If they've found a safe place for Aya, her job here is paused
for a while, too, and I don't think she's very comfortable
sleeping on the couch. It wasn't designed for someone her
size.'

I phoned Jane's mobile when we got back out on the street,
but she didn't want to leave right then. Aya was still with her
and being clingy, and Jane was trying to convince her that she
would be safer and happier with a Muslim family.

'I understand, Jane. But I'm going to miss you a lot, so
come home as soon as you feel you can. You're my very best
sounding board; you keep me from flying off on impossible
tangents.'

'If she does that,' said my loving husband after I'd clicked
off, 'she's a miracle worker. Can you hurry a little? I just
checked the schedule, and the next train's in fifteen minutes,
with an hour's wait after that.'

England's rail system puts America's to shame, and there
are usually trains between Sherebury and London every twenty
to thirty minutes, but not on Sundays. I walked as fast as I
could and made it with at least thirty seconds to spare. Thank
goodness Alan had bought return tickets and had given mine
to me, or I'd have missed the train; there was a queue even
at the ticket machine in Victoria Station.

Once settled in my seat, I had a little leisure to think about
all that had transpired in the last – could it be less than 48
hours? Yes, two days ago Alan and I were looking forward to
Messiah and the little party afterwards, where we could get
to know those delightful people better. Now three of them
were who-knew-where, and perhaps – probably – in grave
danger. That sweet little boy who wanted to sing like an English

treble! His cosmopolitan, sensible parents, so concerned that their children grow up in an atmosphere of tolerance and respect for those with different beliefs. I absolutely rejected the idea that they could be involved in any evil enterprise.

What then?

I dug out my trusty little notebook and turned to the pages where I'd made notes about our present trouble. The train was very hot, which made intelligent thought difficult. I mentally cursed faulty air-conditioning and persevered.

I skipped over the points about abduction. I was convinced that Husam's appearance in Bethnal Green was proof that they were not being held against their will.

Except – oh, dear God!

What if they had been abducted, and Husam had escaped temporarily, only to have Rahim turn up? And then, what if both of them had been recaptured – and that's why nobody had been able to find them?

I knew that speculation without a scintilla of factual evidence was futile. I knew that. But what else could I do?

We passed meadows full of sheep, the lambs by now half-grown and not as playful as they had been earlier. This pastoral scene, usually a source of great pleasure, failed to ease my mind. It only reminded me of the close bond between parents and children, and spiked my worries about the Ahmad children. I wrenched my mind back to my futile speculations.

We'd talked about possible reasons for abduction, but hadn't got around to wondering who might have done the deed. If it was for ransom, then it could have been anybody who wanted lots of money and didn't care how they got it. The world is, unfortunately, full of such people. I passed on to the next possibility, a hostage situation. That, too, opened up a well populated field, but at least one could list possibilities. Groups like those called variously ISIS and ISIL and the Islamic State came to mind. But so far no demands had been sent, at least no legitimate ones. I was sure Alan would have called me if something new had turned up.

Of course reception wasn't always great on a train. I pulled out my phone and looked for missed calls or voicemail. None of either.

There was, I realized, one possibility we had failed to consider, and that was sheer hatred. They might have been taken by a person, or a group, who hated them and all they stood for, and intended to kill them – probably very publicly.

I shivered, despite the oven-like heat of the train. I was reminded of what Sue had said about the persecution of Christians in Iraq. Radical Islamists could have got wind of the Ahmads' interest in Christian churches and decided the family needed to be eliminated.

The heat and the motion of the train and my thoughts were making me feel very sick. Mostly my thoughts. The terrible, destructive power of hatred was overwhelming. Fear was at the root of it, of course. Fear was at the root of most sin, and hatred was one of the worst sins of all. The hate-filled cling to their way of thinking and acting. They fear anyone who threatens their beliefs, anyone who is 'wrong' by their definition. If those who are wrong cannot be forced into changing, they must be disposed of: either sent far away or killed.

I thought of the Spanish Inquisition, of the witch burnings in seventeenth-century Europe and America and, with increasing nausea, of the shameful treatment of Muslims in twenty-first-century America. If the persecutions inflicted by modern-day Muslims were horrific, we Christians had much to repent as well.

And then another thought crossed my mind, and my stomach lurched. Some years ago I'd had the misfortune of encountering, in Sherebury, the nastiest group of people I'd ever met. They called themselves the Chapel of the One True God, and believed, as far as I could tell, in self-righteousness, bigotry, punishment for what they decided was sin, and burning hatred of everyone who did not believe as they did. As always in these fringe cults, a great deal of hypocrisy ran under the surface; investigations had uncovered skimming of communal funds, sexual irregularities, and everything one might expect from those whose guiding principle was sheer hatred.

I was reasonably sure that the organization – I refused to call it a church – had been disbanded after their leaders had been involved in criminal activities. It might have collapsed under its own weight of enmity. But its members were almost certainly still around, poisoning Sherebury with their vile distortion of Christian doctrine. What if they were among those who attended *Messiah* and grumbled at the presence of Muslims? What if they had decided these infidels had to be disciplined? Or destroyed?

The meadows rolling past the train windows gave way to houses, and the spires of the Cathedral appeared on the horizon. I was nearly home, and seldom have I been so relieved to exchange the gritty, toxic prison of my thoughts for the fresh, sane environs of the Cathedral and her people.

It was usually Jane who met me at the station, when Alan was away, but of course she was still in London. I was looking around for a taxi when a car pulled up next to me. 'Where to, lady?' asked a man in a terrible attempt at a New York accent.

'Nigel! You darling! But shouldn't you be at the university doing whatever esoteric things you do?' Nigel is top man in the mysteriously named IT department, and though I use a computer, I find their inner workings baffling. Nigel can make them turn handsprings, I think.

'Peter called me. Alan had called him to say you were on your way, and since the pub is really, really busy just now, Peter asked me to play chauffeur. And as our students are on recess, I'm not quite so pushed.'

By that time I had settled myself in the passenger seat and was being whisked along Sherebury's narrow, inconvenient, beloved streets.

'So I'm almost twenty-four hours behind on the saga, and the way things are going, that could cover a lot of action. Bring me up to date.'

'You may not know the details of Rahim's disappearance.' I recited them, briefly. 'Other than that, I'm not sure anything momentous has happened, except that all the authorities who could get into the act have done so, including MI5.'

'And I suppose they're throwing their weight about.'

'Territorial wars are imminent, although Alan managed to achieve an uneasy truce last night.'

'He's rather good at the oil-on-troubled-waters bit, isn't he?'

That from a Brit, I thought with an inward smile, was the equivalent of the Medal of Honour. 'He is, but I don't know how long the truce will hold. The various groups have different goals. MI5 want to ensure the security of the country, and they're under a lot of pressure. The Met wouldn't mind finding the lost, but that's not their chief concern, either. London, her people and her infrastructure, must be protected, and incidentally the reputation of the police must not be blackened. Of course the rest of us are frantic to know what's happened to the Ahmad family, so that's what Jonathan is working on for us, but he has to be careful not to get in anyone's way. And Alan and I are trying our best to work out possible scenarios, but there's so little to go on, it's really just sheer speculation.'

'Your speculations have been known to be spot on,' my driver said, 'to the benefit of a number of people. Far be it from me to try to counsel my elders—'

'Hah! Since when?'

'—but as I'm very nearly an honorary grandson, I think I'm entitled to suggest that you're discouraged because you're tired. I'm going to drop you off at the Rose and Crown and let my in-laws take you in hand.'

'Oh, my dear, I can't think of anything I'd like better. At least, is the place crammed with tourists?'

Nigel grinned and waved a hand out the window. 'On a June day straight out of Eden? They're hanging from the chandeliers. But Peter and Greta told me – you've guessed this is their idea – that they could put you in their own parlour, and you could be alone with your thoughts and a glass of something rejuvenating, or Greta could keep you company if you like.'

He drove through the gate into the Close and stopped the car at the Rose and Crown's front door. 'I might even join you for a drink, if you don't mind, that is. The Nipper and Greta Jane are both down for naps after a strenuous round of drive-Mum-bonkers, so I don't feel guilty about leaving Inga for a bit.'

'In that case I'd be delighted to have your company.'

'Be with you in a sec, after I park the car round back.'

Greta, who was at the front desk surrounded by guests checking in or out, smiled at me and nodded toward the back premises. 'Be with you when I can,' she said cheerily. 'Just let Peter know what you'd like.'

The day was far too warm for my usual bourbon to sound good. I walked into the bar, where Peter was just as busy as Greta. 'Ah, Dorothy. What can I get you?'

'G and T, please, Peter. Lots of T, and please may I have ice?'

'As if I didn't know, after all these years. One American G and T coming up. You know your way. Your Glenfiddich, sir,' he said, turning to another customer.

That's Alan's favourite whisky. Just hearing the name made me miss him.

The Endicotts' private parlour looked out on the Rose and Crown's lovely back garden, where flowers ran riot. With the French windows wide open, the fragrance filled the parlour. I dropped into one of the squashy chintz chairs and closed my eyes, the better to enjoy the peace. So quiet, just the sound of bees buzzing among the flowers, and the occasional bird singing to the sun. So peaceful . . .

'Oof!' A soft, heavy weight landed in my lap. I opened my eyes on Max, the British Blue who had ruled the pub for some time. He was the father of both my cats, and indeed of most of the kittens in the neighbourhood. I like Max, but I could have done without his attentions just then.

'Oh, for pity's sake push him away, Dorothy.' Peter put my drink and a little plate of cheese biscuits on the table next to my chair. 'Max, go chase a rabbit or something. He never catches any of them, you know. He's far too fat and slow, but he has great ambitions.'

Of course Max knew he was being talked about, and it was Peter's comments about his weight that caused him to jump down and stalk out of the room, tail indignantly erect. He doesn't care to be criticized.

'Sorry about that. He was asleep in the garden, but of course he had to come and pay his respects.'

'It's all right. I was just about to fall asleep.' I took a sip of my drink. 'This is perfect, Peter. Exactly what I needed.'

'I'll leave you to it, then. Sorry, but you know how it is.'

I relaxed back against the cushions, even while knowing

that if I stayed there very long I'd fall asleep again, and if I slept I'd dream, and they would not be the kind of dreams I would enjoy. I was just trying to struggle out of the chair's embrace when Greta came in.

'Oh, is there something you need? I'll get it for you.'

'No, I was just going to get a magazine or something to keep me awake. This room is far too comfortable.'

'It is, isn't it? It's a real oasis when we're so busy.'

'And you're still busy, and I feel awful about taking you away from your duties.'

'Not to worry. Nigel came in just now, and I asked him to stay at the desk. He's perfectly capable of dealing with that side of things for a bit. The fact is, I wanted to talk to you. Peter and I have a problem, and we don't know what to do.'

'In that case, do sit down. That sounds funny from me, when it's your own house! But I hope I can help, though my mind's turned to cream cheese.'

TWELVE

S he sat, far more gracefully than I had, in the chair opposite me. The sun from the garden lit her hair, now more silver than gold, like a halo. Her face, with a few more lines than when Frank and I had first met her, was still beautiful. Her beauty was in the bone; she would be beautiful, and glamorous, in her shroud.

She was having a little trouble getting started. I finished my drink and waited.

'It's a question of money, you see,' she said finally.

'Oh, dear. Of course the Ahmads left their bill unpaid. I'm sure Alan will—'

'No, it's not that. We're not worried about that. This is . . . well. You'll understand we've had to pack up their things to store.'

'I'd have thought the police might have taken them away.'

'No, they looked through everything, of course, very thoroughly, but when they found nothing of interest, they told us we could keep it here in case the couple returned. That's the way they put it: "In case they return."'

'Well, it's the job of the police to be sceptical. I'm sure myself that they will come back.'

'I hope you're right. I like them very much, and I admire them for what they're trying to do, restore a little sense to the attitudes toward foreigners!'

Greta, born in Germany in the fifties, knew exactly what it was like to be treated like an enemy alien. When her parents brought her to England, they could not find any work suited to their qualifications. She and her siblings were, Greta had told me, sneered at and bullied at school. Eventually the family moved out of London to Sherebury, where people were kinder. Her father was hired at the university to teach German and her mother found work as a baker, and the family survived. She met Peter, whose family had owned the Rose and Crown for generations, and gradually she lost her accent and was accepted. But the pain was still there, under the surface.

'So I trust them,' Greta went on, 'and pray for them every day, and we will keep their belongings as long as necessary. But when the police came, we had forgotten about the other bag that Husam had given us. He said he wouldn't need it while he was here, and asked us to lock it away in the luggage storeroom. We found it when we were putting away the other bags, and Peter wondered if we should tell the police.'

'I think you should, if that's what's bothering you. They'll understand why you didn't mention it earlier.'

'No, that's not it. I thought we should take a look first, to see if it was worth bothering about. Because the police might not . . . well, anyway, it was locked, but with a combination lock. Those are usually very easy to guess. People use their address, or phone number, or birthday.'

'And you had much of that information from their registration.' I tried to sound neutral.

'Please! It was not prying. You do not understand, I think.' She was sounding more German by the minute. 'You have never been afraid of the police, never had to hide. I did not want them to come back and scold us, just for nothing.'

'So you opened it.'

'Yes, and oh, how I wish I had not! Because what was inside was money. A great deal of money, in different currencies. Pounds, euros, dollars, and what I suppose to be dinars. At least they're printed in Arabic. But Dorothy, what should we do with it? I haven't counted any of it. I haven't even touched it, but the stacks of the different currencies were side by side and I could see that there was a very great deal of money. And the police will be very angry, and I don't know what to do!'

'What does Peter think?' I asked, stalling for time while I tried to process this unexpected and most disturbing development.

'He doesn't know. The storage room is in the attic. He was down working in the bar when I opened the case.'

'And this happened when?'

'Early this morning, before opening time.'

'And you closed it up again?'

'But of course! And put it back where I had found it.'

'All right. Now, Greta, this is important. Did you touch any of the money at all?'

'No. I opened the lid and saw it and closed it again as fast as I could.'

'Good. What did you touch on the outside of the case?'

'Let me think.' She closed her eyes, picked up an imaginary suitcase, laid it on an imaginary surface, made some rather odd poking motions, ran both hands around the invisible object, twice, and opened her eyes again. 'Well, the handles, of course, to pick it up, and the padlock itself, and then the zip tabs.'

'So it's a zippered bag. Well, I suppose they all are nowadays. Canvas?'

'No, some heavier fabric, a sort of brocade. You're thinking about fingerprints, of course.'

'Yes. I imagine the handles of the bag are leather. What about the padlock itself? Shiny metal, I suppose.'

'Probably, but encased in leather. Something like morocco. Textured, anyway. I don't think it would take fingerprints very well. And I used the tip of my nail to move those tiny wheels with the numbers.'

'And to spin it closed, I hope.'

'No. For that I used this.' She pulled a two-inch eraser out of her purse. 'It's wide enough and tacky enough to do all three at once.'

I sat back with a sigh of relief. 'Then, my dear, you're home free. You and Peter have every right to have fingerprints on the handles. One or the other of you had to carry the bag up to the attic. The only other surfaces that could conceivably take prints are those tiny little number wheels, and even those might not – but anyway you didn't touch them. So as far as the police are concerned you never opened that bag and have no idea what's inside.'

'But if they think we hid something from them . . .?'

'They won't, I promise. What I'm going to do right now, if you will allow me, is to call Derek. I don't know if he's still in London, but he gave me his mobile number. I'll tell him about the forgotten luggage and say you and Peter are worried about it, and he'll take it from there. He knows and trusts both of you.'

'But when they open it . . .?'

I sighed. 'Yes, when they discover all that money they're going to go ballistic. Especially MI5. It won't look good for the Ahmads. That money could be destined to support a terrorist attack almost anywhere in the world.'

Greta opened her mouth and I held up my hand. 'We don't think so. You and I and a few others who know them believe they are fine people, firmly on the side of the angels. But for agents who don't know them, even I have to admit that it looks extremely bad for them to be carrying a fortune in mixed currencies. I think, on second thought, I'll call Alan before I talk to Derek. He might have some ideas about how to minimize the fallout.'

Greta stood. 'I wish,' she said quietly, 'that I had thrown the bag into the river while I still could.'

'I can sympathize. But have a little more faith, Greta. In God, and in the English police. They're very good, you know.'

'I do know. Perhaps the best in the world. But they are human and they do make mistakes, and there are sensitive international issues involved. Who is to say they may not leap to conclusions in their eagerness to find a solution?'

And to that question I had no answer.

Greta took over from Nigel at the desk, thanking him for his help. He gave me a sideways grin. 'Sorry. I did mean to join you, but it's been crazy out here. Ready to go home?'

'Yes, but I'll walk, thanks. It's a lovely day, and I need to think.' I waved to Greta, who was deep in conversation with an arriving guest, and walked out into the Close, surely one of the most beautiful and serene places in England on a sunny summer afternoon. Tourists chattered, children screamed at their play, a couple of teenagers shouted as they tossed a Frisbee back and forth. The noise didn't interfere with the essential quiet.

I thought about going through the Cathedral on my way home, but the odds were good I'd run into someone I knew, and right then I didn't want to talk to anyone but Alan. Or

Jane. And both of them were far away! Well, about fifty miles, but it seemed a long way from the peace of Sherebury to the pandemonium of London.

Telling myself to stop being silly, I shied from a stray Frisbee that was heading my way and walked out of the Close into the street next to my house. My mobile was out of my purse before I even got in my door.

And it rang before I could place the call to Alan. I answered eagerly.

'Dorothy. Jane.'

'Oh, Jane, I've been wanting to talk to you. But is something wrong? Has something happened?'

'Got Aya safely housed. Coming home on 4:17.'

'Oh, dear, I can't meet you. Alan has the car.'

'Taxi.'

'Yes, well, I'll have tea ready for you, anyway.'

'Need it.'

She ended the call without a further word. Hmm. Even terser and more abrupt than usual. I wasn't sure what that implied. Was she upset, or preoccupied, or just tired?

I was all of those things, but before I did anything else, I had to talk to Alan.

He answered on the second ring. He, too, was eagerly awaiting developments. 'It's only me, dear. I just heard from Jane. Is there any other news?'

'Nothing momentous. Anything at your end?'

'Yes. Are you near a landline?'

'I can find one. Security?'

'Perhaps. I'm at home.'

Thank goodness Alan didn't need to have the I's dotted and the T's crossed. I waited by the phone in our kitchen for him to call back, which he did in a very few minutes.

'All right, love. Mind you, I don't know with any certainty that this line is any more private than the mobile.'

'Maybe not, but it makes me feel safer. Because what I have to tell you is absolutely not for anyone else's ears.'

'Ah. Will it wait for a couple of hours?'

'Oh, dear, I suppose so.'

'Then I'll head for home. There's nothing at this end that

absolutely requires my presence. Depending on the traffic, I should be there in a bit over an hour, two at the most.'

I am not the most patient of women. It was a good thing I had several chores to keep me busy. First the animals, of course, ours and Jane's. They all got rather short shrift, food, a toilet break, and a little petting with promise of more later. The cats were indignant about such treatment, the dogs mournful (and if there's anything more mournful than a sad dog's eyes, I don't know what it is). I found myself apologizing to the bulldogs, who clearly showed that they had expected better of me. Watson's eyes were less pleading; he knew he'd talk me round soon.

There wasn't a thing in the house for tea, and I didn't have time to shop. I threw together a quick batch of scones. Jane has shown me how to make them properly, and while mine will never equal hers, they're not bad. I also got a box of gingerbread mix out of the cupboard. Jane might scorn the use of a mix, but at least the kitchen would smell good from the baking. I had just finished a lemon sauce for the gingerbread when Jane rapped on the back door and walked in.

'Jane, are you too tired to take the dogs for a quick run? I haven't done that yet, and they're very disappointed in me. I'll have tea ready when you get back.'

She nodded and went back out the door. I felt bad about sending a woman her age out the moment she got home, but she was devoted to the dogs and would enjoy spending time with them, and it would give me time to decide exactly what to tell Alan, and how much to share with Jane.

The decision cost me a brief struggle, but in the end it was obvious. Throughout our marriage I have sometimes been cagey with Alan about what I was going to do, thinking he'd stop me if it sounded dangerous. But I have never withheld important information about a case. I trust him implicitly. I would tell him everything Greta had told me. As for Jane – yes, I would tell her, too. Jane knows how to keep her mouth shut, and with her concern for the children, she was in this mess just as much as Alan and I.

She got back before Alan arrived, trudged into the kitchen, and sniffed with seeming approval.

'Dogs okay?'

'All over me. Might have been weeks instead of days.'

'Yes, Watson was like that too, and Alan and I were gone less than a full day. Sam and Emmy, of course . . .' I shrugged.

'Cats.'

'Are not dogs. Right. Now – tea or a drink? Alan will be here soon.'

She sat down heavily in a kitchen chair. 'Drink now. Tea later.'

I poured her some of Alan's Glenfiddich and got out a box of assorted crackers, 'biscuits' to the English. I was concerned about her. She was looking her age and more, and seemed to have lost her combativeness. I poured myself a small tot of Jack Daniels to join her, and we sat for a few moments in a weary silence.

Watson put an end to that. He bounded in the door Jane had left ajar and threw himself ecstatically at her feet. 'Fool dog,' she said affectionately, reaching down to pull his silky ears. He rolled over on his back, all four paws in the air, and she gently massaged his belly with her sensibly-shod foot.

'Jane, I'll bet you've never met an animal that didn't fall in love with you. Or a child.'

She waved the remark aside. She finds praise embarrassing. 'Know who likes them.'

'Yes, they usually respond to love. So tell me, what's happened with Aya? You said she's found a safe haven.'

'Didn't want me to leave her. Clung and cried.'

Of course. 'Oh, dear, that must have been very hard for you. She's with a Muslim family, then?'

Jane nodded after a restorative sip of whisky. 'Police family, both of them. Carstairs found them; Duncan checked them out. Police can move fast when they want to. Perfect record.'

'Did the police take her to them, then?'

'Unmarked car, with me. Good people. She'll do.'

For Jane, that was quite a speech, and 'good people' a ringing testimonial. So Aya was safe, and with people who would understand her much better than any of us could, even Jane.

But what about her parents, and Rahim? Where were they? And were they safe?

THIRTEEN

I heard Alan putting the car in the garage and turned on the kettle. He might want a strong drink later, but I've learned over the years that his preferred stress reliever is tea.

'All right,' he said, after he had embraced me in a bear hug, 'what is this highly confidential information you're pining to pass along?'

'Come into the kitchen and have your tea. Jane's here, and I can tell you together.'

I poured tea and passed goodies and then settled down at the table. 'Alan, I need your advice. I also need you to decide whether you're going to take any official notice of what I'm about to say.'

He put down his cup and gave me a searching look. 'I'm still a sworn police officer, you know.'

'I do know. I also know you don't have to answer to any authority anymore, unless you choose to. So here's the story, at the moment for no ears but yours.' I included Jane in that remark; she simply nodded.

Taking a deep breath, I told them about the suitcase and the money, not leaving out the fortunate circumstance of the lack of fingerprints. 'Greta's frightened. We think of her as English through and through, but she remembers a time when Germans were hated in this country. She also remembers the stories her parents told about the terrible time, during the war, when the *Polizei* were the enemy. She is afraid that she and Peter will be reprimanded, at the least, punished at worst, for forgetting about the suitcase. I've told her they must report it now, but I said I'd talk to you first.'

'Oh, lord.' He passed a hand over the back of his head. 'Damned if they do, damned if they don't. When MI5 get hold of this, it's going to set the cat among the pigeons with a vengeance. You know what they may think.'

'I've got a pretty good guess.' I made a face. 'I suppose they do have to be told?'

Alan just looked at me.

'Okay, dumb remark. Can we do anything for damage control?'

'I'm not sure anyone can do anything about that. The money is a fact. The conclusions that can be drawn are horrific, at best. I'll do what I can. I'll report it myself, and only to Derek. I'll tell him the exact truth, that Greta told you about the suitcase and you told me, not sure of what to do.'

'But not the whole truth?'

'I'll not lie, Dorothy. I won't mention Greta opening the bag, but if he asks, I'll have to tell him.'

'Yes.' I put down my fork. Another bite of gingerbread would have choked me. 'Jane, what can you and I do to help Greta? She's pretty frantic.'

Jane's answer was a nod, as she stood and headed for the front door. I didn't know what she was going to do. I didn't have to know. I trusted her to find a way to comfort Greta and allay her fears, with very few words. She's a woman of action leavened with kindness and good common sense. Which isn't all that common.

Alan stood, too.

'You're going to call Derek?'

'I'll ask him to call me from a landline. The secure connection question again. He may be able to tell whether our line is under surveillance.'

When Alan reverts to officialese, I know he's under stress. I barred his way to the kitchen door and gave him a hug.

'What's that in aid of?'

'Just for being you. And as encouragement.'

'Why is it,' he asked in a tone halfway between amusement and irritation, 'that you come out with a comment like that just when I've decided you're becoming a very great nuisance?'

'I know, I know, your Helen never got you involved in the sort of messes that seem to crop up with me. Truly I can't help it, my dear. It's just that—'

'Just that you take an interest in people and have to come to their aid when they're in trouble. You'd be surprised how much trouble my first wife got me into. You're a lot like her in some ways. Now, out of my way, woman, and get yourself busy thinking up a thumping good dinner for a hungry and irritable man.'

I'd planned on defrosting the leftovers of last week's lasagne, but plainly that wasn't going to do. I looked at the kitchen clock. There was just barely time to run to the supermarket for a roast and vegetables and something really good from their bakery. But I was tired and a bit irritable myself. I'd probably burn the roast and scorch the potatoes, or something equally disastrous. I had a better idea.

Watson was under the kitchen table, half snoozing, but when I reached for his leash he was instantly wideawake. I called to Alan, 'I'm taking the dog out for a little run.' We headed straight for the Close and the Rose and Crown.

The inn doesn't do take-away meals as a rule, but for their special friends they've been known to stretch a point. I unclipped Watson's lead and let him run ahead. He's very fond of the Endicotts, partly because they always have a handout for him, though he keeps clear of Max, who doesn't appreciate dogs and has well sharpened claws.

The front door was hospitably open on this beautiful summer day, but I saw Max lounging just inside, so I put Watson back on the leash and tied it to the bench outside the door. He's usually very good about 'stay', but if Max decided to taunt him, fur might fly.

Greta was at the front desk, but at the moment there were no guests needing attention. She looked up from her paperwork as I came in, and instantly looked anxious.

'It's all right,' I said quietly. There was a buzz of conversation from the bar, and I was quite sure no one could hear. 'Alan's dealing with it discreetly with Derek. Police will come, and they'll take away the bag, but there shouldn't be any trouble for you and Peter.'

'That's what Jane said, but I'm still worried.'

'Don't be. That is, worry all you want about the Ahmad family, but not about yourselves. You'll be fine. Where is Jane, by the way?'

Greta smiled a little. 'I think she went to the kitchen after she soothed me. Two of our helpers are her god-daughters, or grand-god-daughters, or something like that, and she wanted to visit them. Is there anyone in Sherebury she doesn't know?'

'Not that I've heard. She taught two or three generations of them, and now there are the children and grandchildren of the last pupils. She keeps track of them like an old-fashioned nanny.'

'That's just what she is! She wants everyone to be happy. Truly, she did make me feel better, with just a word or two.'

'Yes, I don't know how she does it. But I didn't come to talk about Jane. I'm begging. Alan wants a "thumping good dinner" – his words – and I don't have anything to give him, and we're both too tired to go out. You wouldn't have any of the Sunday roast left, would you?'

She took me to the kitchen and packaged up enough beef and roasted potatoes and gravy for an army, and a bag full of raw Brussels sprouts ('because they cannot be reheated, you know') and a whole summer pudding. And she wouldn't let me pay for any of it, overriding my objections with claims of repayment for favours. I was still arguing about it when my mobile rang.

'Love, Derek will be here in a few minutes, and he wants to talk to you before he sees the Endicotts.'

'Oh. Okay, I'm just bringing dinner. Home in a jiff.'

Greta packed everything in a sturdy canvas bag, well wrapped in plastic against Watson's eager nose, and sent me off with a hug.

'Just let me put this stuff away. I got what you commanded, straight from the best chef in town, and I need to get it out of Watson's reach.'

'You were at the Rose and Crown? You didn't—?'

'I didn't say anything about anything, except to reassure Greta that you were on it and everything would be all right.'

'We hope.'

'You're almost as bad as she is. I already told her she needed more faith.'

'There are certainly some large mountains to be moved. Look out!'

Watson had crept quietly up to the bag I had let droop too

close to the floor, and was drooling. He spoke sharply when I pulled it up out of his way, and that brought the cats from wherever they'd been lazing away the afternoon. Sam began expressing her imminent starvation in piercing Siamese profanity, Watson continued barking, and Emmy joined the chorus in her very own dialect, peremptory yips like a cross between puppy and duck. Alan put his hands over his ears, turned around, and stepped on Derek's foot.

'I did ring,' he said apologetically, 'but . . .'

Alan kindly took him to the parlour for a drink, while I stashed the meat and gravy in a high cupboard with a latched door. Even Sam hadn't figured out how to get into that one. Yet.

I put some dry food down, which all of them rejected, telling me plainly That Wasn't It. Emmy and Sam tried to cover up their bowls. 'Well, it's all you're going to get right now. I do appreciate the comic relief, but I have other fish to fry. Now beat it.' Sam and Emmy looked hopeful at the word 'fish', one of the bits of English they understand, but when none was forthcoming they stalked off to dream up new ways to punish me. Watson just flumped down on the kitchen floor, the picture of an unloved dog.

I took a deep breath and went into the parlour.

'Dorothy, I can see you have your hands full at the moment.'

'Not as full as I'd like them to be. Ah, thank you, dear.' Alan handed me a large cold gin and tonic, complete with a slice of lime on the edge. I pushed the lime down in and took a revivifying gulp. 'Okay, better. Fire away, Derek.'

'Alan has given me the bare bones of your story. I'd like to hear it from you. You went to the Rose and Crown when you got back from London earlier today. Was there any particular reason you went there instead of straight home?'

'I had planned to go home. But Nigel, who picked me up at the station, thought I looked tired, and heaven knows I was. So he dropped me at the pub instead for some TLC from the Endicotts.'

'What happened then?'

I frowned, trying to be accurate, trying not to get irritated. Derek was just doing his job. This was routine. Just the facts, ma'am.

'I went in. Greta was at the desk, very busy, and Peter was at the bar, also very busy. He asked me what I wanted to drink and told me to go to their private parlour, where it would be nice and quiet and peaceful. It was so peaceful, in fact, that I was nearly asleep when Greta came in – no, that's not right. Max came in and jumped on my lap. He must weigh twenty pounds. Then Peter came in with my G and T and some snacks, and chased Max away, and then Greta came in.'

'She had dealt with all the guests?'

'I don't think so. She said Nigel had come in and was handling all that for a little while. You know Nigel helped out there after he and Inga were first married, so he knows the ropes.'

'Yes, I remember.' Derek was being patient. 'What did you and Greta do then?'

I took another long pull at my drink. This was where I had to be careful. And if Derek was as good as Alan at reading body language, he'd know I was stalling. Well, it couldn't be helped. Tell the truth as far as I could. 'I'm sorry, Derek. I'm a little nervous, and my throat's dry. I've never been questioned like this before, you see.'

'Take your time.'

Oh, lord, that was what they said to the chief suspects in all the crime novels. I tried to smile. 'And tell it in my own words? As if I could use someone else's. Well, Greta seemed upset, and said she wanted to talk to me about a problem. "Peter and I have a problem, and we don't know what to do," was the way she put it. I thought it would be about money, the Ahmads' bill, and started to say Alan and I would help, but then she got even more upset and told me about the bag. That is, she said your people had searched everything and then left it all here for the Ahmads when they returned, since you didn't find anything incriminating.'

'Nor anything that gave any hint of where they might have gone, or why.'

'Yes, okay, I know you weren't just trying to find evidence of a crime, or . . . well, anyway, she told me about the bag they'd overlooked, since it was stored in the attic, and I told her she had to produce it now, and she showed me how afraid

she was, so I said I'd talk to Alan first before we told you.' I
picked up my drink and finished it, wishing there were more.
My throat still felt like sawdust.

'And that was the entire conversation? For example, did she
say why she was so afraid?'

'Oh, I left that part out, didn't I?' I explained about her
post-war traumas, and her parents' stories about the terrible
conditions during the war. 'She knows it's different here, really,
but I think it was the idea of her house being searched that
brought it all back. Alan, is there any more tonic? Without
gin, please.' I handed him my glass.

'I see,' said Derek smoothly. 'I must say, in their position I
would have opened the bag, to see if it was anything important.
Did they?'

I sipped from my refreshed drink. 'I believe it was locked.'

'Most luggage locks are easily defeated,' Derek said, and
waited.

FOURTEEN

Alan looked at me. Derek looked at me. The silence stretched out.

'Damn!' I put my glass down. I was in exactly the position I'd tried to avoid. 'Derek, you know me too well. I had no intention of telling you, but yes, Greta opened the bag. Peter knows nothing about it.'

'I assume there was, indeed, something interesting inside, or you wouldn't be so reluctant to speak about it.'

'There was, according to Greta. I haven't seen for myself. And Alan can glare at me all he wants, but I'm not going to say another word. You're going to have to see for yourself. Greta said what she said in confidence, and I refuse to betray it any further.'

'Ah, well, we'll know soon enough. Thank you for the hospitality.'

Alan rose with him. 'I'll come with you, if I may.'

Of course Derek agreed. What else could he do? I knew, and he knew, that Alan was going along to assure fair play. What Derek didn't know was what he was going to find, and how big the bombshell was. I was happy Alan was going to be there. I suppose I should have gone too, to support Greta, but I couldn't face it. Irrational though it was, I felt like a rat fink, not only to Greta, but to the Ahmads.

The animals were back, having decided to forgive me. Watson lay down at my feet and I pulled Emmy up into my lap (with some difficulty; she weighs almost as much as her daddy) and sat trying to think. Why, why, why would the Ahmads be carrying around a small fortune in cash? And in the cash of various nations, furthermore?

It might not be a small fortune, of course. These days it takes an awful lot of money to earn that designation. But the bills might be of high denominations. Greta hadn't said, and I hadn't thought to ask. But even if the total were only, say, £20,000, that was still a lot of cash.

They were travelling. Perhaps to various countries where they would need various currencies.

Right. In this age when cash is almost obsolete, when plastic pays for anything from dinner to a new car, when, if cash is needed for some small purchase, your debit card in an ATM will generate the money used in that location.

Anyway, whatever purpose the cash was intended for, they no longer had it with them. They hadn't kept it on their persons, but in a locked suitcase in the attic of the Rose and Crown. And when they left so precipitately, they hadn't come back for it.

What could I deduce from that? Hmmm. Either they'd gone to some place where the money wasn't needed, or the summons was so urgent they couldn't afford even the few minutes to stop for it. Actually, it might well have been half an hour or so, if both Greta and Peter had been busy – which was likely, on a Friday night in high summer, and a music festival night at that.

What could have been that critical?

And that got me back on the same old squirrel-wheel, going round and round and getting nowhere. Abduction. Murder. But he was seen in London. Maybe. If Rahim was right.

And where were they all now?

And, it suddenly occurred to me, what were they doing for money? London is one of the most expensive cities in the world. The Ahmads were wealthy, of course, and they might be carrying quite a lot of cash. But they had left behind a lot more. If they were in hiding somewhere, they wouldn't use their credit cards or go to an ATM. All these things are readily traceable.

It's really, really hard to disappear in this electronic age, and yet the Ahmads had apparently done it.

How? And most importantly, why?

The squirrel kept up its relentless, pointless race.

Eventually I pushed Sam off my lap (to her annoyance) and went to the kitchen. Doubtless Alan would be back soon, and that dinner he wanted was still hidden away. I put the meat and potatoes into the warming oven of the Aga and started water boiling for the Brussels sprouts. I couldn't steam them till Alan was actually here; overcooked, they are fit for nothing but the compost heap. I would have liked another drink, but I'd already had two, and there'd be wine with dinner. Alcohol-induced anaesthesia might sound like a good idea, but it didn't solve anything and would in fact lead only to a headache later.

Alan and Jane came in together a few minutes later. Watson appeared magically in the kitchen, awakened from his snooze in the parlour. He's getting quite deaf, but his nose is still in good working order, and he had just smelled dinner and his two favourite people. He roamed about, getting very much in my way as I put the sprouts on to steam and set the table.

'Well?' I asked, handing Alan three sets of knives and forks. It was understood that Jane would eat with us.

'Not very well, actually.' He set the silverware out precisely, as if the exact alignment of each knife were critical to the future of civilization. 'Derek was as courteous as anyone could have hoped, and tried to be non-threatening, but his reaction to the money was rather . . . um . . . intense, and Greta became somewhat upset.'

I mentally translated: Derek went all stern and official and Greta had a panic attack. I sighed and checked the sprouts. 'And Peter?'

'Peter's furious with Derek and all his works, including me. He lost his temper. Jane and I didn't wait to be thrown out.'

'A portent of things to come, but it can't be helped. And letting our dinner get ruined won't accomplish anything. Alan, if you'll pour us some wine, and Jane, could you serve the stuff from the oven?'

We ate. The excellent food might as well have been sawdust. We talked resolutely of other things. How much money the Cathedral had made from the music festival. (Just about broke even, which was better than some years.) The lovely weather. (Sure to change soon.) In the end we resorted, in desperation, to talking about the animals. This had the effect of chasing away the cats, who do not care to be discussed, but as Watson couldn't hear much of it, he continued to be a begging nuisance under the table.

Jane's contribution to the conversation was a nod here and there.

She helped clear away and wash the dishes, still without a word, then went home with a brief expression of thanks, and Alan and I were left to deal with our thoughts.

'What did Derek think about the money?'

'He didn't say, but one can imagine. Why were the Ahmads carrying so much money about? How did they get it into the country, through customs? What, above all, did they plan to do with it?'

'And we don't have answers to any of those questions. There's nothing much we can do, is there? About anything.'

Alan shook his head. 'Not much.'

I sighed and took a sip of my coffee. 'So much hatred and fear. Fear, most of all. You know, Alan, the other day I read a newspaper column by an American man, who reminded his readers that fear kills thought, that when you're scared your brain stops working and you act on sheer fight-or-flight instinct. I think that's what's happening all over the world. The fear and the anger were always there, smouldering beneath the surface, but they've been fanned into flame by the rhetoric of demagogues, even in my own homeland, to my sorrow and shame. Now half the world seems to fear the other half, and they're reacting with mob violence.'

'Yes, and the demagogues seem to have no regard for truth. They seem to know that if what you say is sufficiently frightening, your audience won't stop to check your facts or put your actions into historical perspective. Indeed, they may not know or care enough about history to be able to do so.'

'Who was it said that those who fail to learn history are condemned to repeat it? It's true, anyway. Tragically true.' I shook my head in frustration. 'And the trouble is, so many people these days seem to be not only ignorant, but proud of it. It's a bad combination.'

We spent the rest of the evening in silence. I, for one, was thinking of parallels in history, when demagoguery led to events too horrific to contemplate. Surely we weren't headed for another Holocaust.

Surely not.

*   *   *

Sometimes things look better, brighter, in the morning. Sometimes not. I woke, far too early, to a raging thunderstorm. The bedroom floor was wet and slippery with rain, and Watson, who had been trying to hide under the bed from the thunder, was also wet. When I got out of bed, bleary-eyed, I stepped on his paw, where-upon he wriggled out from under the bed frame and shook himself, giving me an unplanned shower. I should have given up on the day then and there.

For once I was up before Alan. I pulled on the terry-cloth bathrobe to help me dry off and stumbled down to the kitchen to start coffee. I was grateful for the warmth of the Aga. It can be a great trial in the heat of summer, indeed had been for the past few days, but on this wet, very chilly morning it was a blessing. So was the coffee. I was well into my second cup when Alan appeared, greeted by yips and mews.

'Ignore them. They've been fed. And Watson's been out.' Alan grunted something and poured himself some coffee. We're neither of us chatty in the morning, thank the Lord.

After a while I made some toast. Alan's the breakfast chef most of the time, but I didn't feel like anything more and neither did he.

'Any plans for the day?' he asked when we'd both imbibed enough caffeine to be more-or-less human. Most of his attention was on the very damp newspaper he'd retrieved from the front stoop.

It was one of those non-questions, exactly akin to a grocery clerk's 'How are you today?' spoken with her eyes fixed on the items she's scanning. I surprised myself as much as him by answering, 'Yes. I just decided. I'm going to Matins. You?'

He shook his head. 'Not today. I'm expecting calls from Derek and the Keystone Kops.'

'They do sort of tend to run around in circles and get in each other's way, don't they? That's why I'm heading for church. I need some peace.'

An especially loud thunderclap rattled the coffee cups in their saucers. Watson whined and scooted farther under the table. 'I shouldn't think you'll be able to hear the choir if this keeps up.'

'Maybe the storm will be over by then. Anyway, several tons of solid stone should keep out some of the noise.'

The storm was still carrying on its tantrum when I ventured out, clad in all the wet-weather gear I possessed. An umbrella would have been blown inside out in seconds. I clutched at the hood of my raincoat as I splashed across the Close in my wellies, looking, I suspected, quite a lot like Paddington Bear. I could hear the bells only in fits and starts above the clamour of wind and rain and thunder.

Only a few other worshippers had braved the elements, among them the dean's wife. The choir raised their voices valiantly against the tumult, but occasionally in the quieter passages the thunder overwhelmed them. Everyone was glad when the service was over, but I remained for a few moments on my knees after the others had left, trying to find the peace I sought.

It eluded me. I sat back with a sigh. I knew perfectly well that I would find no respite until I'd done what I could to find Rana and Husam and Rahim and untangle the web of mystery surrounding them.

Until I'd done what I could. There was the rub. What could I do? At least three official agencies were working night and day to find them. Alan was collaborating with them and trying, subtly, to guide them.

The question was, what would they do with them when they found them? It all depended on what they had been doing. Angels of peace, or demons of insurrection? MI5 weren't saying what they believed, but I had a feeling they were thinking the worst. As, I reluctantly admitted to myself, they had every right, even a duty, to do.

And here I was, one elderly individual, with no training, no qualifications except a certain understanding of people and a willingness to ask a lot of nosy questions.

Whom could I ask? Who might be able to point me in any helpful direction?

The thunder roared, rattling the stained glass and startling one of the bats that, in the grand tradition, inhabited the belfry. It swooped rather aimlessly around the amazing fan-vaulted ceiling, its echolocation mechanism apparently disturbed by the clamour. I felt a strong sympathy with the poor thing. I, too, was without direction. I needed a strong dose of common sense to set me on the right track.

Jane? She would usually be my choice, but she was caught up in the web of confusion, too. The dean? His advice about spiritual dilemmas was always spot on, but he was not the most practical of men.

In a momentary pause from the tumult of the storm, I heard two of the ladies from the flower guild. I didn't recognize either voice, but one of them sounded very old indeed and probably rather deaf: a high, cracked voice complaining about something.

Aha! That old lady – what was her name? – who'd given me valuable information about that dreadful church, the one I'd remembered just recently. She'd had a voice like that. Margaret Allenby had described it, quite accurately, as sounding like a cross between a creaking gate and a Siamese cat. The Chapel of the One True God, that was the name of the place, and the woman's name was . . . was . . .

'Are you all right, Dorothy?'

'Oh, Margaret, you're just the person I wanted to see. I thought you'd gone.'

'Only to the gift shop. How can I help?'

'There was a very old woman a while back. You told me about her, in connection with the murder of that awful man at that awful church. Do you remember?'

'Simmons,' she said promptly. 'Miss Simmons.'

'I visited her a time or two after that, but it's been a while. Is she still alive, do you think?'

'I suspect she'll never die, though I shouldn't say so. You must admit there's something definitely witch-like about her. I haven't heard from her lately, but someone would have told us if she'd gone. She's a fixture in this community, even though she almost never leaves her house now. I don't think she even goes to church; the Baptist minister is a good friend of ours, and he mentions visiting her now and again. You want to talk to her?'

'Yes, I'm not sure why, but she strikes me as the sort of person I need just now.'

Margaret reminded me of her address and how to get there, and I slogged home through the rain to get the car.

Alan had gone, leaving me a somewhat cryptic note on the kitchen table. I gathered he and Derek were off on some mission and I was to expect him when I saw him.

Fine. The animals were all dealing with the storm, the cats under the covers, Watson under the bed. Later we would get their reproaches for doing nothing about the Terrible Thing, but for now I could ignore them. I got out the car and headed out, my first stop the best bakery in town to get an appropriate bribe for Miss Simmons.

She greeted me with the same graciousness I had experienced before. 'For the Lord's sake come in and shut the door! I've no fancy to be drowned.'

'Miss Simmons, I don't know if you remember me. It's been some time—'

'I still have my memory, thank you very much. You're that nosy American woman who married the chief constable and kept your own name. Faddy. You can put that cake in the kitchen. I suppose it's edible, even if you didn't bake it yourself. Thought it'd soften me up, did you?'

'I hoped so, because I've come to ask your help again.'

'Only reason you ever come to see me, isn't it?'

'Not true. I've visited, now and then.'

'More then than now. Oh, sit down, sit down. I'm too old to stand and chatter.'

She did, indeed, look much older than the last time I'd seen her. She was a bent old crone now, her hair totally white and grown thin. Her assortment of clothes would have made a punk rocker look well groomed. She hobbled, with the aid of a stick, to a chair in front of the fire. I shed my rain gear, looked around for a place to hang everything, and finally left it on the floor.

'Right. You can make some coffee later. Tell me what you want.'

I went straight to the point. 'What can you tell me about the Chapel of the One True God?'

'You still harping on that? They're long gone. After Rookwood stole them blind and then decamped, the ones who were left got to infighting, and the whole thing collapsed.'

Miss Simmons had once been tangentially connected with the group, through her father, but she had never espoused their beliefs, and had left for the Baptist church when her father died. She knew the inmost heart of the despised sect very well.

'Just what I would have expected, actually. Those people were very good at hating, if at nothing else. But what happened to them? I can't see them joining normal churches, but some of them must have wanted some other group to bully.'

'Hmph. Smarter than you look, aren't you? Yes, some of them banded together after a while and got up another sorry excuse for a church. This one's called the Temple of Truth.'

'Oh, dear. That almost certainly means that they peddle lies.'

'Complete bilge. And hatred. You're right about that, too. Twice in a row. Don't let it go to your head.'

I grinned. 'I'll try not to. So who's in charge of this new incarnation, and where is it?'

'Same building. I suppose they couldn't find an uglier one. And it's all women this time. They call themselves deacons. Mixed lot of acidulated spinsters. Oh, I can see you trying not to laugh. I was never a "spinster". Could have married a dozen men. Weak-kneed imbeciles, all of them. I chose to stay with my father. He could be a bully, but at least he wasn't a milksop. Now this lot, at the so-called Temple, pretend they hate men, because no man ever looked at any of them twice. Pah! I'll have that coffee now.'

The kitchen, surprisingly, was relatively clean, if cluttered. The jar of instant decaf was sitting next to the electric kettle, along with sugar and a few little plastic containers of cream, and there were clean cups on the drainboard. I cut the cake while the water boiled, found a tray, and carried everything to the sitting room, where I had to put the tray on the floor while I cleared a space on a small table.

Miss Simmons watched my discomfiture with obvious enjoyment. 'Should have done that before, shouldn't you?'

'I'll never make a proper parlourmaid, will I? Do you take sugar and cream?'

'Both, and I'll put the sugar in myself.'

She did so, as I watched in amazement. I hoped she wasn't diabetic.

'Don't like coffee,' she commented briefly as she stirred the syrupy mess. I forbore to ask the obvious question. 'You didn't take any cake. I'm not so fierce as all that, you know.'

'I don't like fruitcake. Many Americans don't. I took the risk that you did.'

'Most English do,' she mimicked me. 'Sit down, girl. I like you. You don't mind me being rude, and you're not afraid of me. Makes a nice change.'

'And I like you. I don't care for pretence. Of course, you do pretend to be more wicked than you are, but that's greatly preferable to smarminess. Another piece of cake?'

She held out her plate. 'I suppose,' she said after a bite or two, 'you're wanting to know about the nest of nasties because of that business at the Cathedral.'

I long ago accepted the fact that the Sherebury grapevine reaches even those who seldom get out. 'Yes. It occurred to me that Muslims would probably be among the many groups they hate, so of course I wondered if they might have had anything to do with what happened.'

'You think they've been kidnapped?'

'I don't know what to think, but it's obviously a possibility.'

She chewed on the dense, rich cake. 'Hmm. I'd not have thought Dulcie Robinson would have the brains to organize something like that. Or the will.'

'She's the head of the Temple?'

Miss Simmons cackled. 'Not a good name for a hatemonger, is it? She's the very opposite of sweet. Calls herself a deaconess. I hear she preaches sermons against the Muslims, all lies and insults. Stirs up fear and hatred against them. But then, she preaches sermons against Anglicans, too. And Baptists. And of course Catholics. And Jews and Hindus.'

'And, in short, everyone who doesn't look like her and believe exactly what she believes.'

'Which is the entire civilized world. But, given all that, you're barking up the wrong tree. They're a small group at the Temple, all at least middle-aged, and nearly all women. They rant and rave, but action is too ambitious for them. No, they like to sit like spiders in their nest and hug their superiority to themselves.'

'And suppose some of the despicable Other came to the nest?'

'They'd sting, and drive them away. How could they keep their purity if anyone from outside tried to intrude?'

'Not exactly evangelical, then.'

Miss Simmons cackled again. 'Oh, no. The number of the elect is already made up, you see, and it's them.' She took a gulp of the despised coffee and made a face. 'Take it as medicine. Got to stay awake somehow. But you know, I may be wrong about those Temple witches. There are one or two, new to the group, who . . . ah, well. Probably they're as ineffectual as the rest.'

I noticed something that had escaped me before. 'You're not smoking. And I don't see any ashtrays.'

She gave me a malevolent look. 'Fool of a doctor forbids it! I told him I'd smoked for well over eighty years and if it was going to kill me it would have done by now. I'm a tough old bird. But he wouldn't listen to me.'

'I admit I'm a little surprised *you* listened to *him*.'

'Not got a choice, do I? I don't get out, and no one will bring me cigarettes. I don't suppose you – no, I thought not. You're an upright, follow-the-rules sort. You're not going to take away the rest of the cake, are you?'

At that extremely plain hint I rose and started putting cups on the tray. 'Wouldn't dream of it. I'll leave it here where you can reach it easily.'

'And make me another cup of that ghastly coffee while you're in the kitchen,' she called out. 'Witch's brew for a witch. Hah!'

I left her looking very tired and old. She paid no attention when I left.

FIFTEEN

The storm had rumbled itself away while we were talking, the rain settling down to a steady shower of the determined sort. I sat in my car and ruminated.

Had I wasted my morning?

It had been a treat to see Miss Simmons. (If she had a first name, I'd never heard it, and I didn't know anyone who had.) I had told the truth when I said I liked her. Not everyone's cup of tea, perhaps, but refreshing to me. I made a note that when this was all over, I had to come back and tell her all about it. But it had better be soon. She had looked, when I left, as if her next breath could easily be her last. Tough old bird or not, she must be nearly 100. She should be in a care facility, or at least have someone to look after her, but it was obvious that she'd never tolerate that.

But aside from an interesting visit, had I learned anything? I had hoped for some hint that the 'nest of nasties' might have had something to do with the disappearance of my Muslim friends, or might at least know something. Now that didn't seem at all likely. I thought of the graphic image of the spiders sitting in their toxic nest spewing venom on everyone who didn't conform to their warped, bitter doctrine, and I shuddered. I hate and fear spiders. Real ones, the eight-legged variety, can be useful, I admit. They eat flies. The two-legged variety are simply disgusting and terrifying.

However. It was possible, barely, that some of these human spiders might know something to the purpose. Alan wasn't home. It was a rotten day to do anything. My instinct was to go home, curl up in bed with the cats, and snooze the day away. I most emphatically did not want to go visit the Temple of Truth.

I have a fixed notion, shared I think with many people from Saint Paul on down, that if I don't want to do something, it's probably exactly what I should do. I started the car, paused for a moment of memory searching, and headed for the Temple of Truth.

I got lost, of course. Even after living in Sherebury for years, I still find parts of the town confusing. I can't quite shake my American idea that a city ought to be laid out on a grid, but medieval cities followed natural paths like rivers and hills, and the walls encircling the city set up other byways. In modern Sherebury, although some roads were widened and even straightened a bit, the basic street plan was still circa 1200 or so. The old Chapel of the One True God was in one of the less salubrious sectors of Sherebury, an area of drab little houses with no gardens, the occasional dusty shop (often closed), and a few empty buildings. I thought I remembered that the Chapel had been in the largest building on the street, a depressing pile of brown brick that looked more like a disused warehouse than a church.

I made a wrong turn somewhere along the way and ended up approaching the place from the back. The gaudy sign on the roof that had marked the Chapel was gone, but the deliberate ugliness was unchanged. I turned the corner to find a place to park, and nearly ran into a small crowd of people.

Huddling under umbrellas, they were gathered in front of the door to the building, and were spilling out into the street. What on earth? A planned service gone awry? Someone had forgotten to unlock the door?

There was no place to park, so I turned a few more corners, found a small car park by a shuttered shop, and walked close enough to see and hear, but, I hoped, far enough away to remain unnoticed.

Not a group waiting to enter. No. A protest group. And what were they protesting?

As I began to make out words, my blood ran cold. 'Down with the infidel devils!' one woman was screaming. 'England for the English!' a man bellowed. 'True believers unite!' And the worst of all: 'Satan is a Muslim! They must all die!'

The rest of the crowd picked up on that one. 'They must all die! They must all die! All die! All die!'

A hand touched my shoulder. I screamed and thought my heart would stop.

'Good job they're making too much noise to hear you,' said a familiar voice. 'I'd advise you to make yourself scarce before they see you. This is going to turn ugly in a matter of seconds.'

'Derek! Thank God you're here! It's already quite ugly enough for me.'

'They haven't started throwing things yet. Let me escort you to your car before they do.'

He sat in the car with me for a little, till he could see that I'd regained some of my composure.

'Derek, who *are* those people? Members of that horrible sect?'

'Infiltrators intending to lift the Temple to new heights of bigotry and savagery. A few neighbours called in complaints, saying the protesters arrived, started hammering on the door, and then began to shout insults about the Temple doing nothing about the "Arab menace" and so on. That was when I called out a small force of riot police. They'll be breaking it up about now.'

'Then you didn't know I was here?'

'Good grief, no. I might have guessed, though. You do seem to find your way into the most extraordinary situations.'

'Well, I can't tell you how glad I was to see you. I was getting really scared. But I thought you and Alan were off somewhere together.'

'We were, and I can't tell you much about what we were doing. MI5 stuff. I had to leave when I heard about this little melee, but I suspect Alan will be occupied for the rest of the day. Now, if you'll turn left here and then just keep on following the road down to the river, you'll fetch up at the King's Head. You know your way home from there?'

'I do. Thank you. Left to my own devices I might well have ended up back in the middle of that mob.'

'And the chief would have had my guts for garters. I'll leave you then. Got to see how my troops are faring.'

I was shaking when I pulled into the pub's car park, and not entirely from nerves. It had been a trying morning, I'd had nothing in my stomach since my sketchy breakfast except for a cup of very bad coffee, and the King's Head did an excellent lunch.

It was the middle of lunchtime, in high tourist season. The weather had kept people from touring the lavish gardens in our area or just walking the town, so those who hadn't simply stayed in their lodgings had gone out for sustenance, many of them in this attractive old pub. I didn't see a single unoccupied table.

As I stood hesitating, a woman not far away stood and waved. 'Mrs Martin! Over here.'

Who on earth? The woman looked vaguely familiar, but I couldn't place her for a moment, nor did I recognize the man with her. They had an empty place at their table, though, and were apparently asking me to join them.

'This is very kind of you,' I said when I got close enough to be heard over the many other conversations, 'but I'm afraid I can't remember . . .?'

'Amanda,' said the woman. 'You knew me as Amanda Doyle.'

I smote my forehead. 'Of course! How stupid of me not to recognize you, but—'

'She's changed a good deal, hasn't she?' Her companion beamed. He was a pleasant-looking man, a little older than Amanda, I thought, balding, with a little paunch. A comfortable sort of man.

But Amanda! She'd had her mousy hair cut and styled, and I thought given a brightening rinse. She was wearing a little discreet make-up, along with small, tasteful earrings. The biggest change was her clothes, which were smart and well fitted to a figure that had filled out into slim but pleasing outlines.

She watched my survey of her with a shy smile. 'You would never have known me, would you? It's all Tom's doing. Mrs Martin, let me introduce my husband, Thomas Wright. And do please sit down.'

'May I get you a drink, Mrs Martin?'

'It's Dorothy, if I may call you Tom. And yes, please. A pint of whatever their best beer is here.'

'And to eat? We've ordered ours already, but what would you like? They do excellent fish and chips, or there's a very nice fish pie on today.'

'Oh, fish pie, please. Thank you!'

He left for the bar, and I said, 'Amanda, you're right. I wouldn't have known you. I've been really shameful about keeping in touch, I know, but truly you're a different person! When did this miracle happen?'

'When I met Tom. You're right, it was a miracle. I was driving Miriam home from one of her last therapy sessions, and I had a flat tyre. My sister had moved back to London, and I couldn't think of anyone to call, when a car stopped and this man got out and asked how he could help. I was still rather easily upset, and he saw that, and told me he'd take care of everything, I wasn't to worry. We were near that little tea shop in the High Street – you know the one – and he took me in there and bought me tea and a pastry and said he was Tom Wright, and told me he'd take the tyre to be repaired and be right back. I hardly knew how to act. I wasn't used to being pampered that way.'

'Well, it's about time someone treated you right!'

'That's what Tom said when I'd told him a little about my life. And he's been treating me like a queen ever since.'

'How long have you been married?'

'Just over two years, the most wonderful years of my life!'

They would not, I reflected, have had to be all that great. Amanda Doyle had been married to a cold, self-righteous, bullying philanderer, a pillar of the Chapel of the One True God, and when he was murdered Amanda had been the prime suspect. She, in turn, had been terrified that their daughter Miriam had killed her father, whom she hated and feared. Before the wretched business was resolved, Amanda and her sister and Miriam had been involved in a nasty car smash that injured Miriam badly, requiring months of therapy. Almost any sort of life had to be an improvement, but Amanda did look truly radiant, and Tom did seem to be a good sort.

He came back with my drink, followed by a waitress with our meals, and for a few minutes we concentrated on the joys of good food. Mine was very good indeed, with just the right balance of fish to sauce to potatoes. When my hunger and thirst were partially satisfied I said, 'Now tell me how Miriam is doing. She must be quite a young lady by now.'

'We're very proud of her.' It was Tom who answered. 'She did brilliantly in the eleven-plus and got admitted to St Margaret's Grammar School in Wadhurst.'

'And that after the bad start she got at that horrible school! Oh, I'm sorry, Amanda! I shouldn't have reminded you of that.' For Miriam's early education had been at a school run by the unspeakable Chapel, a place where she had been brow-beaten, repressed, and frightened into a pale ghost of a child.

'It's all right; don't worry. She's tough. Thanks to you and your husband, all that's behind us. And my sister helped so much to turn her into a normal little girl. And then Tom came along, and he's wonderful with her. They really love each other.'

'She's a great kid,' said Tom, turning slightly red, the usual Englishman's reaction to a complimentary remark.

'And don't I remember that your sister was suggesting a puppy? How did that work out?'

They both burst into laughter. 'I decided we'd try it,' said Amanda when she could speak again, 'so we went to a kennel I thought looked reliable. The cages were clean and the puppies looked healthy and happy. I was really taken with a sweet little Cairn terrier, but Miriam had a different idea. She fell in love with a fluffy little creature that looked like an animated dust mop.'

'Very animated,' put in Tom with a grin. 'And rather large for its age. The creature turned out to be an Old English Sheepdog pup.'

'Oh, my!'

'Indeed. You remember the size of our house then. I was about to say it was impossible when the puppy turned its head on one side and gave a little, low whine. It had the funniest face, black fur over one eye, white over the other, with a little black button nose, and the most imploring look in its eyes. Together with the look in Miriam's eyes, I hadn't a chance.'

'She weighs eighty pounds now,' said Tom, still grinning. 'Eats us out of house and home.'

'And she's utterly devoted to Miriam. She'd go to school with her if it were allowed. As it is, she – Annie, the dog – goes up to Miriam's room as soon as she leaves for school, and stays there moping all day. The moment she hears Miriam come home, she's galumphing down the stairs. And believe me, eighty pounds of dog can galumph to some purpose!'

I found myself beaming in response to their enjoyment. 'I'm so glad! There's nothing quite like the love of an animal for a child – or an adult, for that matter. So where are you living now? The house I remember would be pretty cramped for a dog that size.'

'I always hated that house anyway. John would never . . . anyway, our house now is bigger, with space for a lovely big kitchen garden *and* a flower garden, which I've always wanted. We have to try to keep Annie out of the gardens, but we're right at the edge of town, so there's plenty of room for her to run on the heathland. She gets very messy, of course. That long fur collects mud and burs and goodness knows what, so the house is never really tidy, but it's a real home.'

'Which you've never had before.' I didn't mean to say it aloud, but Tom heard and nodded. 'I'm trying to make up for that,' he said quietly. 'I don't like talking about Miriam's father, but that horrible church of his did its best to root all the joy out of her life, and Amanda's, and very nearly succeeded.'

'But not quite, thank the good Lord,' I responded. 'And He is good, no matter what those warped cultists believed. And speaking of them, they seem to be out to ruin some more lives. At least, I know it's not all the same people, but the sect that's taken over the building was attracting some sort of nasty demonstration today. I happened to be driving past, and there was a little crowd shouting slogans and so on. I couldn't quite make out what it was about, but it looked like it was getting ugly, so I was very glad when the police came to break it up. I don't suppose you two know anything about what might be going on?'

Amanda shook her head with a little shudder, but Tom said, 'I've made it my business to keep an eye on them. They were a vindictive bunch when Doyle was associated with them, and the ones who remain still are. I'd steer well clear of them if I were you, Dorothy. They've branched out, you see. They're still preaching a religion based on hate and fear, but now they're also espousing a political agenda on that same basis, and they're attracting some of the worst element in Sherebury. Practise what you preach, I suppose.' He grimaced. 'Many of them are none too well balanced, emotionally, and most of them are either stupid or wilfully ignorant, or both. They're dangerous people.'

'Dorothy.' Amanda sounded hesitant. 'Those people who disappeared, the Muslim couple – you know who I mean?'

'Yes,' I said, equally hesitant.

'Well, I haven't wanted to go to the police with this; it's too vague. But I heard some women from that awful place talking yesterday in Tesco. I didn't hear everything. I moved away as soon as I saw them, because I didn't want them to see me. I guess I'm a coward, but—'

'Good grief, Amanda! You just heard Tom say they're dangerous. Me, I would have high-tailed it out of there. But you did manage to hear something?'

'Well, they were shouting, and they didn't seem to mind who heard. It was something about Arab infidels deserving what they got. It was dreadful! I heard the phrase "burn in hell", and then one of them laughed and said, "That's probably where they are right now!" I was so glad Miriam wasn't with me. She's learning kindness and tolerance now, and I don't want her exposed to that sort of filth.'

Tom shook his head and sighed. 'She'll hear it at school, I've no doubt. Children these days are so much more aware of the world around them than we were.'

'Ain't it the truth!' I exclaimed. 'Back when I was little, somewhere around the Jurassic era, we were kept away from the horrors. Of course that was in America. Over here, during the war and just after, children were exposed to far worse than any of us have ever dreamed of. It does seem, though, that the issues may change over the years and decades and centuries, but the fear and hatred are constant. One is almost tempted to believe in original sin.'

We finished our beer in silence.

SIXTEEN

Alan wasn't home when I got there. The rain was still pelting down, and I was cold and wet. I got out of my wet clothes and took a hot shower, and then, since I was in the bedroom and clad in a bathrobe, lying down to rest for a moment seemed a good idea. I pulled up the eiderdown and the animals settled around me. Blissful warmth. Ten minutes . . .

Alan woke me at teatime. 'Good rest, darling?'

'Oh, dear. I hadn't meant to go to sleep.' I yawned and stretched. 'How did it go with Derek and co today?'

'Not well, I'm afraid. Get dressed while I make tea, and we can talk.'

'Can you actually tell me anything? I ran into Derek briefly and he was very close-mouthed about the whole thing.'

'I can give you some general outlines. Not much more. I'm sorry.'

'Goes with the territory. I'll be down in five minutes.'

Well, it was ten, because I had to dress, and then the cats decided they needed some extensive cuddling, but when I got downstairs Alan had made the tea and set out some jam tarts. 'Heavens, I just had a big lunch!' It was a ritual comment; Alan paid no attention, but put two on my plate and poured my tea. 'Shall I recount my day first, or you?' he asked.

My mouth full, I pointed to him.

'I met Derek and we went to MI5 headquarters to meet with Carstairs and Duncan.'

'And Jonathan?'

'No. Jonathan's unofficial. They allow him to meddle, up to a point, but Duncan in particular is pretty testy about him.'

I sipped my tea. 'Duncan is pretty testy about a lot of things.'

'As well he might be! Dorothy, think of what he's facing. He's under enormous pressure because of the escalation in terrorist activity, not just here in England, but all over the world. His job is to be suspicious of everyone, and that suitcase full of money points suspicion squarely at the Ahmads.'

'But—'

'We, you and I, want to believe them innocent. And perhaps there are innocent explanations for the money, but I admit I find few of them convincing. And I know and like the family. I can't blame Duncan for his attitude.'

I held up both hands in concession. 'Okay, okay. So you met. At MI5 HQ, I suppose. Where is it, by the way? Or can you not tell me that?'

'My dear girl, you can find it yourself online. There's no secret about it. It's just across the Thames from Lambeth Palace.'

'Ah. So the archbishop can keep an eye on them. Good.'

'I doubt my Lord of Canterbury has much influence over Duncan's domain. However. We met. We told both the bigwigs about the infamous suitcase. Duncan was furious with Derek for not finding it earlier, and with the Endicotts for "concealing" it. I had a bit of trouble holding onto my temper at that point.'

'I should say so! As if any of them were at fault!'

'Duncan is the sort who has to blame someone when anything goes wrong, and things have gone badly wrong. Carstairs calmed him down a bit, and we went on to discuss the implications and what should be done about it.'

He stopped.

'And that's the part you can't talk about.' I sighed and absent-mindedly picked up the last tart.

'I can't go into details. But I'm allowing myself to pass along broad outlines. I know I can trust you not to broadcast them widely.'

I was touched. Alan's response meant not only that he trusted me – I knew that already – but that he thought I might be able to help somehow with this terrible, convoluted problem. 'I suppose Duncan is all for hunting down the Ahmads as spies and terrorists.'

'Of course. He can see that money from only one angle.'

'What has become of it, by the way?'

Alan was able to smile a little at that. 'That's one of the questions you mustn't ask. It's safely locked away.'

'And if I can guess where, I'd better not, right? Was Carstairs, or anybody, able to broaden Duncan's views at all?'

'We all came up with alternative notions. I suggested that, if the money was intended to fund terrorist activities, it was uncommonly careless of the Ahmads to leave it in the care of an innkeeper, protected only by a flimsy lock. He accepted that with only a token protest. He's not a stupid man.'

'No, I suppose not. He wouldn't have risen to his exalted position if he were. But he wears blinders. To an intelligence officer, everyone looks like a potential terrorist.'

'The old hammer/nail bias. Yes, I agree. But sometimes the hammer's right. And we all know there really are terrorists out there.'

'Sadly. But they're not the only bad guys, not by a long shot. Let me tell you about *my* day.'

Alan hefted the teapot and raised his eyebrows at me.

'No, thanks. But I wouldn't say no to a sherry.' So he poured glasses for us both and sat down with me on the sofa, and I told him about calling on Miss Simmons and learning about the new incarnation of the Brethren of Hatred. 'That's what I've decided to call them. Though now they're mostly Sistren, or whatever the feminine form would be. And I don't think there's much familial feeling uniting them. Hatred of a common enemy can seem to unite people for a little while, but it's awfully unreliable glue.'

'Yes. Coppers used to talk about the "criminal fraternity", but when criminals work together, it's for strictly pragmatic reasons. Greed always wins out over any pretended affection. And that's how we get them, in the end.'

'The trouble is, they may get a lot of other people in the meantime. I learned more about this unholy confederation, more than I want to know. Did Derek tell you where he was going when he suddenly had to leave your meeting?'

'Only that there was trouble brewing in Sherebury. His super thought it was urgent enough for Derek to take a car and driver. We'd taken the train up, but a police car can often get there quicker.'

'It *was* urgent, Alan, and if he hadn't got there when he did, I might have regretted it.'

'You don't mean to say you got yourself involved in something dangerous! Dorothy, how many times—'

I held up a hand. 'Not guilty this time. I wanted to see what the place looked like now. You know, the one that used to be called something about the One True God. Now it's the Temple of Truth, and it's in the same building. I don't know what good I thought it would do just to drive past, but that's what I did. I got lost—'

'What a surprise.'

'Sarcasm is the tool of the devil. Not badly lost, but I was coming at the place from the back, and when I rounded the corner I saw there was trouble, so I kept going and parked far enough away that I could see without being seen. And hear, unfortunately. It was awful! They were spewing hatred and death threats against Muslims, and the crowd kept growing and getting closer to me. And just when I was wondering how I was going to get out of there without them seeing me, Derek turned up like my guardian angel and got me out of there.'

'Thank God for that. Don't you realize those people are dangerous? Any mob is trouble, but when they're representatives of a hate group to begin with—'

'I do realize, even more so after my last little discussion of the day. I decided I deserved a little R & R after that rather frightening incident with the mob and all, so I dropped in at the King's Head for lunch, and ran into – you'd never guess – Amanda Doyle! Only it's not Doyle anymore, she's found herself a lovely new husband named Tom something. Alan, you wouldn't have known her! I didn't. She's gained enough weight to have a really good figure, and she was wearing nice clothes and make-up, but it's mostly happiness that's changed her. She positively glows. I'm so happy for her.'

'She deserves some happiness, after all she's been through. But you were saying . . .?'

'About that awful church, yes. Though even calling it a church seems blasphemous. Anyway, Tom – Wright, that's his name – Tom's been keeping an eye on the place because of Amanda's past experiences with them. He didn't say so, but I think maybe he's afraid that they'd try to get Miriam back in their clutches. Oh, and she's been admitted to St Margaret's Grammar School and is doing well, isn't that great?'

'Dorothy . . .'

'Yes, I'm coming to the point. Two points, actually. Tom has discovered that they, the Temple of Truth people, are now preaching a political message as well as a religious one, and it's the same old stuff – hatred and fear, and we're right and everybody else is wrong. But the worst thing, the scariest thing, is something Amanda overheard when she was shopping. A bunch of women from the Temple were using pretty loud voices and talking about "infidels burning in hell".'

Alan made a face.

'Yes, but that's not the end of it. One of the women laughed at that – *laughed*, can you imagine? – and said that was probably where they were right then.'

'Sorry, I'm not following. Where who was, when?'

'The implication was that some unspecified "infidels" were at that very moment burning in hell. Which would mean they were dead.'

Alan put his hand over mine. 'And you think . . .?'

'I don't know what I think. I'm not really thinking at all, just being fearful. But doesn't it sound like they were maybe talking about the Ahmads? And they think, or maybe even know, that they're dead?' My voice shook in spite of myself. I took a steadying sip of sherry.

'You know, love, that's always been a possibility.'

'Not always. We had that call from the Abdullah person. And Rahim saw his father on Saturday.'

'He thought he saw him.'

'I'm sure he did. He's not a half-baked kid. He's smart and savvy, and he'd know his own father! And we've been over this and over it, and no matter what anyone says, I believe Husam was alive, and free, on Saturday.'

'And when did Amanda say she overheard this nasty conversation?'

I tried to think. 'Yesterday?'

'Sunday. If we agree to posit Rahim's identification as accurate, Husam was alive in London on Saturday. That doesn't give a group from Sherebury a great deal of time to find him in London and kill him, does it?'

'Oh. If you put it that way, no, it doesn't.'

'I suggest that what Amanda heard was wishful thinking on the part of the speaker. Nasty, ugly, appalling, but not in any way truthful. They were leaping to conclusions. The Ahmad family is missing. They might have been killed. That is, to the hatemongers, a desirable outcome, therefore it is true. It follows that, since the Ahmads are Muslim and therefore wedded to Satanic principles, they are in hell. QED.'

'That logic is as full of holes as their so-called religion.'

'Of course it is. Didn't Sayers, in one of her novels, say that fancy religions led to a deterioration of the intellect? Something on that order.'

'Yes, and she was right. It begins with accepting without question a doctrine someone preaches on no evidence whatsoever. That leads to "I say so, so it's true." And that slippery slope eventually guts the critical abilities. So you think those bigots are indulging in pipe dreams. That makes me feel a little better, but only a little. The family may be alive, for the moment, but we've uncovered another group of people who hate them and want them dead. Alan, it's frightful! I can't even imagine what it must be like to be hated that much by people who don't even know me.'

'Try to remember, love, that most Muslims have lived in that climate of hatred and prejudice most of their lives, given the instability of the Middle East. They've probably developed an extra shell, as other minority groups have had to do – African Americans, for example.'

'Muslims are not in the minority in Iraq,' I objected.

'No, but the various Islamic sects have been warring with one another ever since the death of Muhammed, nearly fourteen hundred years ago. Muslims have been persecuted by each other, by Christians, by Jews, for all I know by Buddhists and Hindus. It's amazing, really, that people like the Ahmads can keep their dignity and their commitment to peace in the face of all that.'

I sat silent.

'I know you're frightened for them, Dorothy, but—'

'Wait!' I ran my hands through my hair. 'Wait a minute! I'm trying to pin down an idea.'

Alan patiently waited.

I spoke slowly, thinking out loud. 'They're committed to peace through understanding. What do they do about that commitment?'

'Teach their children, mingle with people of other religions—'

I waved agitated hands. 'Yes, all that. But what would they try to do in the face of the recent terrorist attacks here in England?'

SEVENTEEN

Alan considered. 'You think they would play some sort of active role?'

'I do think so. I think that their dedication to peace is more than a simple belief. I think it's a pillar of their religion, the root of their being, supporting an absolute obligation to do whatever they can to destroy hatred and bring about harmony and concord.'

'And so?'

'And so, if I'm right, they've come to England to try to deal with the terrorists, not to aid them, but to help stop them.'

Alan looked at me in alarm. 'Dorothy, do you have any idea what you're saying? ISIL, or whoever is behind the most recent attacks, is extremely well organized and well funded, and desperately dangerous. If the armies of several countries have been unable to stop them, how could Ahmad? I'm sorry, love, but it's a non-starter.'

'Alan, I'm not a child! I do know that. I know they can't do a lot, on their own. But suppose . . . suppose they got word that something awful was planned in London for the queen's birthday. If I were a terrorist, I'd think an occasion like that would be a perfect opportunity to kill a lot of people and get my point across. And if I were Husam Ahmad and learned that something like that was about to happen, I'd get to London as fast as I could. And if I were his wife, I wouldn't let him go alone. Of course the children would stay here, where they were relatively safe.'

'And just what, Husam Ahmad, were you planning to do when you got there?' His voice dripped with sarcasm.

'*I* don't know, but that doesn't mean *he* didn't have a plan, so don't sound so snarky. If you want to know what I think might have been in the works, I think all that money was involved somehow. Maybe – how's this? Maybe it was meant to help peaceful Muslims get to places where they'd be safe, where the killings wouldn't touch them and the reaction wouldn't redound upon them.'

'Then why didn't they take the money?' He still sounded sceptical, but at least he was beginning to consider the idea.

'I can only suppose that there was no time; the danger was so imminent that they had to get to London as fast as they possibly could.'

He sat silent, absent-mindedly petting Emmy, who had jumped into his lap in hopes of a handout, but was willing to settle for attention. At last he said, 'You know this is all the purest speculation.'

'What else can we do? Neither of us has forces at our command; we have only our own brains. And not to brag, but we both of us have pretty good brains, and quite a lot of experience with the way people think. If we can come up with some ideas to present to the guys who do have personnel at their beck and call, we're helping the only way we can!'

I had begun to sound combative. Alan shook his head, but with the kind of half-smile that concedes a point. Not quite 'I'm in,' but several degrees above 'Yes, dear.'

'And what, precisely, do you propose to do about this brilliant idea of yours?' he asked.

'All right, it's time you climbed off that high horse, my love. What I propose to do is write this up like a report. You'll have to help me with the jargon; I've never mastered officialese. Then we'll present it to Derek and see what he says. If he thinks the idea has merit he'll pass it along to Carstairs, who can decide whether it goes to Duncan. Given the level of animosity between those two, I'm not placing any bets either way.'

'Oh, he'll cooperate with Duncan. He has no real choice. With the world political climate what it is, everyone's paranoid. Everyone, Dorothy. The good guys, the bad guys, everyone. I hate to have to say it, but the Ahmads are in almost as much danger from some overzealous MI5 agent as from Islamic terrorists or pseudo-Christian hate groups. The world is a perilous place.'

I sighed. 'I know. I just read that guards on both sides of the American–Canadian border have been seizing people's cell phones, sometimes forcibly, and searching them for all kinds of information, regardless of whether that's legal. I swear it's like living in a police state.' Suddenly furious, I pounded my fist into a sofa cushion. 'And I am not, Alan, I am *not* going to put up with it! My native country has gone mad, I think, and there's nothing I can do about that. I can't even vote the idiots out anymore, now that I'm a permanent resident here. But I can't bear to see England descend into the pit of hatred and fear and injustice. I may only be one old lady, but what I can do and what I will do is everything possible to find the Ahmads and make sure they get out of this country safely!'

'"The only thing necessary for the triumph of evil is for good men to do nothing,"' Alan quoted softly. 'Good men and women. You've never been the sort to do nothing, my love. I've often wished you were more cautious, but I'm with your courage, all the way. You write up your idea and give it to me, and I'll put it in impressive police language and pass it along to Derek with my strong recommendation that he act on it. And then we'll sit down and do some more concentrated thinking about where the Ahmads might be.' He reached over and kissed me on the cheek. 'You are a remarkable woman, Dorothy Martin, and I think I'll keep you.'

I couldn't think of a thing to say, and I couldn't have said it, anyway, over the lump in my throat.

I went to my computer and sat down to labour over the wording of my idea. I was more and more convinced that I was on the right track. Now I had to convince sceptical officials to follow that track.

I wrote and discarded, wrote and discarded, blessing Bill Gates for making it so easy to rewrite. I made extensive use of the online thesaurus, changing words like *hypothesis* and *theory* to the more positive *premise* and *postulation*. I especially liked that one; it sounded scientific and oh-so-intellectual. I used sub-heads and bullet points wherever possible, and tried to avoid any suggestion that my construction was almost entirely unsubstantiated by any concrete facts.

I finally sighed, printed out what I'd written, and took it to Alan. 'I don't like it, but I can't do any more with it. My head is stuffed with hay. If you can make it sound less like a children's fantasy and more like solid fact, you deserve a Pulitzer Prize. I'm going to take Watson out for a walk. The rain has stopped, finally, and I need some fresh air.'

I also wanted to get away from Alan for a little while. I didn't want to hear his opinion of my little opus.

I put on my wellies; the rain had left puddles everywhere. Watson was going to get himself gloriously wet and muddy. I picked up one of his towels in the hopes of capturing the worst of it before he came back into the house, and we set out.

Half the sky was still covered with sullen clouds, but as they receded the sun appeared suddenly, turning every clinging raindrop to diamond and setting a brilliant bow over the Cathedral. I caught my breath. If there were ever an auspicious sign when I badly needed one, here it was. I stood spellbound and watched until it faded and Watson whined in impatience.

I went into the Cathedral Close and let him off the leash. A well-behaved dog, he wouldn't bother anybody, and I always carried a scooper and plastic bag in case some of the bushes proved too tempting. Later I'd tether him to the bike rack near the west door and drop in to pray for a little, but right now I just wanted to let my thoughts wander, leading me where they would.

I was strolling aimlessly, keeping half an eye on the dog, when he uttered a volley of delighted woofs and ran toward a figure just emerging from the church. I went after him as fast as I could and tried to call him back, until I saw that the figure was Jane, who wouldn't mind even if he jumped up on her.

He was too well trained to do that, but he licked every part of her that he could reach, his tail wagging as frantically as if he hadn't seen her for weeks rather than hours.

I caught up with him and clipped on his lead. 'Sorry about that. I wasn't paying attention.'

'Never mind. Good dog, aren't you?' She caressed his head, and he wriggled with joy.

'One thing about a dog: you're never in any doubt about their feelings. Some humans could benefit by their example.'

'Mmm. Busy?'

'No, just thinking out a course of action.'

'Talk about it?'

'That's just what I've been wanting to do.'

Watson tugged me along, knowing where he was headed. Life with two adored humans and two cats was good, but a visit with an equally adored human and several canine friends was a special treat. Besides, there might also be some edible treats going.

Jane let her dogs out to roughhouse with Watson, and we sat down at her scrubbed kitchen table with a nice wine in front of us. 'Alan?' she asked.

I hesitated. Did I want my husband to join us? It felt like the two of us had already talked the subject to death; I wanted a fresh perspective. On the other hand, it felt mean and petty to leave him out. I shrugged. 'I suppose.'

She gave me a sharp look as she pulled out her phone. 'No trouble?' she asked when she had made the call.

'No. Just we've talked ourselves out about the Ahmad situation. I think we're both tired of worrying about it, but we can't leave it alone. Or it won't leave us alone.'

'Time to stop talking. Act.'

'Yes, if we could figure out what to do!'

Alan walked in on that. 'I've emailed your report to Derek, and spoken with him about it. He seems to be persuaded, but of course the next step is to get MI5 and the Met to act.'

So I had to explain my theory to Jane, who nodded in agreement. 'Makes sense. More sense than anything *they've* come up with. Need Jonathan to work on it.'

'Yes, and I've emailed him, too.'

'Talk to Aya,' said Jane.

Alan looked startled. 'She's only a child. Would she know anything useful?'

I started to think, really think instead of just fretting. 'She's nine. That's fourth grade, in America. I remember my fourth-graders as sensible, intelligent people. They were my favourite pupils, in fact. Old enough to be interesting, too young to be smart-aleck. Back then, anyway. Nowadays they probably carry guns to school.'

'All right,' said Alan, ignoring my grumpiness, 'I'll accept her intelligence. I also thought I saw a level of sophistication that would be unusual in an English child that age. But would her parents have entrusted her with any of the details of what they planned to do in England? Surely it would be safer for all concerned if the children didn't know.'

'Possible to know too little. And kids listen.'

'So they do,' said Alan reflectively. 'I remember my own. We were careful about what we said in front of them, but somehow they picked up the most amazing things we'd never told them.'

'Atmosphere,' said Jane.

'Yes,' I added eagerly. 'And the younger they are, the more they can sense just by the way the situation feels. I never had any of my own, of course, but the kids at school would know something was up, often before I did. And they were so perceptive, they could usually guess what was amiss. And Jane, you're quite right. They would have wanted the kids to know enough, not to frighten them, but to protect them. They might even have told Rahim where to go in an emergency.'

'And he would have told Aya?'

'Maybe. Maybe not. He's part of a culture where men are in charge and women and girls simply follow orders.'

'But westernized,' Jane said firmly.

'Yes, and fond of his little sister,' I replied. 'When their parents vanished, I think he would have told her enough to calm her fears.'

'Including a meeting place?' asked Alan dubiously.

'I don't know!' I was suddenly impatient. 'We can't get into their heads. All we can do is make guesses and see where they lead.'

Jane went to the door and whistled for the dogs. They came charging into the kitchen, where she filled their bowls, including one for Watson, and picked up her purse. 'Train's fastest,' she pronounced, and led the way to her car, parked down the street. She barely gave us time to lock up our house and placate the cats before we were off to the station.

The train, for once, left on time, and arrived in London only a few minutes late. Jane snared a taxi and gave the driver an address. I thought about writing it down and then decided

to try to remember it. The paranoia about security was beginning to get its grip on me.

'Should you call and tell them we're coming?' I asked Jane.

'Don't want their number on my phone,' she said, and I
was silenced.

We arrived at a street of modest terraced Victorian
houses, the sort that we Americans used to call 'row houses'.
They were tall and narrow and now almost certainly made
into flats, cramped, inconvenient, and in London ruinously
expensive.

Jane had the driver stop at a corner; we walked the rest
of the way. Jane rang the bell in a complicated rhythm. I saw
the front curtain twitch, and then the door opened on a chain.
Jane held a low conversation with the person on the other
side, then the door closed, the chain rattled, and it opened
again. A dark man with a beard murmured, 'Come in, please.
Quickly.'

There was no sign of Aya. We were led into a small room
at the back of the house. It was lined with bookshelves and
had a minute fireplace with an electric fire in the grate. It was
not turned on, nor did the man turn on the light, and the room
was stuffy, chilly, and damp.

My apprehension was growing. I was beginning to believe,
based on all that had gone before, that we would be told Aya
had disappeared, or been abducted, or killed, or that terrorist
threats had made their way into this supposed sanctuary . . .

The man spoke. 'I'm sorry it's so chilly and close in here.
We thought it best to keep the windows closed, and we don't
like to have the fire when no one is in the room. I'll light it
for you.'

'Actually, sir, we'd like to talk to Aya. I should introduce
myself.' He did so, introduced me, told him why we were there,
and added, 'I'll understand if you don't wish to give me your
name.'

'It is not that we don't trust you,' said the man quietly. 'I
know who you are, of course, and I believe you have Aya's
best interests at heart, but we live in difficult times, and the
safety of the little girl is our primary concern. It will be better
if you go upstairs to her room, and I will ask you not to turn

on a bright light. We must make sure that no one suspects she is here.'

I grew more and more uneasy and glanced at Jane, who seemed perfectly at ease. I shrugged mentally and followed the rest up the stairs.

EIGHTEEN

Aya was sitting in bed reading. The small lamp on the bedside table was the only illumination, so the room was dim. She looked up when we entered, and her face split in a broad smile when she saw Jane.

'Miss Langland! Have you come to take me to Mama and Papa?'

'No, child, only to see you, ask you some questions.' The two looked at each other. Jane's look was searching. She said, finally, 'No need to ask how you're doing.'

'I'm fine,' she said, but she sounded listless. 'Mr and Mrs—'

'No names, dear,' Jane interrupted.

'Oh, I forgot. They – the people who are looking after me – are very nice, and good to me, and I am comfortable and, I think, safe. But I miss Mama and Papa and Rahim.' Her voice shook a little and she blinked hard.

'Of course you do,' I said. 'That's why we came to see you. We're hoping you might be able to help us find them.'

'How?' Her voice was wary.

Alan sat down in the small chair in the corner. 'It's like this, Aya. We think your parents have gone to help other people who might be in trouble in London.'

'People like us?'

'Yes. Did they ever tell you that they might have to do such a thing?'

She closed her mouth firmly.

'Ah. They said that you mustn't tell anyone. Aya, I don't know how to convince you that you should tell me, how to make you believe that I'm trying to help find your family and that I wish them no harm. You and I follow different faiths, but we in this room are all children of Abraham, with many of the same beliefs, and I swear to you, by all that I hold holy, that what I tell you is the truth.'

The man said something to Aya in what I assumed was

Arabic. She replied with a single questioning word, and the man nodded.

Aya turned to Alan. 'I will answer your questions,' she said gravely.

'Thank you, Aya. I hope and believe that your answers will help us find your parents and your brother. First, did your parents tell you and Rahim what they planned to do in England?'

'Papa told Rahim. He is a boy, and I am a girl, but Rahim knows that I am intelligent and can be trusted. Also he loves me and does not want me to fall into danger. He thought I should know what might happen.'

'That was very sensible of him. What did your father tell him?'

Aya took a deep breath. 'Papa said that he was taking us to England because there were many important things to see here, palaces and castles and places where battles happened and treaties were signed. Papa and Mama both think history is very important to know.' She stopped and chewed her lip.

Jane laid a hand on her arm. 'You're safe, child. Don't worry.'

'But Mama and Papa and Rahim . . .' She blinked again.

'We are working very hard to make sure that they are safe, too,' said Alan in his gentlest voice, 'and you are helping us. Rahim told you more, didn't he?'

She sighed. 'He said that Papa said that he might have to go to London without us for a day or two. Mama, too. And Papa said that if . . . if anything happened to them, or we were afraid, we should have someone take us to his uncle Abdullah, who lives in London. But Rahim didn't tell me where Uncle Abdullah lives, so I can't go to him!'

This time the tears won. She put her head down on her folded arms and tried not to sob.

Jane couldn't stand it. She sat on the bed and put her arms around the little girl and made those little cooing sounds, the universal wordless words of comfort.

Alan looked at me and raised his eyebrows. I shrugged in indecision. We needed more information, but if Aya didn't have it, there was no point in disturbing her further.

Jane took the matter out of Alan's hand. 'Your Uncle Abdullah, child. What is his other name?'

She drew a shaky breath and looked up, wiping her eyes with the heels of her hands. 'He has many other names. Our names are longer and more complicated than yours. But in England I think he is known as Abdullah ibn Rashid.'

'And do you have any idea where in London he lives?' That was Alan, persisting while Aya was quieter. 'London has many different neighbourhoods. Did Rahim say anything that might help us to find Uncle Abdullah?'

Aya thought hard. 'He said something about a big shop. I can't remember anything else.' She slumped down into her pillow. Jane gave her one last pat, kissed her on the cheek, and stood up.

'Yes,' said Alan, also standing. 'Aya, you have helped us a great deal, and I hope we haven't disturbed you too much. You are a very brave girl and I know your Mama and Papa are very proud of you. Rahim, too! Now you settle down and go to sleep.'

'Are you going to find Mama and Papa and Rahim?' Her voice was suddenly strong and steady and most unchildlike. The question was a clear challenge.

Alan accepted it. 'Yes, Aya, we are. I can't promise when. But we will find them. Goodnight, now.'

The man surveyed the street carefully through the window before letting us out, and we heard him put the chain back on the door.

Alan let out a soundless whistle, but made no other comment until we reached a busy intersection where street signs were prominently displayed on the corners of buildings. He pulled his *A-Z*, the comprehensive London street guide, out of his pocket and found our location. 'Good! There's a tube station just two streets away.' He led us confidently to it, chose the line he wanted, and shepherded us to the right platform. I consulted the list of stations on the wall; it didn't enlighten me to any great degree. I had no idea where we were, and I'm not familiar with the Northern Line.

'I don't suppose you'd like to tell me where we're going,' I said, trying to sound meek and, I'm afraid, not succeeding.

'We'll change at Embankment,' he said, pointing to the schematic. I gave up. Either he was continuing the cloak-and-dagger routine, or he was being obscure to annoy, because he knew it teases.

We duly changed at Embankment to the District and Circle Line, where the list of stops was much more enlightening. 'Ah!' I spotted Victoria Station a few stops along. 'We're going home!'

'Not quite yet.' And he said not another word until we reached the St James's Park station, where he ushered us out.

'We're going to the park? Isn't it a little late? It'll be closed by now.'

'No, my dear, we're going to a place that never closes.'

'Give me that *A-Z*!' I demanded.

He handed it over with a grin. I found the park, and nearby – 'Oh! But why?'

'Because, my dear, I think I know where to find Uncle Abdullah.'

'With just a name? There aren't very many Arab names. If we had the full name, with the man's whole ancestry built in, there might be a chance, but how many hundred men do you suppose there are in London with the names Abdullah Rashid?'

'But we have one other clue, remember?'

'Big shop,' said Jane, beginning to look happier than she had all day.

'Precisely. Now, my dear, when you think "big shop" in London, what do you think? What's the biggest and most famous of them all, owned until recently by an Arab?'

'Well, Harrods, of course, but – oh, of course! I *am* being stupid! Knightsbridge. You think Uncle Abdullah lives in Knightsbridge.'

'I do, indeed. And here we are, ladies. I doubt they'll let you in, but there's a reasonably comfortable place to wait.' And after a few formalities, we entered the renowned precincts of Scotland Yard.

Waiting is not my best thing. Jane, I could see, was also impatient. 'I want to put on my armour and get on my horse and go find him,' I whispered.

'Find *them*,' she replied in a low growl.

'Yes. Especially Ra– the youngest.'

I wanted to talk about what the Ahmads might be up to in this vast metropolis. I wanted Jane to convince me that they couldn't possibly be in any danger. I wanted to *do* something to make it so.

Walls have ears, even perhaps in the most famous police station in the world. The vast personnel of the Metropolitan Police are all human, with human failings. Certainly the majority of them are decent and honest. There have, however, been policemen and -women all over the globe who went bad. We couldn't risk a conversation that might be overheard and used to hurt our friends. We sat silently fuming.

When Alan reappeared, it took every bit of my self-control not to ask him what had happened, how Carstairs had responded, what was being done. I kept my mouth shut until we got outside, and then, when I opened it, Alan didn't let me talk.

'Love, I do understand. And I do want to tell you all about it. But I'm afraid it's going to have to wait until we get home. I'm sorry.'

I ground my teeth. 'I hate it, but all right. There's one thing I must know right now. Is anyone going to do anything about it?'

'Oh, yes. Yes, indeed. Now, do you want to walk to the station, or shall we find a taxi?'

'Walk,' Jane and I said together.

If we'd been closer to the park we'd have had a prettier walk, the park on one side and, presently, Wellington Barracks on the other, in the delightfully named Birdcage Walk. Then Buckingham Palace and the Royal Mews and on to Victoria Station. The way we chose, down Victoria Street, is less picturesque but more direct. It's a busy commercial street of small restaurants and shops. It's a part of London I've known well for years, and despite my anxiety and eagerness for information, just being abroad in the city I so love raised my spirits. I quoted Sam Johnson to myself: 'When a man is tired of London . . .'

Alan heard me and finished the quote: 'He is tired of life.' He smiled and took my arm.

We had just missed a train to Sherebury. Of course. There was no place to sit and wait except in a pub or café, and the smell of food reminded me suddenly that we'd had no supper and I was starving. So we bought baguette sandwiches from Au Bon Pain and ate them leaning against pillars near our platform, washing them down with bottled water and throwing the wrappings and napkins on the floor. My housekeeper's mind rebels at the practice, but the station abolished rubbish bins years ago in the days of IRA bombs and has never reinstated them. Cleaners circulate constantly to sweep up the detritus. Oh, well, it all gives work, I suppose. By way of dessert I got an almond croissant to eat on the train, and then it was announced and we boarded.

There was only one other person in our carriage, but that was one too many for a private discussion. I ate my croissant, scattering flakes of pastry everywhere, and then picked up an *Evening Standard* someone had discarded and read depressing news for part of the way home. I finally cast it aside and just stared out the window at the darkening landscape, wishing desperately that we could talk about our problem.

Even the weariest river winds somewhere safe to sea. Even the longest journey comes to an end. This one was long only in our minds, and we were eventually decanted onto the platform at Sherebury station and found the haven of Jane's car.

'Whew!' I said. 'I feel like I've been holding my breath for hours. Tell, Alan.'

He was prepared. He'd probably been outlining his ideas all the way home. 'Carstairs was impressed with your thinking, Dorothy. He had, of course, considered the possibility that the Ahmads had fled to London on some sort of errand of mercy, but he had not considered that the children might have some information. It's a pity we didn't think to ask Rahim when we could, but events were moving a little too rapidly for logical thought. Carstairs gave orders, while I was still there, to find Uncle Abdullah, beginning in Knightsbridge.'

'They won't arrest him or anything like that, will they?'

'The orders are to find him, question him, and search his home for the Ahmads.'

'If they're there, I'm sure they'll be hiding.'

'Of course, love. But the Metropolitan Police are well trained in search procedures. If they're with Abdullah, they will be found. If they have been there, the police will find evidence of their presence.'

'What then?' Jane's voice had sunk to a growl.

Alan sighed. 'When – if – they find the Ahmads, I'm afraid they'll be taken into custody, if only protective. I know, I know, but they can hardly do anything else, given the political climate. They may be entirely innocent of any wrongdoing. We believe they are on the side of the angels. But the authorities can't afford to assume any such thing. And even if, *especially* if, their aims are merciful, there are certainly a number of groups who would like to make sure they don't carry out their intentions. Hatred is an enormously powerful force.'

'And Rahim?' She sounded even more menacing.

'I think I can answer that one, Jane.' I swallowed hard. 'Much as I hate to have to say it, children have been involved in terrorist plots before. Rahim is eleven, quite old enough to understand the stakes. And he ran away to his father. They'll have to question him, too.'

We reached our street and got out in silence. Jane didn't even say goodnight before she stumped into her house.

The night had turned chilly. Alan laid a small fire in the parlour, and we sat, drinks in our hands and friendly animals nearby, and brooded.

NINETEEN

I was too tired and out of sorts to wake early the next morning, even with a boisterous chorus of birds outside and a trio of hungry animals within. Alan shook me awake when I would much have preferred to snuggle deeper in my pillow. His voice was grave. 'Developments, my dear. Here's your coffee.'

The caffeine was not enough to restore my good humour, but a second cup at least brought me to full consciousness. 'Yes. What?'

'Uncle Abdullah has decamped.'

I tried to process that. 'Explain.'

'The Met had no trouble finding his house. Elegant Georgian townhouse in Wilton Place. They send their most diplomatic officers to talk to him. They found no one at home, not even a servant. The neighbours on either side, approached with all the tact the officers could muster, claimed no knowledge of where he might be, and indeed little knowledge of the man himself. Quiet, pleasant neighbour. No, don't know him except to say hello when arriving or departing. No trouble at all, officer. Goodnight. And a firmly closed door, with no excuse at all to inquire further.'

I sagged back into the pillows. 'Dead end.'

'Not quite. We now have a name and address to run through the system. We'll find out if the man is a British subject, whether he was born in this country or the Middle East, what his business is, or his source of income.'

'A whacking big income, if he lives in a townhouse in Knightsbridge.'

'Indeed. We'll also trace his ties to the Ahmads, his ties if any with other Muslim families, including Muhammed al Fayed, the former owner of Harrods. He's Egyptian, of course, but there still might be some connection. With a name and address, it's truly amazing what the Met can find out.'

I shivered. 'Amazing. And scary. There's no privacy in the world anymore.'

'Well, of course not. Electronics have done away with privacy. Especially if one is extremely wealthy and a member of a sometimes despised minority. Unfair, of course, but true. And useful to the police.'

'Or anyone else who wants to spy on you. I think I'm happier being an ordinary person.'

'You still leave an electronic trail wherever you go, whatever you do, love. You know that.'

'Yes. It's just that with me, nobody's much interested. Oh, all *right*, Watson!' He was whining and tugging at the sheet. 'Haven't you been out?'

'Of course he has. And he's had his breakfast. He just wants your love and attention. Don't you, mutt?'

Apparently he did. He continued to whine till I was up and dressed and downstairs, where he got his petting and settled at last on my feet to let me have some toast and another cup of Alan's excellent coffee.

'Do we have an agenda?' I asked, as Alan scrambled eggs and fried bacon.

'Not a very ambitious one, but I've done a bit of thinking. I wonder if there's anyone we've overlooked who might have some clue about the whereabouts, or the plans, of the Ahmads?'

'Let's see. We don't know where they were before they came to Sherebury. Can the Met trace that? Or MI5, or anybody?'

'Probably. Probably already have done.'

'Would they tell us what they found out?'

Alan shrugged.

'No, I don't suppose they would. Well, then. We've talked to the Endicotts. Everybody's talked to them. I'll try again, in case there's some little something that they forgot to tell the cops. Jane – we know everything she knows. How about Nigel and Inga? I don't know if anyone's asked them anything, except on that first night when they disappeared. Heavens, it was only a few days ago, and it seems like weeks. Oh! They talked a bit to Margaret and probably to Kenneth. I wonder if they're been questioned.'

'I doubt it,' said Alan thoughtfully. 'You know, I very much doubt it. The dean of a cathedral and his wife are Very Important Persons, though we sometimes forget that, as they're such dear friends. And I don't know if any of the authorities realized they'd had some conversations with the Ahmads.' He slid bacon and eggs out of the frying pan onto two plates. 'As soon as we've got outside that lot, let's go and find them.'

Matins were over long ago, so the dean might be in his office, or talking with the bishop or the organist/choirmaster or city officials, or attending one of the meetings which were the bane of his existence. Margaret was an extremely busy lady with more guilds and committees than any woman ought to be burdened with. Either of them might be almost anywhere, but the Cathedral was the obvious place to start.

We slipped first into the chapel set aside for private prayer, and then waylaid the first verger we saw. No, he hadn't seen either the dean or his wife. Had I tried his office? Or Margaret might be at home.

The office and the deanery were in separate buildings in the Close, one nearby, the other at the far corner. We were about to split up and go in different directions when we ran into Jeremy Sayers, the organist/choirmaster. He was on his way to choir practice and was about to wave and pass on when I stopped him.

'Jeremy, I know you're in a hurry, but we're looking for the Allenbys – either or both.'

'You're in luck, dears. You'll find them in the gift shop. Something about a grandchild's birthday? Must run – ta-ta.'

The shop is in a corner of the Cathedral itself, near the main entrance, the better to trap souvenir-hunting tourists. The dean and his wife were just coming out, carrying parcels, as we approached.

'Jeremy told us you were searching for birthday presents,' I said. 'Looks like you were successful.'

'Yes, they're for Colin. He's going to be nineteen on Friday – hard to believe!' Margaret relieved the dean of one of the parcels, a book, by the weight of it. 'He's studying to be an architect; we're so proud of him! So we got him the book about the building of the Cathedral. It's quite new; have you seen it?' Taking it out of the bag, she laid it on a convenient table and showed us some of the pictures, while her husband showed signs of wanting to slip away.

'It's a beautiful book,' said Alan, 'and we'd enjoy looking at it properly before you send it on its way. Right now, though, I'm sure you both have things to do, and we need to talk with you, if you can spare a moment.'

The dean's face instantly took on his priestly expression of kindly concern. 'Of course. Shall we go to my room?' There's a small room in the Cathedral itself set aside for urgent pastoral counselling when time constraints or inclement weather make the walk to the administrative office inexpedient.

'It's nothing like that,' I assured him, watching visions of various disasters cross his mobile face. 'We just have some questions about the Ahmads.'

'And we'd like to talk to both of you, if you have the time,' added Alan.

'I've a meeting in a quarter of an hour, but my time is yours until then,' said Kenneth. 'Have you anything urgent on, my dear?'

'Nothing more urgent than this,' Margaret assured him. 'Those dear people must be found, and if we can help, we must. Though I don't know that we have any real information.'

Alan looked around at the tourists, vergers, and others nearby. The choir was warming up, the ladies who look after the altar linens were chatting in a corner, the flower guild were conducting a *sotto voce* argument near the font. The dean led the way to his room.

'It's a question of why they came here,' I said when we had sat down in the shabby, squashy old armchairs that provided comfort to the distressed who came here seeking counsel. 'We think – that is, I think, and Alan's beginning to agree – that they came to England for a specific purpose, having to do somehow with aid and comfort to English Muslims who are under persecution because of the terrorists. That could be what all that money is about. You've heard about the money?'

Margaret nodded gently and I realized what a foolish question it was. 'Oh, yes. The Shereburg grapevine. I suppose there's no one in town who hasn't heard.'

'What my wife is trying to ask,' said Alan, 'is whether any of the Ahmads, including the children, said anything to you that might give a clue to their plans.'

I was about to apologize for wasting time, but Alan caught my eye and I desisted. No need to waste any more minutes.

Margaret frowned in thought. 'They walked into the Cathedral, and I happened to notice them. We don't have many Muslim visitors, and I wanted to make sure they felt welcome, so I talked to them for a bit. Nothing of any substance. He told me they were Iraqi, in England for a visit. They said complimentary things about the building. I asked about their family. The usual. And then Mrs Ahmad said they wanted to come to evensong, and that's when I saw you and asked you to play hostess. I was just a little nervous about how they might be received. Not by the regulars, I don't mean, but one never knows about the tourists. And in the current climate . . .'

'Yes.' Alan nodded. 'Well, not much there. Did either of you talk with them on any other occasion?'

The dean nodded slowly, wearing his professional face again. 'Yes. Mr Ahmad came to me a few days later, saying he had a question and wanted my advice.'

'He said exactly that?' Alan leaned forward, suddenly alert.

'Exactly that. I inferred that he needed to talk to a man of God. I wondered why he didn't go to the imam, but it was none of my business, after all.'

'And did your inference prove to be true?'

'I think I can say that it did. Alan, he spoke to me in confidence. I have been wrestling over what my duty might be. I'm not at all sure I can repeat what we discussed.' His head bowed as if in prayer.

My heart sank. I'd run into Kenneth's scruples before. If he felt he would be betraying a trust by telling us what Husam said, nothing including torture would drag it out of him.

Alan waited a moment, and then said, 'Kenneth, you know I won't ask you to ignore your conscience. You wouldn't, anyway. You couldn't. But please consider that you may have information that could save the lives of that family. If we, that is the police and MI5, don't find them soon, there's a very good chance that someone else will.'

He let that dark possibility reverberate in the room while I held my breath.

The dean sighed. 'What he said was not, of course, in the nature of a confession. I will give you his exact words, as nearly as I can remember them. He said he had determined, as a matter of conscience – he used that phrase – to embark on a course of action that was certainly dangerous and might involve breaking the law. He said that his purpose was to preserve lives, both English and Arab.'

'He said that, as well?'

'Yes. He said that the Prophet, like Jesus, commanded that we love our neighbour and love peace, and that he was committed to promoting peace in any way that he could. He had already spoken about his plans to the imam at the local mosque, he said, but the imam, while a well-respected man, is an émigré from the Middle East, with his own agenda. Mr Ahmad wanted now, he said, to consult with someone who was less personally involved in the problem, and who was thoroughly familiar with England and its customs and laws. I told him my knowledge of the law was only general, but I would be happy to listen.'

'And his question? That is, what was the advice that he sought?'

'He asked whether I thought he was justified in risking, not only his life, but the lives of his family and perhaps many other people in this pursuit.'

'And what did you say?' I broke in. I couldn't help it.

Kenneth looked at me with a weary smile. 'Only what anyone would have said. That I could give him no intelligent advice without knowing more exactly what he planned to do, but that every man must follow his own conscience. I suggested that he pray about it, and reminded him that this Cathedral is a place of prayer for everyone, not just Christians. And he thanked me, and blessed me, and I him, and that was the last time I spoke to him.'

He rose. 'I'm sorry, but I must go. When my bishop calls a meeting, I have no choice but to attend. I know I have left you with more questions than I have answered, and with great anxiety, as well. I'm sorry,' he said again, and went out the door.

I just sat there. My ideas were confirmed, in a way, but Kenneth was right. Now there were more questions, and terrifying possibilities. And we were no nearer finding the family who, it now appeared, were almost certainly in grave danger.

Alan stood. 'The next step is obviously to speak to the imam, but I must consult Jonathan first. I don't want to do anything official just yet. This is privileged information, and I don't feel justified in spreading it about yet, but Jonathan needs to know. Excuse me.'

Margaret released herself from the clutches of the armchair. 'Tea,' she said firmly. 'We need to talk.' She gave me her hand and tugged me to my feet.

'But don't you have something you should be doing?'

'My meeting, unlike Kenneth's, was not called by the bishop. I am therefore free to ignore it in favour of a more pressing duty: friends in deep distress. Come along.'

TWENTY

The Deanery is a most restful place. It's many centuries old, so the floors are uneven and the ceilings low, and nothing is square or plumb anymore. Before the dissolution of the abbeys, it was the home of the abbot, and when the defunct abbey was given new life as a cathedral, the house fell to the lot of the dean and his family, so generations of clergy wives have impressed upon it the stamps of their personalities, and for the most part they must have been generous, kindly personalities. The place has a serenity that can't be entirely explained by the soothing blues and greens of the furnishings or the patina of ancient panelled walls and oaken floors.

Margaret put me in the front parlour where I found myself, this time, immune to the soothing influence.

She went to the kitchen, returning in a remarkably short time with a tea tray. 'Prince of Wales,' she announced. 'This crisis calls for strength.'

I was bemused for a moment until I realized she was referring to the tea, Prince of Wales being one of the more robust blends.

She handed me a cup. The scent of fragrant steam made me feel a little better, but the tea was too hot to drink, so I set it aside and picked up a piece of shortbread. Margaret makes the best I've ever tasted. Buttery and just slightly sweet, it melts in the mouth.

'I phoned Jane and asked her to join us. She always looks at things from a slightly different angle and can help us think.'

There was a knock at the door. 'Come in,' Margaret called. 'It's open.' She waited for Jane to sit, handed her a cup of tea, and said, 'Dorothy, I didn't tell her what Kenneth told us. Will you fill her in?'

I tested my tea. Still too hot, but I took a sip anyway, to buoy me up. 'Husam told Kenneth he was going to walk into danger, in the interests of peace.' I spoke as unemotionally as I could. 'He said that his actions might be illegal and would certainly be hazardous not only to him but to his family and perhaps others as well. He asked for Kenneth's advice.'

Jane considered this. 'Nothing else?'

I put my cup down carefully so my shaking hand wouldn't cause a spill. Margaret noticed and answered Jane's question.

'No. He said nothing specific about what he planned to do, or where or when.'

'And it's the "where" that we desperately need to know. Jane, we have to find them! And before the police do, if they're going to be breaking the law. In the present climate of hatred and fear, you know the police would throw the book at them.'

'Have to know what. That'll tell us where.'

'Maybe.' I was stuck in a rut of hopelessness.

Jane ignored that. 'Said it was for peace. What?'

'What could one man do to promote peace? Well.' Margaret rested her chin on her hands in the classic 'thinking' position. 'One man with a lot of money. He could . . . hmm . . . bribe the terrorists?'

'That would take more money than even the Ahmads have. Millions. Billions, maybe. And don't forget, the family isn't involved in politics. Or maybe you didn't know that. Alan found out.'

'Okay, scratch that. He could help other Muslims, peaceful ones, get out of London. Only where would they go? There's even more danger back in their home countries, and outside the Middle East, few countries welcome Muslims. The fear is worldwide.'

'And don't forget he was worried that his actions might be illegal. Why only "might", I wonder?' I mused.

'Doesn't know English law.'

'Oh. Yes, you're probably right, Jane. As a multinational businessman, he'd know the laws about trade and so on, in various countries, but maybe not criminal law.' I thought about that for a moment. 'He could have asked Alan.'

'No. Couldn't talk about it.'

I rubbed my temple, where a faint headache was beginning to issue nasty little warnings of worse to come. Margaret opened a drawer in a small table, pulled out a bottle of ibuprofen, and handed it to me. I gulped a couple with my now lukewarm tea and nodded my thanks. Really, Margaret was the ideal wife for a priest. Kind, helpful, and observant.

'All right, ladies,' Margaret said with a smile, calling us to order. 'Back to possibilities. Let's reason it out. Suppose you were an ambassador of peace, in a country where your motives might be suspect. Suppose your funds are, if not exactly unlimited, at least abundant. What would you do?'

'It would depend,' I said slowly, thinking out loud, 'on what I knew about the country and what contacts I had. If I were familiar with organized groups that worked for peace, I would try to help them. I still can't imagine how that might be construed as illegal. However. I would want to know first that the organizations were legitimate and the money really would go to help intelligent efforts for peace and not just end up in the pockets of the leaders. That's where my contacts would come in handy.'

'Ahmad has contacts. Business, family.'

'Ah, yes, Uncle Abdullah. And of course his company.' I smacked my head. 'I'd forgotten all about them. I wonder if the police – no, forget it, silly question. Of course they've talked to his corporate officers. Who would, I imagine, be very cagey about their answers, expressing great concern while giving nothing away.'

Margaret nodded slowly. 'Yes. Businessmen at that level are very much like politicians. They *are* politicians, in fact, except that their machinations are in the private rather than the public sector. Mostly. I wonder . . .' Her voice drifted away as her mind focussed on something we couldn't see.

Jane could, apparently, read her mind. 'Not me. Not Dorothy.'

I was lost.

Margaret came back. 'Sorry. I was thinking of who might be able to get the UniPetro officers to tell anything they know or surmise. You're right, Jane, none of us, and not an official person like the police, certainly, but – do you know, Dorothy, our bishop can be remarkably persuasive. You wouldn't think of it, just to look at him, but he has a kind of moral authority that can awe the most unlikely people. I've seen him reduce a young man from a London street gang to repentant tears.' She held up a right hand. 'Truth.'

'You'd sic the *bishop* on Ahmad's business associates? But they're Muslims! Would they even listen to a Christian clergyman? If he could even get in to see them.'

'Oh, Dorothy, I'm disappointed in you! Hasn't meeting the Ahmads taught you that not all Muslims are bigoted? Any more than all Christians are. Actually, if they are indeed men who practise their religion—'

'And women,' Jane put in.

'Sorry, and women, they're far more likely to be courteous to a clergyman than some of the harder-boiled English corporate CEOs. Respect for one religion often carries over into respect for others.'

'I stand corrected. But why not the imam? The UniPetro people would be more likely to see him, wouldn't they? And he's apparently much more involved in this mess.'

'That's why not. He may also stand in danger from the crazies.'

'Oh . . . well . . . but the bishop would still have to get past the barricades, and CEOs are extremely well protected.'

Margaret got that dreamy look again. 'I know someone – no guarantees, but I think she could get an appointment.'

I looked at her sharply, but she gave me a serene smile and would not say one more word.

'Well, supposing they did plan to go to some relief agencies, or whatever,' I pursued. 'I suppose we could come up with a list of possibilities and go and talk to them, but it seems pretty pointless. Because, whatever they planned to do, one thing we know they did not do was distribute money left and right. They left it all behind!'

Jane shrugged. 'Plan went awry.'

I suddenly lost my temper and stood up. 'Then all this discussion about what they planned to do is pointless, isn't it? Because if we're right, they didn't do it. And if we're wrong we're completely at sea anyway. I'm going to leave it to the police. Excuse me.'

It's a very short walk through the Close from the Deanery

to our house, so I was still in a fine temper when I reached home. Watson met me, but sensing my mood as he always does, he backed away and retreated to the safety of the kitchen. I followed him. I needed coffee. Tea is all very well, but when mood adjustment is necessary and it's far too early in the day for alcohol, coffee is what's necessary.

Of course the cats heard me and appeared from wherever they'd been. They can dematerialize at will, I think. They have taught me the rule, however; when a human is in the kitchen, it's time for the cats to be fed. They don't mind if we feed Watson, too, as long as it's clearly understood that they come first.

I am a well-trained housekeeper to my cats. I opened a can of their favourite food and added a little albacore tuna (they won't eat the cheaper kind). Then of course I had to give Watson a little kibble, and then I remembered I'd come in to make myself coffee, and while it brewed I saw that the counter-top needed a good wipe down, and what with one thing and another I was somewhat less irritable when Alan walked in.

'Smells good,' he said. 'But isn't it nearly lunchtime?'

'Oh, I suppose it is. It's been a frustrating morning, and I just really needed some coffee. Alan, I don't think we're getting anywhere – I don't think *anyone* is getting anywhere with finding the Ahmads, and I'm getting more frustrated and worried by the minute.'

'Kenneth's revelation was worrisome, I agree. I've spoken with Jonathan, and he agrees that the imam may have some useful information. He also said he thought I was the one to speak with him.'

I frowned. 'Why? Why not somebody official?'

'The situation's touchy, Dorothy. We're dealing here with the leader of a religion whose adherents have been persecuted for centuries – and who, indeed, have done their share of persecuting. In the current climate of hatred and suspicion on all sides, the leader of a mosque in a predominantly Christian community has to be especially vigilant. In his position, if a policeman or detective came calling, all my defensive hackles would rise.'

'You're a policeman.'

'But a retired one, and a long-time member of this community. I have met Mr Alani on several occasions, and we respect each other. I think he will trust me when I say I seek information solely in order to protect the Ahmads.'

'That may not be the way Carstairs and Duncan, especially Duncan, will look at it.'

'Possibly not. Which is why I'm the one to make the approach.'

I thought about that for a moment while I poured two cups of coffee. 'All right. I agree. But I'm coming with you.'

Alan frowned. 'That might not be a good idea, love. Muslim tradition—'

'Muslim tradition be hanged. This is the twenty-first century, and we are in England, not a theocratic dictatorship. Husam Ahmad is perfectly courteous to women, and plainly does not believe that we are inferior creatures. I won't interfere, but I want to see and hear for myself what Mr What's-His-Name has to say.'

'Alani. Very well. But hurry and drink your coffee.' He consulted his watch. 'It's nearly time for midday prayers.'

'Then we'd better wait, don't you think? We don't want to rush this. Could you phone him and make an appointment for after lunch?'

So while Alan made the phone call I put a salad together and we dutifully sat down, but every time I tried to take a bite, I saw Rahim, eyes bright, filled with desire to sing like an English choir boy, and my throat closed up. Surely he was safe! He had to be safe! But where was he, and where were his parents?

'What did you do when Margaret spirited you off?'

'Jane joined us at the Deanery, and we sat and drank tea and tried to make some sense of the mess, but all we managed to come up with is what the Ahmads might have planned to do with the money. Margaret thinks the bishop might be able to get some information out of the CEO of UniPetro.'

'The police have already been there, you know. Why on earth send the bishop, of all people?'

'Apparently he's a very persuasive man. I don't know; Margaret made it sound plausible. She's a persuasive person, too. But it's all pointless, because he didn't do what he had planned; the money's still here. Or wherever the cops took it. So his plans are irrelevant!'

'Not quite irrelevant, love. If he's free but in hiding, knowing his plans might tell us where he went. And we know, or we believe, that he was free last Saturday, because Rahim saw him. Are you going to eat something? Low blood sugar starves the brain cells.'

'I don't know that lettuce contributes much to one's blood sugar!' But I drank another cup of coffee; lack of caffeine starves my brain cells, too.

TWENTY-ONE

don't know what I expected the mosque to look like. I suppose I had some vague idea of onion domes and minarets and elaborate tile mosaics. In fact the building, which I had passed many times without paying attention, was simply a converted house in a neighbourhood of similar houses. A third storey had been added to the original building, and a small dome, surmounted by a crescent, was the only sign that it was no longer a residence. Alan managed to find a minute parking space, and we went to the door.

It was opened immediately by a man in standard European dress. His beard was neatly trimmed, and his expression was cordial. 'Mr Nesbitt, sir, it is good to see you again. And this is Mrs Martin?'

He got the names right; a point in his favour. We shook hands and he led us into a room that had plainly been constructed of several rooms made into one. It was rather bare and institutional, with long wooden tables and benches set out school-cafeteria style. 'You have not visited here before, I think? This is where we have our meal after Friday prayers, and on other occasions. You see it is adjacent to the kitchen. Our prayer hall is upstairs, and later I will take you there if you wish, but you would need to remove your shoes, and I think you would not want to do that just now.'

'"Put off thy shoes from off thy feet, for the place whereon thou standest is holy ground",' I quoted softly. I hadn't intended to be heard, but Mr Alani smiled.

'Exactly. The tradition goes back to Moses and beyond. It is practical as well, of course. We kneel on the floor to pray, as you probably know, so the carpet must be kept clean. Now, if you will come through here, we can be comfortable and talk.'

The room where he took us was small and rather shabby, a lot like the dean's little office in the Cathedral. Mr Alani closed the door and gestured to us to sit. He cleared his throat and the atmosphere changed.

'I am glad that you came to me, Mr Nesbitt. Had you not, I would have come to you. I have been much torn in my mind about what to do, but now I am certain. You wish to know if I know anything about the disappearance of the Ahmad family.'

'Yes,' said Alan simply.

'I will tell you what I can. You know, of course, of the family's strong belief in peace through understanding. You may not know the extent of their efforts to spread that peace. You probably assume that, given Mr Ahmad's position in the oil industry, the family is extremely wealthy. That is not the case.'

I frowned, and the imam held up his hands.

'Yes, they live well. They dress nicely and can afford to travel in comfort. But compared to some of those in his position, compared for example to your Bill Gates, Mr Ahmad is a pauper. That is because he donates most of his income to the cause he espouses.'

The imam paused for a moment. 'If you will allow, I'd like to tell you a story.'

I hoped I didn't look as impatient as I felt. Alan took it in his stride. 'Some of your people have been great storytellers,' he said.

'Yes, it is a great tradition in my part of the world – centuries old. It is of course the way the Hebrew scriptures were preserved, handed down from father to son over generations. Your Christian teachings were also largely carried orally for a time, though of course Paul's letters were written documents. The Quran, as well, was transmitted in part through the oral tradition. So we of the Abrahamic peoples are accustomed to telling stories. Think of Jesus and his parables.'

He sat back and folded his hands. 'Once upon a time,' he said. 'That is the beginning for all good stories, is it not? Once upon a time there was a good man, a man so good that he was loved by everyone. He was kind and generous, forgiving, compassionate. But he had one flaw. He was so good himself that he was not able to understand evil. He could see others behaving badly, doing things that caused injury and sorrow, doing things that engendered hatred, but he was sure that if these evildoers were only made to understand the error of their ways, they would change.

'It is, in this world, a dangerous thing to be too good, to have no understanding of the dark side of human nature. The wise man tries to follow the ways of Allah, but he knows that there will be many obstacles in his path. This man did not know that. Not at first.'

He let the silence stretch itself out before he resumed.

'Now this man had been well provided with the world's good things. He often used his wealth to help those less fortunate than himself, but he was not gifted with discernment, so he sometimes gave to the undeserving, even to criminals who were simply stealing from him with their pitiful, false stories, and laughing at him behind his back.'

I wasn't sitting near enough to Alan to take his hand. I wished I were.

'This man had a brother, a younger man who was as dear to him as anyone could be. The man would do anything for his brother, so when the brother asked for a large amount of money the man gave it to him, never asking why it was needed or to what use it would be put.

'The brother, who was not overly intelligent, was a member of a body of men who seemed very religious. They prayed every day at the appointed times, and at other times as well. They read the Quran ceaselessly. They met in groups to discuss the Quran. They discussed other things as well, but the brother did not always listen or understand. And when the brother was not there, they made plans.'

I swallowed hard and moved my chair a little closer to Alan's. I didn't think I wanted to hear this.

Mr Alani's tone changed. The pace of his narrative quickened. 'The group used the brother's money to buy arms and explosives. They persuaded the brother that he would be doing a wonderful thing if he went to a large gathering of people in a marketplace to "frighten them into greater devotion to Allah". They assured him that the box strapped to his body was harmless, that it only looked like a bomb. They lied.'

I grasped Alan's hand so hard, he told me later, that he was afraid one of us would break something.

'Most of us in the Muslim community all over the world know this story. Mr Ahmad's brother Faizan was seventeen years old when he died. Three other members of his family died that day as well, two women who were shopping in the market, and the three-month-old baby of one of them. Mr Ahmad was twenty-two. It was an appalling way to learn, in one horrible moment, about the evil in the world.'

I released the breath I didn't know I'd been holding.

'I told you the story to help you understand the man you have befriended. In your religion he would, I think, be called a saint. My tradition is somewhat ambivalent about the term, but no one could argue that Mr Ahmad is a supremely good man. He seeks out the poor in every country he visits, learns what their greatest needs are, and works out ways to supply those needs, believing that a full belly responds much more readily to joy than to hatred and resentment.' He listed that item on a forefinger. 'He contributes largely to Médecins sans Frontières and other health organizations, believing that it is much easier to be at peace when one is not in pain.' The second finger. 'He supports mission schools all over the world, believing that education is a vital weapon for peace.' The third finger. 'I could go on, but I'm sure you see the point. This is a man with a mission, and he gives to that mission his whole soul.'

'And that is why they came to Sherebury?' I was still somewhat at sea.

'They came to England to continue their work for peace, but they came to Sherebury for a holiday, Mrs Martin. Mr Ahmad is not always concentrated on his mission; he cannot keep that focus for too long a time without some relief. So they came to see the Cathedral and the other beauties of the area and let the children see a small English city and its people. They came here, of course, for Friday prayers, and introduced themselves to me. I was delighted to meet him, because we have here the beginnings of a problem.

'One other aspect of Mr Ahmad's work is to help young Muslims who may be confused by terrorist propaganda. Our mosque here is small, but we are close enough to London that we have also been – infiltrated would be the word, perhaps – by certain extremists. I was able to persuade Mr Ahmad to speak to our young people, let them see the danger of extremism and the beauty of the peace of Allah. I could see that they were impressed and hoped that his point of view would counteract the poison of hatred that was being fed to these young men.'

'But something happened,' said Alan, and his face was full of foreboding.

'Something happened. Early last Friday evening a young man came to me, one of the ones who worried me the most. He has never told me his real name; he has adopted the name Fahd, which means panther. It would be pathetic if it were not so dangerous; he is a frail boy who has been bullied all his life and is now trying to fight back, but in all the wrong ways. He was full of defiance, full of plans to commit some act of spectacular destruction. I tried to talk to him, but he paid no attention; he was determined to go to London.' He paused. 'This was, you will remember, the evening before the Saturday of the queen's birthday celebrations.'

Alan spoke with some difficulty. 'You thought . . .'

'I thought he planned some violence in that connection, yes. That was why I called Mr Ahmad. He had developed some rapport with the boy. It seemed possible that he could stop him.'

'And did he?' I asked, also with some difficulty.

'I do not know. I have heard nothing more. I am extremely worried about all of them, the boy and the Ahmads. In their various ways, they represent a threat to both terrorists and law enforcement.'

'There was a phone call on Saturday,' Alan said, 'saying that the Ahmads were in London and were safe. However, as nothing is known about the caller, we don't know how reliable that information is.'

And with that, unsatisfactory as it was, we took our leave.

Just as we got home, Alan's phone rang. He answered, listened for a few moments, said 'Right', and clicked off. 'That was

Margaret. I must say, she's a force to be reckoned with. She walked into the bishop's meeting, hoicked him out, and persuaded him to go with her to London to storm the citadel. In other words, he's going to try to talk with UniPetro's CEO. And Margaret wants us to come along.'

'Good grief, the woman has no fear, does she? I love our bishop, but I wouldn't dare interrupt him in a meeting. And what about Jane?'

'I didn't ask. I imagine her blunt approach might be counter-productive.'

'Oh. I suppose. But whatever does she want us for? We can't go along with Bishop Smith to beard the lion.'

'No. But if the bishop is able to find out anything about Husam's plans, we – you and I and Margaret – can then visit people he might have talked to. And they might lead us in the right direction.'

I groaned. 'It's all so iffy. Even given Mr Alani's information, there are a lot of wild geese to chase up blind alleys, leading to mare's nests.'

'After a fine meal of not only mixed, but chopped and diced metaphors. Yes. Get your hat.'

It was another of those beautiful days that the tourist brochures would have you believe are the rule in England, rather than the exception. The sun was shining and there was so little breeze that the temperature was, in fact, hot, even to an American. We have different internal thermostats from the English, I've discovered. The *Telegraph* will refer to 'blistering heat' on a day that I would describe as pleasantly balmy. But today was definitely hot, and it would be worse in London. 'No hat,' I said firmly. 'I don't care if I am accompanying a bishop. We're not going to church, and I'd melt in a hat.'

Alan raised his eyebrows. The common perception is that I wear a hat everywhere but in the shower. Never mind.

I was almost sorry for my decision when I saw Bishop Smith. He had arrayed himself in the full dignity of his office. His black suit was impeccably tailored and very conservative in cut. His shirt was bright purple, and he wore not only a large, rather ornate pectoral cross, but the ring of his office, also large and ornate.

'I thought a cassock was a bit much,' he said with a smile as he caught my glance. 'Especially in this heat.'

'But you wanted to impress them.'

'You could say that.'

Bishop Smith is a quiet, humble man. I was touched that he was stepping so far outside his usual persona to help the Ahmads.

We took the train, mindful of horrendous traffic and the ever-annoying congestion charge. Once at Victoria Station, we elected for the Tube, again considering traffic. 'Where is this place?' I asked Alan as we made our careful way down the rubbish-strewn steps to the Underground station. (I had slipped once on a discarded sheet of newspaper there and taken a bad fall. Now I took it slowly and watched every step.)

'In the City. Where would you think?'

'Oh, of course.' Fortunately, the nearest station to the UniPetro building was on the District and Circle lines, a straight shot from Victoria. I was already hot and dusty, and hoping the air would be a bit cooler near the Thames.

It wasn't. The City of London is one of the business and financial centres of London and is also home to St Paul's Cathedral, so the streets were packed with cars and vans and buses and taxis and tourists and bankers and lawyers and clergy and choirboys, along with London's ubiquitous pigeons and squawking gulls from the river. The place was noisy and, on a hot day, redolent of fish and too many people. The walk from the station to our destination was only a couple of blocks. That was many steps too far.

The building we approached was ultra-modern and indescribably ugly. It was also air-conditioned. I entered with a sigh of passionate relief. I headed for one of the twisted metal benches that lined the walls. At least I hoped they were benches and not pieces of sculpture. Whatever they were, they were cool to sit on and provided respite for my burning feet.

'You all go on and do whatever it is that you're going to do, and I hope it takes a good long time. I could sit here for the rest of the afternoon.'

'Actually, I fear we won't be long at all,' said the bishop gently. 'Mr Mahmoud has agreed to see me, but only for a few minutes. I'm sorry, Dorothy. This may prove to be a futile errand for all of us.'

Now he tells me! I dredged up a smile from somewhere. 'Never mind. I'll just sit and absorb coolth for the trip home. And if you see water anywhere, you might let me know.'

Margaret and Alan followed the bishop up to the reception desk, which looked almost as well guarded as Buckingham Palace. No bearskin-hatted guards, but a formidable-looking secretary sat behind a very solid desk, and the men standing here and there in the lobby looked much like the Secret Service: chosen to fade into the wallpaper, except for the constantly moving eyes and the fully alert posture.

What a world we live in! I thought about the terrifying people who might at this very moment be searching for Husam and his family, terrorists who would blow up themselves and a crowd of strangers out of sheer hatred – and then decided not to think about them. My concern just now was for a family in danger, a family who, I was convinced, meant no harm to anyone.

But what if I was wrong? What if we were all wrong, drawn in by pleasant, charismatic personalities?

I thrust that thought aside, too.

The bishop did not have to introduce himself. Well, he was the only man in the room wearing a purple shirt and a pectoral cross. He was instantly escorted to an elevator. The escort went with him, I noticed.

Alan and Margaret came back and sat down near me on the peculiar benches, which were surprisingly comfortable, considering they looked quite a lot like medieval instruments of torture.

'Alan, did you ask about water?' I said after a while. 'Or anything at all to drink?'

One of the guards came over to me. 'Madam, there is a canteen through that door serving food and beverages. They are provided for our employees, but you are more than welcome to anything you wish.'

I thanked him and asked my companions what they wanted. Alan offered to go, but I was stiff and wanted to walk. The air-conditioning, such a blessing when we first walked in, was beginning to feel chilly enough to freeze up my joints. Tea, I thought, not water – if they had real tea and not just some herbal stuff.

They had a rich assortment of teas, as well as coffee and fruit juices and water, fizzy and still. No alcohol, of course, though a typical English canteen would have had both beer and wine. Well, UniPetro was after all a concern run by Muslims, and I didn't want anything alcoholic just now anyway. I got a tray, chose three cups of tea, found packets of sugar and milk, debated over some odd-looking pastries and decided to try them, and looked for the cashier.

I didn't see one. Was it on the honour system, then? I couldn't find a menu with prices, either. A young man, noticing my questing glance, said, 'May I help you find something, madam?'

'I can't figure out where to pay,' I said, feeling foolish and out of place.

'Ah. The canteen is a service of UniPetro. There is no charge.'

'But I don't work here. I'm just waiting while a friend visits with Mr Mahmoud.'

'No matter. Guests are welcome as well. Enjoy your tea.'

'Uh, thank you.' I guess. Actually I felt very awkward. I prefer to pay my way. But there was nothing to be done about it. I picked up my tray, balancing it carefully, and moved slowly toward the door.

Only it was the wrong door. I had got turned around while searching for the cashier. A man came out of this door and I caught it with my knee before it closed, only to find that it led not into the lobby but into a long corridor lined with doors.

And just disappearing into one of those doorways was a small boy wearing a tunic and a close-fitting hat over dark curls. He turned around for a moment and saw me, and then vanished.

I didn't quite drop my tray of tea.

TWENTY-TWO

Carefully I steadied the cups. I had spilled only a little tea. Carefully I turned around and walked to the proper door. A kind young man – there appeared to be a ready supply of them – opened it for me. Carefully I carried the tray back out into the lobby and gave the cups to Margaret and Alan.

Alan looked at me sharply. 'What's wrong?' he asked in barely audible tones.

'Take this.' I handed him the tray I felt slipping from my hands, and sat down beside him.

'Turn toward the door,' he commanded. 'Your face is too revealing. Can you tell me what's happened? As quietly as you can,' he added. 'These marble walls amplify sound.'

I lifted my cup of tea in hands that I willed to stop shaking, and sipped. It was only lukewarm, but it was wet. 'Rahim is here,' I said, almost inaudibly.

Alan, bless his heart, didn't react visibly. 'Are you sure?'

'Nearly. A boy his age, in Muslim dress, with a face like his. And he ran away.'

'All right. Talk about something else.' He raised his voice slightly. 'These pastries are good, try one. Rather like baklava, all nuts and honey. Were they expensive?'

'Alan, they were free. Everything in the canteen is free. It's really for employees, but I guess they don't mind visitors using it, too. That must run into a bit of money; there must be a lot of visitors. Customers, you know.'

I was babbling, and I went right on. 'You should see it. It's really a fully-equipped cafeteria, with hot dishes, too, though I must say I didn't recognize much except some roast chicken. And of course a salad is a salad, in any culture.'

'All right, love. Don't overdo it. Here comes the bishop.'

From the way the acolytes fell back at their approach, I

assumed the man accompanying Bishop Smith was the exalted Mr Mahmoud, the great man himself. He also had that look of supreme self-confidence achieved only, in my experience, by the super-wealthy.

'It was good to meet you, sir,' said the well-polished man, shaking the bishop's hand. 'I'm only sorry that I was able to be of so little help. I wish you well in your efforts to locate Mr Ahmad. That quest is of course of great importance to us here at UniPetro as well. Good day, sir.'

He sketched a genial wave to the rest of us, and we walked out into the stifling heat and the blessed freedom of the City of London.

I opened my mouth, but Alan quelled me with a glance. 'Wait,' he mouthed.

I was quivering with impatience. 'But, Alan—'

'Wait.'

He herded us quickly toward St Paul's. Bishop Smith gave him an approving nod while I seethed.

Once inside the cathedral, Alan deferred to the bishop, who said, 'The dean's office, I think.' He steered us in the right direction.

The secretary knew him, of course. She rose to greet him and then said with some dismay, 'Oh, I'm so sorry. The dean isn't here just now. Did I forget to record your appointment?'

'I doubt you ever forget very much, my dear. I have no appointment and in fact would simply like to borrow his office for a few minutes. When do you expect him back?'

'Not for at least an hour. You're certainly welcome – you and . . . er . . .?'

'Friends from Sherebury. Thank you, my dear.'

He gestured us in and shut the door. 'Now, Dorothy. We're perfectly private here. Sit down and tell us.'

I couldn't possibly sit. The room was small for pacing, but I managed it. 'I saw Rahim in the UniPetro building. And he saw me, and ran away. Well, not ran, exactly, but went away immediately.' I described what had happened.

'It was just a glimpse, then.'

'Yes, Bishop, but I'm quite sure it was the boy. For that instant, he recognized me. And why are you sitting here talking about it instead of doing something about it? If Rahim is there, then so are his parents, and we need to rescue them!'

'Dorothy,' Alan spoke quietly. 'What makes you think they need to be rescued?'

'Well, because they . . . that's why we . . . but . . .' I ran out of steam and collapsed into a chair.

'Perhaps I should tell you about my conversation with Mr Mahmoud,' said the bishop.

'Him! He sounded like he had no idea where any of them were!'

'That was what he said in public, out in the lobby. You must remember, Dorothy, that the oil business is extremely political; also that there is much suspicion on both sides of the East–West, Muslim–Christian divide. The Iraqis, in particular, play their cards very close to their chest, a necessary precaution in the distrustful world we live in.'

'So he told you something different?'

Bishop Smith chuckled. 'He was very diplomatic, and oblique in his choice of words. What he said amounted to a confirmation of your supposition, Dorothy, that Ahmad had travelled here with the intent of helping organizations working for peace between East and West, Muslim and Christian. He never said so in so many words, you understand, but his meaning was clear.'

'It's more than just a suspicion now,' I said, interrupting. 'That's what the imam told us. We hadn't had a chance to tell you.'

When we had finished relating our brief story, the bishop nodded. 'Mr Mahmoud also implied that Husam had come to him for counselling on the matter. And also, one assumes, to assure him, Mahmoud, that the funds being dispersed were from his own personal fortune, not from the corporation.'

'You know, I wondered about the money,' said Alan. 'He couldn't have brought it into the country legally, and I don't see him as the sort to try smuggling. He could have got the pounds and dollars and euros with ATM transactions, but it would have taken quite a while, since the machines have a daily limit on withdrawals. And I don't know if there are machines in England that supply dinars.'

'And of course the transactions are easily trackable, which he might not have wanted.' That was Margaret, speaking with her usual restraint.

'Indeed,' said the bishop. 'How very much simpler just to write a cheque. And where better to present it than to one's own employer?'

I smacked the arm of my chair. 'But how stupid of me! I never thought of that, and I've been trying and trying to figure out how he came by the money. But the more important question is: has his mission been scrapped because of that foolish young man? And what's happened to the kid, anyway?'

'I don't, at the moment, have any ideas about that, except that he's almost certainly still alive. If there had been a death at the Trooping the Colour on Saturday, we would have heard about it. But as to the Ahmads' mission, that's precisely where Mr Mahmoud became even more obscure. He made some very general statements that I believe had nevertheless a very specific meaning. Let me see if I can repeat what he said with some accuracy. "Of course," he began, "the work of those striving for peace has become much more difficult in these days of terrorism. I am sure you understand, Mr Smith, that those who perpetrate these horrendous acts are not represent-ative of the true Islam, but they create a climate of fear that taints all of us. Some of the agents for peaceable understanding have been forced to lie low for a time." And then he gave me a look I can't quite describe, as if he wanted me to understand something. It isn't always easy to read the face of someone from another culture, but I got the impression that he was giving me a message; I simply wasn't sure what it was. I think I've reported his words accurately.

'He said one more thing before he took me back to the lobby, and I'm sure I can repeat that word for word, because he placed such emphasis on each word. He said, "But great good can sometimes be done, even under great pressure, don't you agree? I think your Jesus was able to do such things, was he not?" I don't know what he meant, but that is what he said.'

I sat trying to make sense of all this. 'So the family is in hiding there, at the office building. But surely hundreds of people would have seen them, would know they are there?'

'The security is very good, Dorothy,' said Alan. 'You happened, by a series of flukes, to see Rahim, but ordinarily the public would not. And any of the employees who might know would be under strict orders to say nothing. Actually, I suspect that Rahim slipped away from where he is supposed to be, and is now being chastised.'

'Yes,' said Margaret with a sigh. 'He's made the situation untenable. Now that his location is known, how can his parents be certain that you won't tell anyone? And that being the case, they need to go elsewhere. But where? Where can they go that will be safe?'

'Mahmoud will have some ideas about that,' Alan said decisively. 'It may become necessary to move them elsewhere not only for their safety, but that of the company and its employees. But he will do nothing in a hurry. We all have to remember that Mahmoud is an immensely, almost unimaginably wealthy man and a person of enormous influence. He will consider not only Ahmad, but the welfare of UniPetro, of Iraq, of his own fortune, and certainly of the political situation. Until he has resolved all those questions in his own mind, he'll stay his hand. And I doubt there's a thing any of us can do about that.'

'Except pray,' said the bishop quietly, and for a few minutes we kept silent and did just that.

'I wonder,' I said as we sat in the train on the way home, 'if they might come back here.'

'That,' said Alan, 'would depend on how much they trust our discretion. It's certainly possible.'

And with that unsatisfactory reply I had to be content.

TWENTY-THREE

Alan passed along the information about young Fahd to Derek, who was able to report back almost immediately that the boy had been arrested and charged with, among other things, possession of an assault weapon. He was now cooling his heels awaiting the next step. No one had been with him at the time of his arrest.

So that was that. He was safely out of the hands of anyone who sought to do him ill, either terrorists who were afraid he would talk, or counter-terrorists who were afraid he would strike, or anyone in between.

Derek also told us that the tight surveillance of all known or suspected terrorist groups in the build-up to the birthday events had driven them underground, where they were now keeping a very low profile. 'For the time being,' he said, sounding weary, as indeed we all were – weary of the constant need to be on the alert, to be afraid.

That meant, I optimistically – naively – thought, that it would be only a short time before the Ahmads were free once more to go about their business. Whatever peacemaking efforts they had planned in England might have to be deferred for a time, or perhaps someone else might be entrusted to distribute that money to groups and individuals who needed it, but all would soon be well.

I had reckoned without Jane.

Jane was profoundly unhappy. We had thought it best not to tell her what we knew; she was a determined woman and, though perfectly sane and sensible about most things, she had a streak of foolishness about children that had grown wider with advancing age. Where children's welfare was concerned, we couldn't count on her to act wisely. It wasn't easy to placate her with bland non-replies, though Alan did his best. It took the bishop, finally, to tell her that the situation was well in hand and she was not to worry.

Of course she went right on worrying and growing more and more angry and upset. She had all but stopped speaking to Alan and me, which naturally made us upset and a little angry, too. It wasn't our fault we had information we couldn't share, and I simply hated the growing rift, especially since there was nothing I could do about it.

The blow-up was inevitable, but I hadn't anticipated the form it would take.

It was two days after our trip to London. June had grown warm and muggy in a way that reminded me of my Indiana home, though the heat wasn't as intense, and there were no fireflies. We called them lightning bugs when I was a child, and I used to delight in catching them in mayonnaise jars and shaking them up to make them light, before letting them go. They do not exist in England, and I missed them.

As Alan and I sat in our back garden sipping lemonade, my memories of home suddenly crystallized into an idea. 'Alan, what day is it? I've lost track.'

'Thursday, I think.'

'No, I mean what date?'

'Nineteenth June. Why?'

'Because I've just decided to have a Fourth of July party! There's plenty of time to arrange it, over two weeks. We'll have fried chicken and potato salad and baked beans and devilled eggs, all the traditional picnic food. And do you think we can get any firecrackers at this time of the year?'

He looked startled. 'I imagine we could, from the Internet if nowhere else. I can't imagine the Cathedral people would be wildly happy about them in mid-summer.'

'You have a point. Sparklers, then. Red, white and blue ones. And I'm going over to invite Jane this minute! This nonsense has gone on long enough.'

I sprinted down the path to her back door and hammered on it.

Silence.

Frowning, I hammered harder.

Nothing. Not even the barking of dogs that always greeted a visitor.

The Cathedral clock chimed the hour. Nine o'clock.

I'd never known Jane to be out that late, unless she was out of town. But if she was going to be gone, she always asked us to mind the dogs.

Something was wrong. I went back to Alan. 'She's not answering. And neither are the dogs. Dead silence.' Hearing the word I'd used, I gulped. 'I'm scared, Alan. What if something's happened to her, carbon monoxide or something?'

Alan rose with a spryness surprising in someone his age, and strode towards not Jane's house, but ours. 'Key,' he said over his shoulder.

I quivered with impatience while he fetched the key to Jane's house. He also brought the CO detector we had bought recently. 'No point in taking chances,' he said as we hurried to the Georgian house next door.

Alan knocked and called out, loudly. There was no response. He fitted the key in the lock, opened the door, and called out again. The small white box in his hand remained silent. So did the house.

'I think it's safe,' he said. 'No CO, at any rate.' He flipped the switch by the back door and we entered, slowly, cautiously, calling Jane every few seconds.

There was a light on in the upstairs hallway, but we searched the downstairs rooms first. A policeman knows how to search; he checked several places I wouldn't have thought of, including the oven and the chest freezer. Everything was neat as a pin, as it always was. Jane is not a compulsive housekeeper, but she hates clutter, so there are few knick-knacks to gather dust, and the furniture is sparse, all of it functional. Only in the kitchen was there the slight disorder that is inevitable wherever there are pets.

Alan went down the steep, narrow steps to the cellar. Thoughts of rats and spiders kept me upstairs, looking anxiously after him until he came back up, shaking his head. Then we went upstairs.

The bedrooms and bathroom were as tidy as the rest of the house. Several cushions on the floors of the bedrooms had indentations and a few short hairs, telling us where the dogs slept.

After a cursory glance into each of the rooms, Alan walked into the largest bedroom and opened the closet door.

I took a deliberate deep breath. There was nothing in the closet that shouldn't be there. A few clothes in the conservative colours and styles that Jane favoured. As her years and her girth increased, she stuck to neutral colours and loose-fitting garments in lightweight fabrics.

Alan noticed what I had not, a few empty hangers. 'Can you tell what's missing?'

I shrugged helplessly. 'I have no idea. All her clothes look pretty much alike.'

'Would she have taken some things to be dry-cleaned?'

'I doubt it. I think almost everything she owns is washable. Most things are nowadays.'

'Do you know where she keeps her luggage?'

Another shrug. 'You think she's gone away?'

'It's beginning to look that way.'

'But the dogs—'

'She's furious with us, remember? She might have gone somewhere and taken the dogs with her, or taken them to someone else to mind, someone she trusts, as she apparently no longer trusts us.'

'Ouch. Well, I suppose we might as well look for suitcases.'

We found one large, dusty one that looked long unused. That didn't keep Alan from completing a thorough search of the other rooms and the small, stiflingly hot attic. There was nothing sinister, nothing unusual, no more luggage, and no sign of Jane or her beloved pets.

The last step was to check on her car, which wasn't quite as easy as it sounds. Jane has no garage – well, we're the only people on our street who do – so she parks her car wherever she can. Sometimes it's as far away as the High Street. There's a place there, a repair garage really, but they'll let Jane keep her car there if she can't find any other space, and in rotten weather or if she has a heavy load to carry, they'll even drive it back and forth for her. They're nice men who, like much of Sherebury's population, had been Jane's pupils long ago.

We went back to our house. Alan looked up the number of the garage, called, and hung up after only a moment. 'Voicemail. They gave an emergency number, though.' He punched it in, asked his question, and listened. 'I see. No, no need. We were just checking. Thank you.'

He turned to me. 'She took the car yesterday. Had a small bag with her. Mike drove her to the station and took the car back to the garage.'

'She didn't say where she was going?'

'He didn't ask. He let her off on the up side.'

'So she was going to London.'

'Going west, at any rate.'

I shivered at that. 'Gone west' is an English euphemism for 'died'. Alan hadn't meant that, but still . . . 'Gone to visit her family?'

Alan just looked at me.

I sighed. 'She's gone to meddle, hasn't she?'

'As an expert meddler yourself, you know the symptoms.'

I was about to protest, then thought better of it. He was right. I did meddle in other people's business. Always with the best of intentions, of course.

The trouble with meddling is that you need to know what you're doing, or you can create havoc. 'Do you suppose she has the slightest idea what she's getting into?'

Alan shook his head. 'Not unless someone's told her where the Ahmads are and why they're in hiding. And none of us has said a word.'

I didn't care to explore the implications of that, and neither did Alan. We went through our usual evening routine with the animals in a depressed silence, and plodded up to bed.

In the morning we woke very early. Neither of us had slept well, and not only because of our worries. The heat and humidity had continued through the night, and the bed was a welter of damply wrinkled sheets. I pulled them off and dumped them on the floor to put in the laundry. 'I do wish,' I said irritably, 'that the English would drop the notion that it never gets hot here, and start using air-conditioning.'

I dared Alan to repeat his usual argument that window units would be difficult in a house with 400-year-old casements, and a central unit impossible with no furnace and no duct work. He was wise enough to say nothing, but picked up the sheets and took them downstairs to the washing machine, starting coffee on the way.

I took a quick shower and donned my very coolest clothes, a loose caftan dating from the sixties, but still serviceable. With all the windows and doors open, it was a little cooler downstairs, but not much. I stayed out of the kitchen, where the Aga was still on, heating our water, but also the room. Alan turned on an electric fan he'd bought last summer and set out cereal bowls on trays in the parlour, still wordlessly.

'Oh, all right, I'm being childish. You know I hate heat, and especially humidity, but that's no reason to lose my temper.'

'One wonders,' he said cautiously, 'how you managed to survive all those summers in southern Indiana.'

'Air-conditioning, dear. Even back in the dark ages of my childhood. Do we have any muesli left?' I'd learned the English word for granola early on; I love the stuff.

'None of your homemade, but there's a packet.'

'I'll have that, then, and a banana if there is one. And I know you'll think me barbaric, but would you pour my coffee over ice? I can't face anything hot, but I desperately need the caffeine.'

Alan, who is the breakfast cook in our household, complied with a grin. 'I knew you'd reach this stage soon, so yesterday I made preparations. Voilà!' He went to the kitchen and pulled a tray of brown ice cubes out of the freezer. 'I made them with coffee, so as not to dilute the brew. Here you are, my barbaric love.'

I saluted him with my glass, and we ate our spartan fare in amicable silence. When we had finished and were clearing away the dishes, though, I sighed. 'Our problem hasn't gone away.'

'I'll wash, you dry. Actually it has gone away. Or rather, she has gone away.'

'I don't suppose you've tried calling her yet.'

'While you were dressing. Voicemail.'

'Which could mean anything. She could be in trouble.'

'Possible, but not very likely. It would take a good deal to overcome our Boadicea.'

'Alan, we may be dealing with terrorists! These people will stop at nothing, literally.'

'True. But Jane is as canny and cautious as she is determined. It's more likely that she's not answering calls from
anyone she doesn't want to talk to. Whatever she's up to, I
think we can be assured she will take no unnecessary risks,
especially where Rahim is concerned.'

'But that's the question, isn't it? What *is* she up to?'

'Oh, we can answer that with one guess, can't we? She's
hared off to rescue those children.'

'Really, Alan! There are some things I can figure out for
myself, but your generality doesn't help much, does it? What
specifically is she trying to do?'

'Here. Dry this cup and put it all away, and we'll sit in front
of the fan and talk this out.'

I took a kitchen chair with me back to the parlour. I love
the squashy, comfortable couch, but the cushions were too
warm. Better an upright chair with air circulation.

'All right, oracle. Propound.'

Alan tented his hands, which usually meant he was about
to deliver a lecture, but occasionally indicated thought. 'You
are Jane Langland. You are angry with your friends and the
authorities, who appear to be doing nothing to find a family
with children whom you love. You decide to take action yourself, since none of the fools are doing so. What do you do?'

'Um. I know where to find one of the children. Do I go to Aya
and try again to talk to her, see if she can tell me anything else?'

'Perhaps. Perhaps not. Jane might feel that going again
might lead others to her, or in some other way endanger her.'

'Possibly. Well, then, I might try to find Uncle
What's-his-name.'

'Abdullah. How would Jane go about that?'

'The police – no. She thinks the police are idiots. Present
company excepted. Maybe. Anyway, not the police. She'd go
to someone she trusts: Jonathan. He helped find Walter, way
back when.'

'Yes. That's quite likely. I'll phone him next. Any other ideas?'

'Oh, Lord, I don't know! Given that it's Jane, who thinks
she's invincible, she could be doing almost anything. I wouldn't
put it past her to try to talk to the queen.'

Alan's phone rang.

TWENTY-FOUR

I looked at the clock on the mantel. A little past seven. Good news seldom arrives that early.

Alan looked at the display. 'Jonathan.' He answered and listened for a moment. 'Yes. We'll be there as soon as possible. Right.'

He stood up, his face a mask. 'You'd better put on something a bit less informal, but hurry. The next train's in less than fifteen minutes. Jane's in police custody.'

His manner told me not to ask questions; in any case he was out the door, getting the car out.

I pulled on the first shirt and pair of slacks that my hand touched in the closet, slipped on loafers, and followed him in less than five minutes. He broke several speeding regulations and at one point took a shortcut down a one-way street, the wrong way. Alan is a conservative driver and a respecter of the law.

Even at that, we pulled into the station car park not a moment too soon, and rushed aboard the train without tickets. He never does that, either.

Our carriage was full of commuters, too full for private conversation. In fact, we couldn't get seats together. I sat next to a young woman whose heavily tattooed body sported gold and silver studs and rings in ears and nose and probably other places as well. She spent the journey playing games on her phone.

That reminded me. I pulled out mine and called the dean's wife. 'Margaret, Alan and I have had to go to London quite unexpectedly, and Jane's away. Could you feed our menagerie? No, Jane's made other arrangements. Thanks so much; I'll tell you all about it later.' Bless the woman, who asked no questions but simply agreed. I was going to have to do something nice for her if our lives ever settled down.

Victoria Station, always busy, is a madhouse at rush hour.

After a brief conversation with the guard at the barrier turnstile, Alan showing his police ID, we rushed across the station and looked at the queue at the taxi rank, where at least fifty people were waiting for far too few cabs. 'Where are we going?' I ventured. 'Would the Tube be quicker?'

'Police station in the City. We're meeting Jonathan there. It's near Cannon Street Underground station, but the Tube will be jammed.'

'Why are we in such a hurry? You haven't told me what happened.'

'I don't know. Jonathan simply said that Jane had been arrested and was being held, and told me I'd better come.'

I nudged his arm. 'And speaking of Jonathan . . .'

The young man came striding toward us, his limp obvious, but not slowing him down much. 'Come on,' he said urgently. 'I thought I'd best come and meet you. I'm parked quite illegally, and we'll be lucky if they haven't towed me away.'

We rescued the car out from under the nose of an official who was about to summon a tow truck, Alan again brandishing his warrant card. 'I thought you weren't supposed to use that anymore,' I murmured in his ear.

'I'm not.'

I thought it best to make no further comment.

Jonathan drove as skilfully and rapidly as possible through the teeming streets, but there was no way to avoid long delays. The heat in London was far worse than in the country. Diesel fumes from buses poisoned the air. I tried to think of icebergs and snowfields and frigid Arctic seas, but nothing helped.

Jonathan told us what little he knew about Jane's situation. 'She rang me up, said she was coming to London to look for Husam and his family. I tried to tell her I didn't know anything more than she did, but she hung up on me. Oops!' He avoided a bus by a hair, and continued. 'She showed up at my flat and asked me – told me – to find Husam's uncle. She knew I'd been working on that side of it, but I told her I had no leads. Which isn't quite true, but—' The brakes screeched and he paused while Alan and I tried to start breathing again. That one had been close.

'I'd better make this brief. I really need to concentrate on traffic. The bottom line is, Jane made me drive her to the UniPetro building, demanded to speak to the CEO, and made a huge scene. They called the cops. Jane resisted arrest. They took her in.'

I groaned and closed my eyes. Bulldog Jane. Boadicea.

The police station, near St Paul's Cathedral, was tiny; so was its car park. We were stopped by a guard who meant business.

This time Alan didn't try any tricks. He got out and spoke to the man. 'We need your help, sir. I am retired Chief Constable Alan Nesbitt, of Belleshire, and a very dear friend is being held here, I don't know on what charge, but almost certainly nothing major. My wife and I have come to talk to her and see what we can do to help. I do quite realize Mr Quinn can't leave his car here, but would you be able to suggest a car park nearby?'

'Quinn. That wouldn't be Chief Inspector Jonathan Quinn, would it, sir?'

'Now retired from the Met and a perfectly ordinary private detective,' said Jonathan from the driver's seat. He sounded annoyed. He hated being reminded that his name was still legendary in police circles.

'Yes, well, it's a pleasure to meet you, sir. I wish I could let you park here, but there's not room for so much as a bicycle. But there's a private car park just round the corner.' He pointed. 'The guard's a mate of mine. Tell him I said it was okay. It's never full.'

Alan had been watching the exchange with a bemused look. His name used to be the one to conjure with; now it was Jonathan's.

Jonathan was back in less than five minutes, his dodgy legs slowing him only a little. 'Should he push himself that hard?' I asked Alan in an undertone.

'He's a big boy now. Let him decide, love.'

Yes, well, okay, I do tend to take people under my wing. So sue me.

I had no idea what we'd find when we got in. Would Jane still be in full cry, or sullen, or upset?

She was none of those things. They brought her to an

interview room. Well, I say 'brought her'. She marched ahead of the guard, arms folded across her chest, mouth set, eyes ice cold.

Oh, dear.

The guard allowed all three of us to join her. Unusual, I was pretty sure, but then we were unusual visitors. Alan gave me a quick, stern look. I thought it said, *Let me handle this.* I hoped so, anyway, since I couldn't think what to say.

Jane sat down. We sat down. Alan let the silence stretch out until Jane finally said, 'Well?' Belligerent. Spoiling for a fight.

'I am waiting,' said Alan, 'for you to explain your outrageous behaviour.'

Whatever Jane had been expecting, it wasn't that. While she tried to collect her wits and frame a reply, Alan pressed on. 'You have gone away without a word to us, your friends and nearest neighbours, causing us considerable worry. You have bullied your way into an extremely sensitive situation, one with international implications. You have assaulted a police officer in resisting arrest, and finally, your unthinking actions may have placed in jeopardy the very family you were trying to help. What do you have to say for yourself?'

His glance at me was ambiguous. Bad cop, good cop? I took a breath, hoping I was on the right wavelength. 'Alan, I think that's a little harsh. I'm sure Jane's intentions were good.'

Jane snorted. 'Bloody fool. That what you're saying?'

'More or less,' said Alan. 'Though you're using somewhat gentler terms than I would have chosen.'

She snorted again. 'Not the only one. Kept me in the dark.'

Alan nodded. 'Yes. We were wrong about that. As you said some time ago, it is possible to have too little information. We did not anticipate that you would take matters into your own hands. Now that it's too late, are you aware of what you have done?'

She looked him straight in the eye. 'Tell me.'

'We can't know for certain, but you may have put the Ahmad family in great danger by leading their enemies straight to them.'

Her face became, if possible, even more rigid. 'UniPetro?'

'We believe they were hiding out there until it was safe to go elsewhere. We know for certain that Rahim, at least, was there two days ago. At that point the situation seemed stable enough that they might be able to leave soon. Now you've changed all that.'

Jane said not a word. She did not allow her lip to quiver. She couldn't do anything about the tear that trickled down her lined face.

'Alan, that's enough.' I stood and turned to the guard. 'What must we do to get Miss Langland out of here? We'll post bond, if necessary.'

'I'll check, madam.'

I very much wanted to give her a reassuring hug and tell her everything would be all right. I didn't do it, first because she would never forgive me if she broke down into sobs, and second because I wasn't at all sure that anything would ever be all right. It wasn't all Jane's fault. We bore some of the blame for not keeping her informed. But she had certainly thrown a monkey wrench into the works.

It took some fast talking on Alan's part, but eventually Jane was released into our custody, with firm promises that she would return to answer to her charges. Nothing very dire would happen to her, probably, given her age and obvious respectability, but you can't go around slapping the police and disrupting the affairs of mega-business without incurring some punishment. I knew that her worst punishment was the knowledge that she might have put her darling little boy into grave danger.

She wanted to spend the rest of the day and the night with Walter and Sue. She said she'd be fine sleeping on their couch. I knew she wouldn't be comfortable, either physically or emotionally, but if she wanted the solace of her family, she would have it. Jonathan took us to her club, where she had left her things, and then drove us all (in silence) to Bexley.

She wouldn't let us take her to the door. Walter and Sue were both at work, of course, but Jane had a key. 'Home tomorrow,' she said as she manoeuvred her bulk out of the car. She paused a moment, suitcase in hand. 'Sorry,' she said.

'So am I,' said Alan, and put a hand out the window. She

shook it gravely and walked up the stairs without a backward glance.

The three of us let out a large collective sigh. 'But, oh, Lord! What now?'

The words were mine. The sentiment was everyone's.

'I have to say,' I went on, 'I can understand Jane's frustration. She wanted to make something happen. Her actions ended up being most unwise, but she thought we were at stalemate, and that's a most unsatisfactory state of affairs.'

'Well, Jane took care of that!' Alan growled. 'Upset the board and sent the chessmen flying.'

'Flying into checkmate, just possibly,' said Jonathan, as he put the car in gear. 'It would have been relatively easy to sneak the family out of UniPetro and reunite them with the girl. Now that Jane's called attention to the place . . .' He shook his head and signalled.

'Wait!' I cried, just as Jonathan was about to head out into traffic. He braked, narrowly avoiding a collision with a taxi, whose driver delivered a pithy comment as he passed.

'You nearly got us killed, Dorothy,' said Alan severely.

'I know, and I'm really sorry, Jonathan, but I've just had a bright idea. You and Walter have become good friends. The kind of people he works with, museum people, are usually sort of eggheads. Well, you know what I mean,' I said in response to scowls from both men. 'Intellectuals, if you prefer the term. The types that might well prefer chess to football as a pastime. Does he, or do you, know any real chess experts?'

Jonathan turned off the ignition. 'Hmm. That Arab chap Walter knew at the BM – no, he's moved to America. But there might well be someone at the Museum of London, or at Bethnal Green.'

'Could you call him and find out? Now?'

'I could. Why do you think it's important?'

'I don't know. I just have a feeling . . . we were using chess analogies just now, and somehow I think a chess expert might help us find a way out of this mess. Didn't chess originate in Persia? Or am I all wet?'

Alan shook his head. 'I believe most historians think it originated in India, but it probably came to Europe via Persia.

Certainly the strategies often resemble the rather convoluted Middle Eastern way of thinking. But quite frankly, I cannot imagine how chess might be of any use in untangling the current situation.'

'I don't know, either. It's just a . . . call it a hunch. Even if it's nonsense, what is there to lose?'

Jonathan was clearly at least as dubious as Alan, but he pulled out his phone and made the call, while I waited anxiously.

'He knows one chap,' said Jonathan when he ended the call. 'Doesn't care a lot for him, though. Says he's a bit of a nerd.'

'Well, if he's a chess player . . .' I said, and the others laughed.

'Now, now, it doesn't necessarily follow,' said Alan chidingly. 'I've known some brilliant chess players who were fascinating fellows.'

'Not this one, apparently,' said Jonathan. 'What Walter actually said was that the man could bore for England.'

'Oh, dear. So the question is, would he be any help? Do you suppose he has the imagination to apply chess principles to a real-life situation?'

'Only one way to find out.' He began to key in the number Walter had given him.

I stopped him and gave him my phone. 'Call from this one, and let me talk to him,' I whispered. He shrugged and handed the phone back when he had placed the call.

The call went to voicemail, a curt, 'This is Gerald Burroughs. Leave a message.'

I went into my schoolteacher mode. 'Mr Burroughs, my name is Dorothy Martin. You don't know me, but I need some information about a matter concerning chess, and I believe you're the only man in London who can help me. Please call me at this number, as soon as possible.'

'I gather we're not going home,' said Alan, suppressing a sigh.

'Do you really mind? I know this is a wild idea even for me, but I just have this strong feeling we've landed in a high-stakes chess game, and maybe this person can help us find our way out. And honestly, I can't see any other approach at all.'

'There's always the outrageous idea of letting the police and MI5 do what they're so good at doing.'

But he didn't say it as sarcastically as he might well have done. 'And we've seen how much they've accomplished, haven't we?' I retorted. 'My dear, I do know how hard their job is. I know the international complications could be horrendous. I know they're walking a minefield, and poor dear Jane has made it worse. But she has my sympathy. I know enough not to roar in as she did, but if I just sit and wait, wringing my hands, I'm going to explode myself. You can go home if you like, but I really think I need to stay and talk to Walter's nerd.'

Alan said, 'Yes, dear,' and then dodged out of the way and grinned. 'Jonathan, when you get around to marrying your Jemima, you need to remember: never argue with a woman when her mind's made up. Take us to the Grosvenor, if you will.'

TWENTY-FIVE

We had no luggage, of course. And we were dressed very informally indeed. Fortunately the desk clerk was the same one who had checked us in on our earlier visit a few weeks before, and remembered us. 'Ah, yes,' he said, 'sudden visit to London, weren't expecting to stay the night – got it. You'd like a few toiletries?'

'That would be very kind indeed,' said Alan. 'We could buy them at Boots, of course, but . . .'

'But there is a limit to how many spare toothbrushes a person really needs. Here you are, then, and enjoy your stay, however brief.'

A small packet included two toothbrushes, a minute tube of toothpaste and a disposable razor. Well, we weren't planning a visit to the Abbey this time, or tea with the queen, or any other occasion that would demand better grooming tools. Alan gave the razor a dubious look, and I laughed. 'Did you ever see *North by Northwest*?'

'You're thinking of Cary Grant shaving with one of those little toys at the railway station, with other chaps looking askance. This isn't much, but it's better than that one, and at least I won't have an audience.'

'Wanna bet?'

'I'll try to be entertaining. Now that we have a place to lay our heads, I want to find something to eat. Breakfast was sketchy and a long time ago. It's a trifle early for lunch, but how would you like to try that Italian place just down the street?'

I hesitated. How far could I push this? My husband enjoys good food, and so do I, but . . .

He got it. 'Oh, very well. I can see it in your face. You'd rather stay close in the station, where we can get quick transport to go meet your nerd. Garfunkel's?'

'If that's okay.' I actually sort of like Garfunkel's, even if

it is a chain. It's several notches above fast food, it's quick
and reliable – and in the station, so we could get out of there
in a hurry.

It's also noisy. I was worried that I wouldn't be able to hear
my phone, so I put it on the table and kept a close eye on it,
watching for the display to light up. As it did, of course, just
when my lasagne had been served. It smelled wonderful, and
I was suddenly ravenous.

I pushed my plate away and answered my phone.

'Is this Dorothy Martin?'

'Yes. Am I speaking to Gerald Burroughs?'

'You sound American. Are you calling from America? What
would you want from me? There are lots of good chess players
in America.'

His voice had an odd quality, rather flat, with little intona-
tion. 'No, no, I'm in London. I'd like to see you for a few
minutes, if that's convenient. I'm in Victoria Station right now,
but I can meet any place that's good for you.'

'Why?'

'I need to talk with a chess expert, and a friend who works
at the London Museum tells me you're the best one he can
think of.'

'What friend?'

Oh, dear. This was getting more and more uncomfortable,
and my lasagne was getting colder and colder. 'His name is
Walter Tubbs.'

'Oh. He doesn't know anything about chess.'

'I'm sure that's why he recommended you. Mr Burroughs,
I desperately need your help.' If he asks why again I'm going
to scream, I thought.

'Oh. Well, I'm going to lunch in five minutes. If you want
to come to the staff canteen, I suppose I could talk to you
there.'

'I'll be there as soon as I can make it. Thank you so much!'

'I only have an hour.'

He ended the call, and I stood up. 'I'm off to the museum.
He wants me there in five minutes.'

'Which is impossible. It's near St Paul's. We were really
close when we were at the police station; pity you couldn't

reach him then. Take a taxi, love. I'll have them keep your lunch warm. Good luck!'

It would have taken special angelic intervention to get me across London in less than half an hour, at midday in high tourist season. My angels were apparently busy elsewhere. We crawled. We were held up once by road repairs, once by a traffic accident (not involving my cab, but blocking the road for a considerable time), several times for what appeared to be no reason at all. 'Tube would have been quicker, madam,' said the driver at one point.

'Yes, but then I'd have had to walk from the tube station, and it's hot and I'm old. I know you're doing your best; don't worry.'

In the end I had to walk anyway, though only a block or so. 'It's hopeless, madam,' said the cabbie with an exasperated shrug. 'Coaches everywhere. It's not legal, what they're doing, blocking the way, but there it is, isn't it? I'll need to drop you here.'

He refused part of the exorbitant fare that showed on the meter and waved me on my way.

The sun beat down mercilessly on me as I half-ran to the museum. Gerald's lunch hour was certainly over by now; I only hoped I could find him, and that he would talk to me. My face was shiny with sweat when I finally got in the door. 'I was supposed to meet one of your employees in the canteen, ages ago,' I said to a guard, panting. 'Traffic was impossible, so I couldn't get here earlier. Is it okay if I call him to say I've finally made it, or don't you allow mobiles in here?'

I think if I hadn't looked so old and frantic, the answer would have been frosty, but this was an understanding man. 'We actually require that patrons not use their mobiles, but since it's an employee you need to contact, I can phone him for you. Name and phone number, please?'

I read the number from my phone and then turned it off. 'His name is Burroughs, Gerald Burroughs.'

'Oh.' The guard gave me an odd look. 'It might be better if you saw him in person. The canteen serves employees only, but I can find someone to take you there.'

'I think he'll be back in his office by now. It took me over an hour to cross London, from the time we made the appointment.'

'Well, then, I'll direct you to his office. He works in our computer services.'

Of course.

'You'll be careful, won't you, madam? He is – he can be – a bit difficult. I don't know how well you know him. He's a brilliant young man, but he doesn't always deal well with people.'

'I'd already figured that out. I don't know him at all, but his manner on the phone was brusque, to put it mildly. I'll watch my step.'

The computers, at least the ones Gerald worked with, were in the basement. He had his own office, which looked exactly like the domain of every geek in the world, except for the chessboard in the corner. I tapped on the glass of the door, and the young man looked up from his keyboard in annoyance. 'I'm busy,' he shouted through the door.

I opened the door. 'I can see that. I'm Dorothy Martin, and I'm so sorry I'm late—'

'I can't talk to you now. I'm busy.'

I was rapidly losing patience with this graceless man. A nerd he might be, but did that entitle him to ignore simple courtesy? I was about to lose my temper when I saw a book lying on the floor. It was dirty and dog-eared, and the cover was torn, but the title, in large letters, said *Asperger's Syndrome*.

Aha.

'May I come in? I can see that you're busy, but I need only a few minutes of your time.' I spoke quietly and made no attempt to come closer. 'I'd like to tell you how I need your help, and then I'll leave you to your work.'

'You can write it out,' he said, never looking up.

'It's too complicated for that. Gerald, I need you to pay attention to me for just a few minutes. I know that will be hard for you. I do understand, at least a little. Many years ago I had a friend in Indiana who, like you, was brilliant but found social interaction almost impossible. I didn't know then that he had Asperger's. Almost no one back then had ever heard the term. Now, I'm sure that was what was going on.

'You'd rather be left alone to get on with work you enjoy. I get that. But I'm trying to help some people who may be in danger of their lives, and I need you to help me. You don't have to look at me, or say anything to me, but I do need you to listen. Will you do that?'

He nodded.

'All right. You may want to write some of this down, unless you have a really good memory. Which you probably do. I came to you because I think my friends are caught in a sort of chess game, but with real people instead of chess pieces. I think they were close to winning, to outsmarting the other side, but then someone stepped in and spoiled their plans. Now I believe they're at stalemate, if I understand correctly what that means. My friends are probably in no immediate danger, but they quite literally can't move from where they are without inviting disaster. Nor can they stay where they are indefinitely. Is that what stalemate means, more or less?'

Gerald shrugged. I took it to be an affirmative shrug.

'All right. I want you to treat this as a chess problem and see if there's a way out.' And then I waited.

His posture, which had seemed bored, changed. I couldn't see his face, but his body became alert. 'How many men?'

'Only . . . oh, you mean chessmen. Three on the defensive side.'

'King and who else?'

'I don't know.' I thought about it for a moment. 'I suppose the answer depends on their freedom of movement and also on their relative power. Does that make sense?'

He nodded.

'Well, then, I can say that all three of the people concerned are highly intelligent. They are also highly principled, which would limit their options somewhat. I mean, they wouldn't do any harm unless they had absolutely no choice.'

'Chess is about war. About harm.'

'Yes.' I was silent. My idea was looking more and more far-fetched. 'Yes, and though this is war, in a way, the goal of the defensive side is not defeat of the other side, but escape. Maybe the chess analogy breaks down. I'm sorry to have bothered you. I'll leave you to get on with your work.'

'Wait. How much room do they have? Physical room, I mean. Are they in a small space where they can move only a little, or do they have the whole board?'

'I don't know. If they are still where they were a short time ago, they have a good deal of room to go almost anywhere. Except out.'

'That makes it easier. Do you know anything about chess?'

'Almost nothing. I know the names of the pieces and how they move. I taught my nephew the rudiments when he was, oh, I suppose nine or ten. In three days he was beating me every time.'

'You don't know anything,' said Gerald flatly. 'I will phone you.'

He turned back to his computer and forgot I was there.

On my way out I bought a sandwich at the café, sat down in a patch of shade outside and made quick work of it, and then called Alan to tell him I'd be back as soon as I could get a cab and the poor overworked driver could get me through the traffic. He asked if I wanted to keep the room or go back home. 'Keep it,' I said. 'I need a nap and a shower before I can even think of getting on a train.'

'Any success?'

'I don't know. Probably not. Oh, and Alan, I'll need a large G&T when I get there.'

He was chuckling as I clicked off.

TWENTY-SIX

I was still starving, of course, so when I made it back to Victoria I got my favourite almond croissant in the station and took it up to the room. Pastry is perhaps not the best accompaniment to gin, and the sweetness goes oddly with the bitterness of the tonic, but I had to have something in my stomach to offset the alcohol, and comfort food was in order.

Alan kindly waited until I had satisfied the inner woman before asking questions.

'I found out why he's a little odd, anyway,' I said, wiping away a stray crumb. 'He has Asperger's. He's found the perfect job, though, doing computer work in a little office all by himself, where he doesn't have to see anybody and it's nice and quiet.'

'I don't imagine he appreciated your presence in his controlled world.'

'No. But he was cooperative, after his fashion, and got interested in considering the situation as a chess game. At least I think he did.'

Alan nodded. 'It's very hard to read a person with Asperger's. Their visible reactions are different from ours.'

'I was thinking it was all a waste of time, a stupid idea, comparing real life to chess, but I'm not quite sure. Anyway, it was all I could think to do, and now I've done it, and I'm out of ideas. And out of energy.'

'Right. Have that nap, and that shower, and then we can decide whether to stay here or go home.'

'Oh, let's stay. If there's nothing we can do for the good of the order, there are more interesting ways of wasting time in London than in Sherebury.' I took my shoes off and stretched out on the bed, and in a few minutes even the noises of London traffic couldn't keep me awake.

When I woke an hour later, I showered in my underwear and then dried the garments with the hair dryer provided by the management. They were still damp when I put them back on, but they were at least clean. There was nothing I could do about my shirt and slacks, but they didn't look too bad, and I hoped they didn't have too much of an odour. Still . . .

'Alan, I've changed my mind. There isn't much we can do here, after all. We can't go out to dinner in these clothes. We can't go to a play; same reason. It's far too hot to walk more than a few yards, and there's no point just sitting here. Let's go home.'

Before I finished talking, the phone rang.

I didn't recognize the number, but it was a London exchange. Oh, dear. Walter with some awful news? 'Hello, Walter?'

'No, this is Gerald Burroughs. You may want to write this down; it's rather complicated.'

I bit back a furious reply. Gerald was just being Gerald, heading straight for his objective, ignoring anything or anyone, in his way. 'Um . . . wait a minute. I have to find something to write on.' Alan handed me the note pad by the phone, and I gestured toward my purse, where I kept my notebook. If this was going to be as complicated as all that, I'd need more than a few square inches of writing surface.

'Okay, right. I've got pen and paper. Tell me what you've worked out.'

'You won't understand if I explain in chess terms, so I'll try to translate.'

There was not a trace of sarcasm in his voice. I knew he wasn't being deliberately rude, just stating facts. 'Yes, please,' I said meekly.

'The situation is this,' he went on in his nearly toneless voice. 'The defenders of the castle can't get out. The invaders can't get in. We have therefore a state of siege, not stalemate as you supposed. There are several classic ways of dealing with siege, on the part of both the defenders and the invaders. One is trickery; the Trojan Horse tactic. You have heard of the Trojan Horse?'

Again I had to restrain myself. 'Yes, Gerald. I think our defenders are a good deal too sharp to fall for that one.' I couldn't see UniPetro letting anyone they didn't know past their defences. The moat was stocked with sharks; the bridge was drawn up, the boiling oil ready.

'I agree. I mentioned it only to discard it. If it were that easy, you would have thought of it.'

Thank you for that tiny acknowledgement of my intelligence, I thought but didn't say. Gerald *was* much brighter than I; he had a right to condescend.

'There's always negotiation, but I discarded that as well. This does not seem to be a circumstance in which compromise is likely. So the best tactic is diversion. Simply put, the defenders create a distraction intended to provoke the invaders to unwise action, either drawing off or making an unwise attempt to enter, one that is doomed to failure.'

Distraction. Hmm. 'What sort of distraction did you have in mind?'

'In chess, the defender tempts the invader by appearing to make a stupid mistake. The invader may then make a rash move to take a critical piece, not seeing that he will then be placed in an impossible position. In real life, one classic diversion was to start a small fire within the castle, small and relatively harmless, but looking large and dangerous to the invaders. Often near a secondary entrance. The invaders rush in, are taken, the castle is freed. Checkmate.'

That might well have worked in a medieval castle, but it didn't sound terribly practical in a twenty-first-century office building. Even if UniPetro would allow it, the smoke alarms would go off long before a blaze had a chance to look effective, and if by chance one did get started, the sprinklers, or whatever fire-suppression system they used, would deal with it quickly. I sighed. 'I'm afraid that wouldn't work in this situation, Gerald.'

'No. I thought not. Mrs Martin, I do follow the news, you know. I know now what you are talking about, and I do have what I think is a workable solution.'

Oh, dear! 'I . . . um . . . I do hope you haven't talked about this to anyone. Because—'

'No. A good chess player never reveals his strategy. No, my plan is this, and I believe it will work. Listen, and write it down.'

I listened, and scribbled furiously. When he had finished I was silent for a little time.

'Are you still there?'

'Yes, I'm here. You are a genius, Gerald. Your plan is brilliant, and it *will* work, if we can persuade a great many people to cooperate. They will all be reluctant, if not downright obstructive.'

'You must persuade them. I must go back to work. This has taken an excessive amount of my time.'

He hung up without a word of goodbye, and I shook my head once again at the oddities of human beings. This man had just conceivably saved several lives, and he regarded it as a waste of his precious time.

'All right,' said Alan, 'what did your nerd, or genius, come up with?'

'You may not like it.'

'Speak, woman.'

'Sit down,' I said. Taking a deep breath, I outlined Gerald's plan.

Alan did not explode. He seldom explodes. His face took on a strong resemblance to granite, and when he finally spoke, it was in his most constabulary voice. 'Do you have *any* idea of the logistics involved in such an undertaking?'

I shook my head.

'Even if all of them can be made to agree, the planning . . .'

'Yes. Do you think it would work?'

'Oh, it would work. If everything came together in perfect sequence, if all the fallible human beings behaved exactly as planned . . . but the risk!'

'Yes. Is there any other way? Jane's actions have made the situation critical. If nothing is done, something truly dreadful might happen, up to and including an international incident that could lead to . . . well, to almost any horror. So is there a choice?'

Alan groaned. 'We'd better go home. I need to change into a suit and come back. The sort of diplomacy this is going to require has to be done in person, and I need to look as impressive as possible.'

Our guardian angels were back on duty. The trip home was quick. We didn't talk much on the train. There was too much thinking to be done.

Alan was back out the door in ten minutes flat, not even taking time for tea or a stiffener. 'I'll be home when you see me.'

'And meanwhile I'll do some serious praying. And Alan, I have to tell Jane.'

He stopped on his way out the door. 'What!'

'Yes. As we learned yesterday, there is such a thing as too much secrecy. She has to know.'

He groaned again and left, not quite slamming the door.

TWENTY-SEVEN

I thought about making a sandwich, but I was too keyed up
to eat. I thought about a glass of something soothing, but
decided I needed to keep my wits about me. I fussed around
the house. I thought about scrubbing the kitchen floor, but
decided that was overdoing it.

I had to tell Jane what was going to happen. I'd learned the
risks of keeping her in the dark. I dreaded the conversation;
she would see the dangers quite clearly, and would blame
herself for the situation.

Courage, Dorothy. She has to know, and she has to be
persuaded to stay firmly out of it. At least I could put it off
until morning when she returned home. I could put off a lot
of things until morning. I changed my mind about a glass of
wine, drank a small one, and went to bed.

Of course my troubles were still with me when I woke up
next morning, hungry and in a foul mood and with a slight
wine-induced headache.

I've learned a few things about myself in a long life, and
one of them is that a real snit can seldom survive hard work.
I fed the animals and myself (in that order) and then went
into a frenzy of the chores I hate most. It was definitely time
to clean the cats' litter box, scrub that kitchen floor, and give
Watson a bath.

I was tired by the time I accomplished the first two tasks,
but still grumpy. Watson came next.

Watson is an agreeable and usually an obedient dog. He
has firm ideas on the subject of baths, however, or perhaps
only one idea, which can be summed up as 'No'. Or as the
saying used to go, 'don't wanna, don't hafta, ain't gonna'. I
carefully did not look at him as I dragged the big washtub out
into the back garden. We use the tub for many things, but our
dog can sense when it's meant for him. By the time I had
filled it with soapy water (nice warm water, not just horrid

cold water from the hose, but with a goodly addition of boiling water from the Aga), the dog had disappeared.

It was Emmy who finally found him, cowering under the wheelbarrow in the garden shed. She, who bathes herself, is contemptuous of the whole dog-washing process. She likes Watson well enough, but she never lets him forget her seniority in the household and her superiority, as to species, over any other creature, including humans. And, sad as it is to tell, she rather enjoys seeing him in distress. So she strolled over to the shed and meowed loudly until I hauled him out and led him to his doom.

Watson is what is kindly known as a mixed-breed dog. In other words, he's a mutt. There's a lot of spaniel in his ancestry, as witness his lovely long silky ears and feathery legs and tail – the better to pick up burs and other assorted debris. But some larger breed went into his making as well, so he's bigger and heavier than a spaniel. Alan usually handles the dog-washing chore, but I can manage it with just a little cooperation from the victim.

Watson submitted, if unhappily. He scrambled into the tub with only a little shoving and stood there trembling as I brushed soapy water over him, taking care to avoid his eyes, and combed out his feathers, all the while soothing him with words of praise. We were nearly done when my garden gate opened and Jane appeared.

That was too much for my dog. He leapt out of the tub, splashing soapy and by this time dirty water everywhere, and headed straight for Jane, who was standing right next to a plot Bob Finch had just dug for a new flower bed. 'Stop him!' I cried, and Jane nobly stepped into his path, kept him out of the lovely fresh soil, and allowed him to shake himself, spraying water all over her clean clothes. Seizing his collar, she led him firmly to her house.

'I'll bring towels,' I called.

So together we dried him off and wiped up the water from the floor. Jane changed clothes while I made us some coffee, her kitchen being as familiar as my own, and then we sank into chairs around the kitchen table, Watson retiring under the table in case someone tried to torture him again.

'Welcome home,' I said. She snorted. 'Not quite what you'd wanted, I imagine. Where are your dogs?'

'Boarded at the groomer's. Collecting them next.' She looked embarrassed, as well she might.

I didn't say that Alan and I had been hurt by her sudden departure without a word. She knew, and there was no point in hashing it over, especially as I had something much more important to say.

'Jane, let the dogs be for a little while. Another hour or so won't hurt them. There has been an important development. Or at least, there will be, soon. Or as soon as it can all be organized. If everyone agrees, that is. What I mean to say—'

'Spit it out.'

Jane is almost never rude. But then, I am almost never indecisive. I took a deep breath. 'We've worked out a plan to get the Ahmad family to safety. It's complicated, and you may not like it.' One last sip of coffee for courage, and I told her, in as few words as possible, what Gerald had laid out.

She was silent for a long time. I got up and made us more coffee; still she said nothing. She finished her coffee and stared into the distance. She reminded me of the cats, looking at something I couldn't see.

Finally she stood and took the coffee cups to the sink. 'Only thing to do,' she said.

'Jane! I thought you'd be . . . well, I don't know what, exactly, but I thought you'd hate the idea.'

'I do. No help for it. Must go get the dogs.'

And she was gone, leaving Watson and me staring after her.

Alan came home that afternoon, looking about as chipper as I felt. I greeted him, but asked no questions until I'd made tea and put it in front of him with some American-style muffins out of the freezer. Even then, I sipped my own tea and waited for him to speak.

'Well, it's done,' he said when his cup was empty. I refilled it and waited. 'It wasn't actually as hard as I'd feared. Duncan was the first to agree.'

'Duncan! But I thought he'd pegged Husam as a dangerous terrorist!'

'So did I, but we were both wrong. He was abrupt and abrasive in his manner because of his fears *for* the Ahmads, not *of* them. I should have realized he'd know all about Husam's reputation as an apostle of peace. He also knew – knows – what an attractive target that makes him and his family. The big, well-organized groups wouldn't bother with him, but the splinter groups would see him as a menace to be disposed of. He's furious with Jane, by the way.'

'Of course. She's made it much easier for the crazies to get at him, or at least much harder to get him out of harm's way. But she's okay with the plan. I told her this morning, when she got back from London, and she surprised me.'

'This last disaster may have joggled her back into her usual good sense. Dorothy, I'm going to go up for a nap. I'm getting too old for this sort of thing.'

'But tell me – when is D-Day?'

'As soon as everything is in place. Tuesday, probably.'

He yawned, patted me on the shoulder, and trudged up the stairs.

As I've said before, I hate waiting, and Sunday was one of the longest days I've ever endured. We woke early following a night of restless sleep, went to the early service, and then tried to find things to occupy our time.

There was nothing in the newspapers. Well, we hadn't really expected it this soon, but I still searched with feverish intensity. Nothing on television.

In desperation I finally decided to do some grocery shopping. I wasn't interested in food. I most especially wasn't interested in cooking, but we had to eat, and getting out of the house seemed like a good idea.

I was at Tesco trying listlessly to get interested in strawberries when a couple of voices caught my attention, only because they were pitched so low and sounded, somehow, stealthy. The speakers were two women, a few feet away by the greengage plums, and they were making the mistake of whispering, a sound that carries. I moved to shelter behind a display of cabbages and listened with all my might.

'It's tomorrow, then?'

'The *meeting's* tomorrow. The march is on Tuesday. And don't talk so loud. Spread the word, but stay quiet about it. We want to take them by surprise.'

'Oh, they'll be surprised, all right. Think they're so rich and famous nothing can touch them. We'll see about that!'

And the two women giggled, a sound that positively made my blood run cold.

They could have been talking about anything at all, but I was quite sure I knew what their secret was, and I was even more sure when they moved apart and I could see their faces clearly. They were devotees of the Temple of Truth, plainly meeting at their usual rendezvous. I thought I might start shopping at Sainsbury's.

I rushed home. Alan's face had changed, had lost its look of nagging worry.

'Things are moving,' I said, and he nodded.

'How did you know?'

I told him about the harpies in the supermarket.

'Good. The rumour mill is working, then.'

'And it's to be on Tuesday?'

'If all goes well. You do understand, love, that there are a thousand things that could go wrong?'

'I do. But . . .' There was nothing more to say, and nothing more we could do. 'Look, Alan, I forgot to buy anything at Tesco, and I don't think there's a thing in the house to eat. Let's walk over to the Cathedral and then have supper at the Rose and Crown.'

'We can't tell them anything,' he cautioned.

'No. Jane is the only one who knows. I tell you, Alan, these last couple of days I've been feeling like 007; I've been afraid to talk to anybody in case I spilled the beans. But it will help to be among friends, with good food. And they'll know soon.'

'We can never talk about it, Dorothy. Not even after it's all over.'

'I know that. But they'll guess, the Endicotts and the Allenbys and anyone else who was in on the affair from the beginning. We won't be able to talk it over, but they'll know. Oh, Alan, the waiting is so hard!'

'It won't be long, now. Let's go say our prayers. We've missed evensong, but that means the Cathedral will be quiet.'

The small prayer chapel is isolated from the rest of the vast building, and is always quiet. We slipped inside and found it occupied by one other person. Jane didn't look around as we sank to our knees.

It doesn't take long to utter a fervent petition for, as the Prayer Book puts it, 'a happy issue out of all our afflictions'. Jane waited for us, and this time her raised eyebrows got a nod by way of reply. 'Thought so,' she said gruffly. 'Rumours.'

'Planted,' said Alan very quietly. Jane only nodded.

'Jane, we're headed to the pub for some supper. Come along.'

She shook her head. 'Too hard not to talk.'

Well, I could understand that, but I wanted her company. 'We can talk about the dogs. Watson has been very naughty lately, and I'm sure yours have been up to something.'

But she still refused. 'Afterwards. A party.' She gave one of her brusque nods and stumped away.

Of course when we got to the inn, the first thing Greta asked was, 'Has there been any news? We've been so very worried.'

'Everyone is,' said Alan. 'I'm afraid I've nothing to tell you.'

Which was, I thought, a brilliant evasion.

We had a drink, and then some excellent fish and chips, and then another drink, and lingered chatting with people we knew, neighbours and fellow parishioners, until Peter and Greta began to send subtle signals that it was time to leave. We strolled home across the Close, which was beginning to quiet with the close of day. The sky was still bright, but the heat was beginning to abate and there was that indefinable sense of hushed peace that sometimes comes at the end of a stressful day. The Cathedral clock chimed ten o'clock, its last utterance for the night, and it felt like a benediction.

TWENTY-EIGHT

A lan was remarkably patient with me the next day. 'Have we touched all the bases?' I kept asking. 'Have we forgotten anything?'

The 'we' was of course pure invention. I had done nothing at all except pass along Gerald's plan and fret, which was one reason I was so antsy. I wanted to be in there doing something, and there was no role for me to play, so I kept on bugging my poor husband. He assured me, over and over, that everything needful had been done, all procedures had been carefully explained to all concerned, the operation planned as thoroughly as was possible. 'You have to remember, love, that we're dealing with human beings: fallible, unpredictable human beings. We've tried to provide for all contingencies, but really that's impossible.'

'I know. With so many people involved, there's bound to be at least one loose cannon. Probably among the protesters. They're crazy, or next to it, and logic isn't their strong point. What if they decide to step up the action a little with a bomb or something?'

'We've thought of that, of course, and taken precautions. But as I said—'

I sighed and bit my lip and dropped the subject for at least ten minutes.

That night we both watched the news intently, but there was nothing of any interest to us, since at that point we had only one interest. 'Shouldn't something be happening?' I asked anxiously.

'Not yet. In this case, no news really is good news. It means everything is being kept under wraps, as far as the public is concerned.'

And then he had to give Jane the same reassurance when she called a few minutes later with the same concern.

We went to bed early on the same principle as children on Christmas Eve, to make tomorrow come earlier. And though we'd both had fairly stiff drinks, sleep didn't come easily to either of us. Did I really want tomorrow to come soon, I asked myself? What will it bring? Good news or disaster? It would be the one or the other, I was sure. There could be nothing in between.

'When is the balloon supposed to go up?' I asked.

'Quite early. When the first UniPetro employees arrive at work.'

I drifted into a troubled sleep, filled with vague images of balloons, huge barrage balloons over London, and toy balloons at a party, balloons that kept encountering candle flames and bursting. One of them burned and burned, flames everywhere, bodies falling, a radio announcer sobbing, and in my dream world the Hindenburg had crashed into the World Trade Center, and I woke with a scream to a dawn that promised a perfect day. For some people.

The usual routine got us through the beginning of the day. A household with animals is not allowed to concentrate on fretting, no matter what the emergency. Let the dog out, feed them all, clean the litter box, administer affection to the dog and admiration to the cats, and only then can human needs be considered. We turned on the small television in the kitchen, but the early news held nothing of interest. If a true crisis popped up, there would be news bulletins.

But there were no bulletins. I managed not to pepper Alan with nervous queries, but it took considerable effort. I knew that Jane was dealing with the same anxiety, but I decided not to walk next door. Trouble shared may be trouble halved, but worries shared have a tendency to escalate into near-panic. We would build on each other's 'what-ifs' and frighten ourselves badly. No, best to wait it out.

I took Watson for a walk to work off some nervous energy. It didn't work very well, because Watson sensed my mood and stuck to me like a bur instead of running ahead. His little whines, meant to ask what was wrong and if he could help, simply intensified my unease.

We completed half our circuit of the Close and were headed for home when Greta Endicott flew out of the pub and hailed me.

'Have you heard the news?' she demanded. 'There's a fire at UniPetro! That's Husam's company! What if—'

But the rest of her question was lost. I dropped the leash and headed for home faster than I knew I could move, with a confused Watson straggling behind me.

Alan was headed out the door. 'You've heard?' he asked unnecessarily. 'I'm going.'

'And I'm coming with you. No argument.' I paused only long enough to drop Watson at Jane's, promising to keep her apprised, and then we were off.

Alan laid down the law all the way to the station. I was not to go. This was no place for onlookers. I would just be in the way. I could get badly hurt, or worse. He would be worrying about me when he should have his mind on dealing with the situation. And so on. I didn't bother to reply, but looked straight ahead and willed the car to move faster. I knew he wasn't really furious with me, just worried sick.

He pulled into the car park with a screech, bought two tickets (scowling at me), and ran for the train as the guard blew his whistle.

The commuter rush was in full swing, but (astonishingly) we found seats together. Alan, in very low tones, was able to tell me what he knew, which wasn't much. The news bulletin had said only that UniPetro guards, at about eight that morning, had notified the police about a suspicious package found in a storage area. A few minutes after that, as the bomb squad were on their way, a bomb threat was phoned in to the UniPetro switchboard. Somehow the public had got wind of the situation – Alan nodded at me at that – and a large and growing crowd had assembled outside the building, including, the news report had said, a small contingent, mostly women, with signs sporting anti-Muslim slogans, and a rather larger group of men in Arab dress shouting angrily in Arabic.

'So far, just as planned,' I said.

'Wait for it. The next thing was *not* as planned. Smoke began to appear, and though the police, according to the news report, thought at first it was just a smoke bomb, flames quickly appeared and the fire grew. It was not clear whether it was inside or outside the building, because of the volume of smoke.

The fire department was on the scene. "Further bulletins will be issued as more information becomes available." Do you understand now why I don't want you there?'

'Yes. I've understood all along. Just as you understand why I must be there. We both have to know.'

He sighed and patted my hand, and we pulled into Victoria Station.

He called Scotland Yard then and requested police escort to the scene. 'Urgently, please,' he added, and in a remarkably short time a police car pulled up just outside the taxi rank, and we were on our way, with lights and siren. Even so, our progress was slow.

We were surprised, or at last I was, to find Derek Morrison in the car. 'They called me straight away,' he said. 'I'm not in this officially, of course, but I gather it's all hands to the pump.'

His question was implicit. Alan answered, 'No, I'm not here to help. I doubt there's anything I can do. I'm here because—'

He hesitated and I interrupted. 'We're both here because we couldn't stay away. This is not the way we hoped things would work out.'

'No. Nor is this one of the possible problems we anticipated.' Derek and Alan sighed in unison.

'Derek, have you heard any more about exactly where the fire is? Or even if it's inside or out?'

'No one seems sure yet. They think it's some sort of oil burning; the smoke is very thick and black. Well, you can see it.' He pointed out the window.

We were nearing the City, and sure enough, angry plumes of black smoke billowed up, filling the limpid blue sky with ugliness, blotting out the sun. The windows of the car were all closed, but the smoke seeped in. I began to cough.

'Here. Better put these on.' He handed us face masks that looked only a little less sinister than something Darth Vader might have worn. 'They're no help against flames, and they're frightfully uncomfortable, but they'll help against the smoke. We won't be able to get very close, I'm afraid.'

Alan said nothing. I think that, until now, he hadn't quite understood the magnitude of the disaster. I know I hadn't, and

I was nearly sick with worry about our friends. About everyone, in fact, who was anywhere near. If that fire was inside the building, hundreds of people could already be dead of smoke inhalation. Alan put on his mask and helped me with mine. I was absurdly reminded of the standard in-flight announcement about the oxygen masks, and started to giggle.

'Steady, old girl,' said Alan, and my rising hysteria was quelled.

The going was even slower now. Our driver was trying to get through the traffic, but lights and siren can't magically open a path when there is no place for the other cars to go, and we were jam-packed. 'Streets blocked off,' he called back to us. 'I doubt I can get you any closer.'

'We'll walk,' Alan started to say, when Derek's phone rang and we turned to him, studying his face as if it could tell us what he was being told.

He rang off. 'Outside. Not near enough the building to pose a great threat, except from the smoke.'

'But the building's air-conditioned, so there wouldn't be open windows,' I said, almost as a question.

Derek and Alan both shrugged, and I realized it was a stupid comment. The ventilation system had to draw in air from the outside somehow, or everyone would eventually die for lack of oxygen. Anyway, everyone inside would have been evacuated in case the bomb threat was genuine.

Almost everyone.

I began to cough again, despite my mask, and looked at the evil black cloud. Was I imagining things, or was the cloud a bit smaller?

'They're getting it under control,' said Derek. 'It's driven away some of the protesters, probably the anti-Muslim crowd. That sort won't usually hold to their convictions long, when personal discomfort is involved.'

I wasn't so sure about that. Some of those people from the so-called Temple of Truth were really scary. And the others, the radical Islamists, would walk through Hell itself to advance their cause, or many of them would.

I craned to try to see what was happening, and Derek gestured toward a nearby office building. 'I know someone

who works in a front office here. We could get out of the
smoke up there, and see better, too.'

So we climbed up to the third floor – second, in Brit terms
– and were graciously received by Derek's friend, who was
in fact ignoring his work and looking out his window.

We had a great view from there. The smoke was definitely
dissipating, aided by the brisk wind that had sprung up.

Bystanders were being shooed away by the police. A few
were taken to the ambulances that had appeared on the scene.
Smoke inhalation, probably. I hoped, viciously, that some of
the stricken were from the Temple of Truth. That'd teach 'em!
It was an uncharitable thought, and one I would have to repent.
Later.

Now the bomb squad, recognizable by their protective gear,
were beginning to leave the building. I watched with intense
attention. Alan gave me a look and shook his head slightly.

Okay, I got it. Turn my gaze elsewhere. Almost anywhere
else.

Now the last few security people were leaving, and a small
trickle of non-uniforms. I wished I could see better, but going
down to move closer would be unwise for a number of reasons.
Now the security guards had stationed themselves at the
entrances and were allowing employees back into the building,
after scrutinizing their credentials. That was a slow process,
but eventually everyone got in. The security staff got in. The
doors were closed. The onlookers were beginning to leave,
going back to their own work or whatever they'd been doing
when the spectacle began. The protesters remained.

Now that the smoke was nearly gone, Derek's friend (we
never did learn his name) opened his window. We thanked
him and turned to his office door. The show was over.

But it wasn't.

We heard a scream from below, then a few more, mixed
with angry shouts. We turned back to the window.

It was impossible from so far away to see clearly, but trouble
seemed to be centred around the bomb squad van. Some of
the protesters were running toward it. The uniformed squad
members were trying to fight them off.

'Alan, what—'

He didn't reply. He looked sick.

Derek's radio spoke. I couldn't understand, what with the static and the departmental shorthand, but Derek paled. 'They got them,' he said, and ran out of the office.

There was no point in even trying to follow him. He would be caught up in official duties. We made our dreary way to the nearest Underground station, and on to Victoria and home.

TWENTY-NINE

Alan went immediately to the Shrewbury police, leaving me to explain to Jane and the Endicotts and Margaret. 'Everything went almost as planned, until the end,' I said, trying not to succumb to tears. 'The diversion – the bomb threat – worked exactly as we'd hoped. It brought both of the hate groups to the scene, so they could see clearly that the Ahmads were not among those evacuated from the building. The fire – well, we still don't know who set that, or why, but it actually helped, because even the stupidest protestor would have assumed that the additional threat would have brought out anybody left inside. Of course they'd fetched Aya earlier, and left her in the squad's van. I know that much; the rest is guesswork, because I was too far away to see clearly, and there was so much confusion. I did see one of the people in bomb-squad uniform trip and fall, and I think it was Rahim, because even the smallest uniform they could find would be way too big for him. They'd got the family into the uniforms inside the buildings, you see, so everyone could leave well covered up. In the confusion, it was very unlikely that anyone would notice more uniforms leaving than went in to begin with.

'But I think Rahim tripped over the pants, and the suit's so heavy he couldn't get up. And the helmet came loose, and . . .' My voice shook. I swallowed and tried again. 'Someone saw his face, the face of a young boy—'

I couldn't go on.

There was a long pause. Peter broke it, finally. 'Why was the crowd allowed to get by with taking them?'

I blew my nose and took a sip of water. We were sitting in Margaret's parlour. She had offered drinks, but water was all I could face. 'It all happened so fast. The bomb squad people couldn't do much. They can't move fast in all that gear. Most of the police had dispersed, along with most of the UniPetro security. I'm guessing Husam and Rana went to Rahim's rescue, but they'd have been hampered by the suits, too. As I said, I couldn't see much.' I blew my nose again. 'Derek's on it, and Alan, and I'm sure the Met and MI5 and the lot of them.'

'Who got them?' Jane had said nothing until then.

'I don't know. Derek ran off before he could tell us, and Alan couldn't get phone service on the train. He'll know by now. Margaret, I think I'll take you up on that drink.'

We were still sitting around, saying the same things over and over, when Alan called. 'Are you alone?'

'No, I'm at the Deanery with Jane and Margaret and the Endicotts.'

'I'll be there in a few minutes.'

The news, when he arrived with it, was not good, and Alan didn't try to sugar-coat it. 'Everything I say will be a supposition, but based on the best evidence the authorities have at the moment. The whole family has been captured, and not by any Islamic group. The faces in the melee were all European, and the only language anyone heard spoken, or rather shouted, was English. The assumption is that the captors are a far-right Christian group.'

'I object to the word "Christian,"' said Margaret firmly.

'Non-Muslim, then, if you prefer. Anti-Muslim might be a better description. Derek's speculation is that the Temple of Truth here in Sherebury may be responsible. Certainly a group of their representatives was among the protesters at the office building; Derek recognized some of them.'

'That's bad, Alan.' I felt actually sick. 'They are bigots of the worst sort; their credo is based on hatred of the "other". Some of them are, I think, not quite sane. They could . . . they could kill the whole family just out of sheer malice.'

'Yes.'

The word fell into the room like a stone.

'What's being done?' Jane was wearing her usual drab clothing. It looked like armour.

'All possible forces are searching for the family. Finding them is the first step.'

'Did anyone see them actually taken away?' There was little hope in my voice.

'Sadly, no. You were there, Dorothy. The scene was mass confusion. One of the bomb-squad people thought he saw several people being bundled into a car, but he couldn't see well enough even to describe the car, never mind note a license number.'

'If it is those Temple people, would they bring them back here to Sherebury?'

'Perhaps. It may depend on what they intend to do.'

I stood; I couldn't sit still any longer. 'Margaret, do you know of anyone in Sherebury who knows that disgusting crowd better than Miss Simmons?'

She thought a moment and then shook her head. 'Not that I can think of. They keep themselves very much to themselves, but having once been connected with them, Miss Simmons hears most of what goes on.'

'Then I think we need to hear what she can tell us. Alan—'

Margaret put out a restraining hand. 'No. Miss Simmons has no use for men. She has no use for most people, actually, but she seems to have taken to you, Dorothy. You might get her to talk, but only if she wants to.'

'I'll go,' said Jane. 'Talks to me.'

'We'll both go. Somebody say a prayer for us.'

'What took you so long?' was Miss Simmons' gracious greeting when she opened her door. 'Get in quick before they see you.'

That remark, from any other elderly person, would have had me shaking my head and thinking sad thoughts about senile paranoia. From Miss Simmons, it scared me. I managed, just, not to look over my shoulder as we scuttled inside.

'No bribe this time?' she asked caustically.

'No time. I'm taking orders for later on. Miss Simmons, we're worried sick. What can you tell us?'

She looked at Jane rather than me. 'Kids are safe. For now.'

'Where?' she barked.

'The building has a cellar. It was a warehouse. The door is hidden. Well hidden.'

'You're talking about their church?' I frowned.

'I won't call it a church. Meeting house. Den of thieves.' She spat, quite accurately, into the fireplace.

'And the parents, Rana and Husam?'

Miss Simmons shook her head. 'Don't know where.'

'Do you know what they plan to do?' I was almost afraid to hear the answer.

'There's infighting. The new members – the ones you saw rioting a few days ago – they're all for killing the lot of them. They'd like to do it in public, like Joan of Arc, for a public example of what happens to infidels, but they know that would probably be stopped. They're crazy, but not stupid. They're talking about locking them in a house somewhere and burning it down.'

I've read, in novels, of people turning white as a sheet. I never believed it until I saw all the blood drain out of Jane's usually ruddy face. I thought she was going to faint. She sat down, abruptly, in the nearest chair, and uttered not a word.

'Get hold of yourself, girl!' Miss Simmons spoke in her usual peremptory fashion, but there was a trace of sympathy in her tone. 'It won't happen. Other faction is stronger, more of them. They want to stand them up before the whole group and make them repent of their evil ways. The adults, that is. The kids they mean to take away from the parents and raise them in "a decent God-fearing home."'

I could hear the quotation marks. I found my voice. 'Which would mean lots of propaganda, lots of discipline, sparing no rods.'

'Right.'

Anger boiled up in me. 'They'd turn those beautiful, sensible, sweet children into frightened rabbits, if they didn't end up beating them to death. And if the kids lived and escaped, they'd probably have the hatred of non-Muslims scarred into them forever. How did these people *get* that way! They weren't born bigoted monsters!' I was pacing the floor.

'You just said it. Scarred into them as children. Abusive parents, whatever.'

'That's no excuse. Lots of people grow up in bad conditions and turn out just fine.'

Jane made an impatient gesture. 'Beside the point. How to get kids out?'

'Back way.'

It seemed to take forever for Miss Simmons to give us the information. Her speaking style could be almost as elliptical as Jane's, besides which, she enjoyed irritating people. However, in her own way she understood that this was no occasion for delay, and bit by bit, she told us. Her father had in his youth been employed in the warehouse that became the Chapel of the One True God. (Her father had been well over a hundred when he died, and Miss Simmons was in her late nineties. Good grief, I thought in some idle portion of my mind, between the two of them they represented close to two centuries of Sherebury history.)

When the warehouse was sold to the sect, in the 1950s, Mr Simmons joined the group and then cannily disguised the entrance to the cellar. His loving daughter wasn't sure why he had done it, unless as a place to store his own stash of the demon drink his new religion disapproved of. He also turned one of the old below-grade loading doors into a concealed exit. He had told a few carefully-chosen members of the sect about the first carpentry work, but not about the second. Miss Simmons believed she was the only one who knew about that.

'Where?'

'Not sure anymore. Could find it, probably, but it won't open from the outside anyway.'

'Oh, this is all so medieval!' I was still pacing; now I was waving my hands. 'Hidden doors, concealed exits. I suppose you're going to tell us it opens with some sort of mysterious mechanism!'

'This is England, Yank. Those things exist. Father studied medieval carpentry and liked to play jokes.'

'Well, it's no joke if we can't get those kids out before the Temple monsters turn them into zombies. We don't have too much time – what, Jane?'

'Mike,' she repeated, and pulled her phone out of her bag. After a brief conversation she put it back. 'Be here in five minutes.'

'Jane, who on earth is Mike? We don't have time for distractions.'

'Mechanic. Can work out anything.'

'Mechanic – oh, your mechanic at the garage. I know he's good at cars, but we don't have a car that needs work!'

'Not just cars. Anything mechanical.'

Miss Simmons cackled. 'One for you, Jane! Should have thought of him myself.'

The penny dropped, finally. 'You think he can find the concealed door and figure out a way to open it from the outside!'

Mike, when he arrived covered in grease and goodwill, was sure he could do that, and was all for starting right then.

'No,' said Jane and Miss Simmons in one breath. 'Not until after dark,' Miss Simmons went on. 'They'll have a watch, but the door's at the back. The passage is narrow now; fools keep putting up buildings. Carts used to back up to unload; no room now.'

'Wait!' I didn't mean to shout, but that's the way it came out. 'Wait just a minute, everybody. The kids may not even be there, but even if they are, we can't just go roaring in there and take them. For one, thing, *where* would we take them? We could lock them up in one of our houses, but that would just be exchanging one prison for another. What they need is their parents, and a resolution to the threats, so they can all go about their business in freedom again. Sorry to drag you out for nothing, Mike, but we need to plan this all very carefully.'

'Right,' said Mike. 'It's okay, Mrs Martin. I'll be ready when you need me. But one thing: Miss Simmons, I could go take a look at the place where you say this door is meant to be, and see what I can find.'

Jane and I left as they were arguing over whether Miss Simmons was to take him there, after dark, or simply tell him where to look.

'I thought she didn't go out at all these days,' I commented to Jane.

Her answer was a sceptical grunt.

Alan and I settled in the kitchen for a small and very belated meal, something between tea and supper. I hadn't even thought about eating for hours; food was the last of my worries. Now that things looked a little better, I knew Alan and I both needed fuel. The young can sometimes go for hours and even days without eating, but people our age aren't as resilient, and the day had been endless. I felt as though I'd lived through at least a week since I got out of bed.

I had a lot to tell him. Between bites I related Miss Simmons' idea of where the kids were and how it might be possible to reach them. I also told him about the plans of the splinter group to deal with the parents.

I put my sandwich down.

'I've learned some things, too,' said Alan. 'Finish your sandwich. We have a lot of thinking to do, and—'

'I know, I know. Low blood sugar starves the brain cells. The adage is engraved on my heart.' But I took another bite of sandwich.

Alan went into his lecturing mode, fingers tented. 'The situation is this: Derek has determined that a contingent from the Temple of Truth is holding the Ahmads, but the police don't know where. If your Miss Simmons is right about the children, that's a big step forward, but as you say, we can't just rush in, even assuming that's possible. The woman is remembering a piece of deceptive carpentry from at least sixty years ago. One's memory dims in that length of time, and at her age—'

'She's all there, Alan. And that secret door was something special, something her father delighted in, something that only the two of them knew. It may have been discovered during those intervening years, or the building may have been altered so much that it's now inaccessible, but I'd bet money that it was once there, just as she remembers.'

'She's all there, is she? And she knows all about this dubious sect. Then why in the name of all the saints doesn't she have any idea where they've hidden Rana and Husam?'

'She isn't admitted to their confidence, Alan. She left the group years ago, and became anathema to most of them. Now they've morphed into another self-proclaimed religion, with a lot of new people who don't even know her, except by reputation. Wait a minute!'

I clasped my head with both hands and stared into space. A stranger would have thought I was having a stroke. Alan knows me well. He just waited, as commanded.

'People,' I muttered. 'Not just a mob. People.' I was silent for a moment, thinking hard. 'Alan, who are the people? I mean, the Temple of Truth isn't just a fruitcake. I mean, they are, of course, but they're made up of individual raisins and so on.'

'And nuts,' said Alan drily.

'Yes, but who *are* they? They must have positions in the community. They have to have jobs of some kind. Butcher, baker, soldier, sailor . . .'

Alan was beginning to have some glimmer of what I was thinking. 'Individuals.'

'I think Miss Simmons can give us some names. She isn't part of them anymore, for which may God be thanked, but she seems to know everything that goes on with that crowd. See, Alan, they're crazy, of course, but some must be more or less sane. They're not like an organized band of terrorists. When we were worried about some splinter Isis-like group, we were helpless. They've been brainwashed, and besides, they're from a culture so different from ours that it's almost impossible for us to think the way they do.

'But this Temple group – they're English. They think of themselves, I suppose, as Christian. They live in this community and buy their groceries at Tesco and shop at Marks and Sparks. They're ordinary people with a deformed conscience, but otherwise ordinary.'

I looked at him, pleading with him to understand.

'And you think we might be able to reason with them.'

His voice, his whole manner, bristled with scepticism.

'Okay, so it's unlikely. But if we can find two or three of them who are less radical than the rest, who still retain some shred of practicality and compassion, it's worth a try, isn't it? What have we got to lose by diplomacy?'

'I don't like it, Dorothy,' he said at last. 'The danger—'

'I wouldn't go alone, of course, and we'd meet in some public place. The Rose – no, they probably think a pub is a haunt of the Devil. Maybe the museum. That's about as neutral as you can get. And I'd take – let's see, who might they respect? Jane, probably. If they grew up here, she taught them at some point. Not Miss Simmons. Not the bishop; they'd regard him as Popish. The Baptist pastor, possibly.'

'And of course I'm coming.'

I rejoiced to hear that. It meant he'd bought into the idea, without even noticing. But I said, 'No, Alan. You're the police. I know you're retired, but you're still Authority in their eyes. You'd be a threat. I want this to be a reasonable discussion between reasonable people.'

'And you think you'll find such people at the Temple of Truth.'

'I think there's some possibility.'

Alan and I have been married long enough that we recognize in each other the signs of immovable resolve. He didn't argue with me. He did point out the probability of success, which in his view ranked with the private sale of the Brooklyn Bridge (though he didn't put it quite that way). I didn't argue, either. I just listened and nodded and waited until he had finished so I could phone Jane.

I explained my idea to her. She wasn't a whole lot more enthusiastic than Alan, but she agreed to phone Miss Simmons and get some names. 'Wouldn't tell most people,' Jane added.

'I know. That's why it's better for you to ask. I'd bet you're her best friend.'

'Only, more like it.'

'No, she can count me, too. I don't know why. She's rude and ill-tempered and demanding, but at least she's real. You know where you are with her.'

'Hmph!'

While I waited for her to call back, I made some plans and shared them with Alan. He has often accused me of getting into danger without consulting him, a charge with which I must meekly agree. My defence on those occasions was that I wasn't aware of the danger until it was too late – and that I always managed to get myself out. This time I did know I was walking into a viper's nest, and I was glad to have him know exactly when and where.

He commented only with grunts (that most irritating of sounds), but at least he listened.

By the time Jane called, I had a full-blown plan of action. She grunted, too, but finally agreed.

'Tomorrow, then, if you can get it organized by then.' A mutter of protest. 'I know, but you're the one to do it. All of them know and respect you. And we do need to move fast; the good Lord alone knows what they might be cooking up.'

I hung up the phone, drained and bone-weary. Alan, who had of course been listening, unbent and fetched me a glass of bourbon. 'I think you're mad as a hatter, my dear, but I think I'll keep you anyway. Drink that and go to bed. You're done.'

'I am that. Thank you, love.'

I never even noticed when both cats went to sleep on top of me.

THIRTY

Morning. I had slept dreamlessly and, I thought, without even moving; I was stiff as old leather when I woke, and far too warm.

'You had Sam and Emmy for your eiderdown,' Alan told me when I complained. 'I suppose they thought you needed comfort.' He handed me a large, steaming cup of the life-giving elixir that's so prosaically called coffee. 'I tried to shoo them away, but they had turned blind and deaf and unresponsive even to a shove.'

'Umm.'

I was somewhat more brilliant after another jolt of caffeine, and with full wakefulness came the awareness that it might be a very long day. 'I suppose it's too late for matins.' I never wear a watch, and I couldn't see the clock without my glasses.

Alan handed them to me. 'Far too late. After ten. You needed the sleep.'

'I also need solace, and strength, and all the help the good Lord can give me. Alan, I'm getting cold feet.'

'Too late now. The die is cast. Jane called a while back. All is arranged. And – careful of your coffee – last night's operation went off smooth as silk.'

It was a good thing he'd warned me. If the cup had been full I'd have poured it all over myself. I wanted details, but the other matter came first. 'When?'

'Six thirty, at the museum. If you want to work out the details with your co-conspirators, you'd best get weaving.'

Once I had showered and dressed and waved away the offer of breakfast, the hours ahead suddenly seemed far too short for all that had to be done. First a call to Jane, to find out exactly whom I'd be facing.

'Teacher, local school. Not theirs; that's closed. Nurse at the hospital. Retired couple, been with the group for yonks, don't like latest developments. And the head. Pretty rigid, but had to include her.'

'And you think these others will be able to persuade her?'

Jane chuckled. 'All big donors to the church.'

Jane is nobody's fool.

The next people I needed to talk to were the Baptist pastor and the imam. We'd made the risky decision to include him. I still wasn't sure it was the right thing to do, but it might just turn the balance. One way or the other. I shivered and decided not to think about that.

I doubted that Jane had spelled out exactly what strategy we proposed to use. That would have used up about a month's ration of words. I went first to the Baptist pastor and talked it out with him.

He was amenable, to a point. 'It is an admirable approach,' he said with a smile. He was a sweet, pink and white man who reminded me of the Gerber baby, all rosy cheeks and dimples and laugh lines. 'And it just might work. However, if it does not, there are other approaches.'

'I don't think bullying will work,' I said with a frown.

'Nor do I. Mrs Martin, you're a good woman – oh, yes, I know all about you, though we've never met. I know all about a good many people in this city.'

He said no more, but I was left with an unpleasant impression. Surely he didn't mean what I thought he meant! Not a clergyman.

I had to wait to see the imam; he was saying midday prayers. I popped into the nearest pub and had a sandwich and some plain tonic. I didn't want to go to a mosque smelling of alcohol; it didn't seem right, somehow.

He was a good deal harder to convince than the Baptist. Well, he had a lot more at stake. 'You are relying on the assumption that these are reasonable people. Our community here has not always found them so.'

I laughed at that; I couldn't help it. 'Mr Alani, you've lived in England long enough to master the understatement. I should imagine you've found these people to be a nasty bunch of bigots, and frankly I've always thought of them the same way. But there's a difference between the group as a whole and its individual members. I'm hoping that dealing with individuals, avoiding the mob psychology, we may be able to appeal to their better side. We think it's worth a try, anyway. If it doesn't work, what have we lost?'

'Time,' he said simply. 'Time is not on our side.'

'We know that. But these aren't an organized terrorist cell. They're just a bunch of people steeped in hatred and fear, some of them perhaps not terribly intelligent, and they are, moreover, a house divided. Some are far more radical, but they are in the minority. We're praying that they're not prepared to do anything drastic just yet.'

He held up his hands in a classic gesture. 'Very well. What do you want of me?'

'Just be there, be the friendly gentleman that you are, listen, and put in a calming word here and there if it seems advisable. I want them to understand that you are not a threat.'

He gave me a half-bow. 'I will do as you ask, and I will pray Allah's blessing on your effort.'

'And also with you,' I said, and the ritual response seemed appropriate.

I made it to the Cathedral for evensong, and never had my prayers been more fervent.

Then the time dragged again. Alan made me sit down for tea, but I declined the beverage. 'No. I've had plenty of caffeine today. It would only make me nervous, and then I'd probably have to go to the bathroom in the middle of the meeting. No tea.'

'Then take a thimbleful of sherry with a few biscuits. I insist.'

He also insisted on driving me and Jane to the museum for the meeting. 'I'll wait for you. I want to make sure you have a quick way out, if things go wrong.'

'Nothing will go wrong,' I said, and the old automated-airplane joke echoed in my head. *Nothing can go wrong . . . go wrong . . . go wrong . . .*

Stop it, Dorothy! I gave myself a mental slap.

We were the first ones there, as planned. Alan had arranged for the building to be opened and the lights turned on. A small room off to the side of the main display area held a table and comfortable chairs, and Jane produced glasses and several carafes of water. Alan went reluctantly to the car, and we dithered, moving chairs an inch or two, arranging the glasses.

Our co-hosts appeared next, also by arrangement, and after we had them comfortably seated Jane went to the door to greet our – what? Adversaries? Victims?

They came in a body, and in no sweet mood. Introductions were made. Mrs Robinson, deaconess. Mr Jeffries, teacher. Mr and Mrs Grant. Mrs Arnold, nurse. Mr Miller, pastor. Mr Alani.

He was given no affiliation, but the Temple people bristled at the name. Jane glared at them and they said nothing. They were now prepared to resist anything we might say.

Well, it was my agenda. I sat down (don't try to intimidate, Dorothy), took a sip of water to ease my dry throat, and began. 'It's very good of you to come. I know this may be an inconvenient time, but I hope not to keep you from your dinners for very long.' I smiled. They did not.

'First, all of us here owe you, and the other stalwarts of the Temple of Truth, our thanks for coming to the rescue of the Ahmad family. As of course you realized, they might have been in grave danger from the group of angry radicals at UniPetro that day. As emissaries of peace, Husam and his family have incurred the enmity of those who would destroy the hope of peace between Muslims and Christians.'

This time the response was not hostile, just bewildered. Blinks, frowns, glances from one to another. Mrs Grant, who looked like the very archetype of the sweet old lady, opened her mouth. Her husband shook his head; she closed it again.

'We also feel it was very wise of you to keep the whereabouts of Mr and Mrs Ahmad a secret. Certainly there are those, even in Sherebury, who would wish them harm. We want you to know, however, that those radical elements in this community have been identified by the police and will no longer present a danger, so it is now safe for the Ahmads to leave sanctuary. We who love them thank you very much for keeping them safe.'

I glanced at Mr Alani, who picked up his cue. 'I, too, am in your debt. Mr and Mrs Ahmad have been very kind to our

community, Muslim and Christian alike. Their kind of understanding and compassion is badly needed in these troubled
times. You and I, Mrs Robinson, call our God by different
names, but we all worship him in love and peace. In His name
I bless you for your kindly actions.'

'And I echo his words,' said Mr Miller. 'You are to be
commended for your prompt recognition of the danger.
We are proud to have such disciples in our midst.'

He sipped his water, perhaps choking on his words.

'Well, that's really all I have to say. Can you tell us where
Husam and Rana are staying, so that we may meet them
when they come back into the community? We want to
welcome them back. And of course we want to take the
children to them.'

And right on cue, Alan entered with Aya and Rahim clinging
to his hands.

'And that completed the demoralization of the Temple people,'
I said as we gathered later at the Rose and Crown for a victory
celebration. Aya and Rahim had been allowed to stay up and
join us; they didn't want to let their parents out of their sight.
'Mrs Robinson was all set to bluster and stand firm, with the
children as her trump card, but when she saw them, she just
folded.'

'No one else on her side,' said Jane, sipping at a glass of
dark amber liquid. 'They don't like her. Don't like her tactics.'

'So you won, without a shot fired,' said Alan admiringly.

'Yes, and with some new ideas in those bigoted heads,' said
Mr Alani. He was enjoying a glass of tonic. 'How long they
will stay there . . .' He gave one of those expressive shrugs.

'Where actually were the Ahmads?' asked Peter, who had
been very busy at the bar. 'Some dungeon somewhere?'

'More or less,' Alan replied. 'Mrs Robinson has a bare-bones
granny flat at her house, not much more than a bed-sitter, with
no outside door. The house is at the very edge of Sherebury,
and the flat faces the river, with no path nearby. She locked
them in. It was unlikely anyone could see them in there, or
hear them cry out.'

'Which we did not do,' said Rana, her arm around Aya. 'We

were quite sure someone would come. Husam prayed, you see.'

'And Allah sent you, my friends.' Rahim wasn't quite clinging, but he stuck close to his father.

'And you are reunited, and no one was badly hurt, just frightened. So all's well that ends well, I suppose.' I polished off my gin and tonic. 'I hope you're going to stay in the area for a while, now that the crazies, on both sides, have been dealt with. Temporarily, at least.'

'Alas, we cannot.' Husam shook his head. 'I wish we could stay and continue to work with the young people at the mosque, but we might serve as a lightning rod for more trouble. It is better that we go elsewhere.'

'Will you be safe?' I was trying to ignore gathering tears.

'Who knows? *In shah'Allah*. And now we had better put the children to bed. They have had a bad few days.'

THIRTY-ONE

The summer sped past. I forgot about my Fourth of July party. We heard nothing from or about the Ahmads, though I kept expecting word. And so, as the poet said, we watched and waited for the light. Prosaically, the first hint of the end of it all was a tiny item in the business section of the *Telegraph*. I never read that section, since I know nothing about business and economics and all that sort of thing, and care less. We have a few small investments, which Alan handles, and unless the world of commerce undergoes a slump like the Great Depression, we should have enough money to last out our days, so I don't worry about it.

So it was Alan, one morning over the breakfast table, who made a small exclamation and handed the paper to me.

The headline was 'UniPetro vice-president to retire'. The five-line story said that Husam Ahmad, senior vice-president for international investment, was retiring on the advice of his doctor, and would be sorely missed. There was no word as to his replacement.

'Alan! What does that mean? Are they covering up something?'

'Almost certainly. The question is, what?'

That remained the question for quite a while.

The Temple of Truth people had gone grumbling on their sour way, not quite sure that they had done the right thing in releasing the Ahmads, and with the uneasy feeling that they had been conned. Their rhetoric had tamed considerably, however, and there were no more demonstrations in the streets.

Autumn had lingered until we thought winter might never come, and then it came with a vengeance. Bitter winds bit off the remaining rosebuds and starred our windows with frost patterns. Watson went out with the utmost reluctance and came back in as soon as possible, to snooze in front of the parlour fire, or the Aga if we were in the kitchen. Jane went to Bexley to help Sue and Walter when their baby boy was born in November, and sent back pictures that threatened to clog our mobiles.

And one day, just before Christmas, the postman delivered a large padded envelope to our door. It was covered with stamps I didn't recognize, and the postmark and return address were badly smudged.

I prodded the lumpy envelope. 'What on earth?' I said to Alan.

'You might open it and find out.' He was patient with me; he knows I go through this every time something unexpected arrives.

There was a card inside, and several parcels; I opened the one with my name on it. It was a lovely shawl of heavy silk, embroidered in my favourite blues and greens. Alan's was an elaborately embroidered coat that would make him an elegant dressing gown. (It was far too nice to be called a bathrobe!) There were small parcels for Watson and the cats as well: a fine new leash for the dog and toys for the cats.

The card, when we finally opened it, said:

> Greetings from your friends Husam, Rana, Rahim and Aya. We will not tell you where we are (this parcel was not posted from where we are living), but we want you to know we are safe and well and think of you often. It has been necessary to change our way of disseminating peace, but we have not given up. We shall never give up. We are sorry we had no opportunity to know you better, but perhaps one day when the world is a better place, we will see each other again. We owe you a great deal, and hope you remember us happily.
>
> I remembered, Dorothy, that you admired my hijab. Perhaps you will enjoy this similar shawl. And Alan, though you would probably not wear the coat outside, it may help keep you warm in your English winter. Your pets might not appreciate Muslim gifts, so theirs are universal.
>
> Merry Christmas!

Below the message was some flowing Arabic script, and a translation: 'Peace be with you. May Allah bless you, until we meet again.'

Through my tears I whispered, 'And may that day come soon. Amen, and amen.'